FIRST BLOOD

FIRST BLOOD

Man and Machine

AMBER

PARTRIDGE

A Penguin Random House Company

To order additional copies of this book, contact
Partridge India
000 800 10062 62
orders.india@partridgepublishing.com

www.partridgepublishing.com/india

Contents

Chapter 1

Introduction

Yanus walked slowly but confidently on the rough floor of the orphanage. It was after midnight and in the isolated area where the orphanage was located, the nights could get very quiet and frightening. The other children would usually turn in just after sunset as there was nothing to occupy their time after dinner. The poorly lit orphanage and the streets outside with their dim lamps offered no recreation for the boys and girls. Most were under ten and didn't like the oppressive darkness and eeriness that set in and went to bed early. Yanus, at eighteen, was the oldest and had never been adopted by a family. At this age, he knew it was never going to happen and did not like to think about it. He wondered how long they would keep him here anyway. Nobody stayed this long in an orphanage and he was sure he was going to be moved out soon. With no apparent skills and education, Yanus thought his future looked bleak.

Yanus paused, listening intently. It was just the guard snoring as loudly as the jets that occasionally flew over their building. A big man with a big moustache, the guard was hardly ever awake. Yanus could not understand whether he had been hired to prevent children from escaping or from thieves breaking in. The children were not going anywhere and there was hardly anything inside the orphanage itself which was worth stealing; except the children themselves. The precious, innocent, and vulnerable children left at the mercy of strangers. Left without care and hope in life until someone adopted them and took them home.

Yanus shook his head. These thoughts always led him to think about his own future. Yanus got to his favourite spot and sat down. He didn't want to think about something that he could not control. Yanus could still hear the guard's snores all the way up to the terrace. The sound drowned out the barking of the dogs up the street. Yanus wondered if the caretaker would be back tonight. He was frequently gone from the orphanage these days and every time Yanus had seen him, he looked in a bad mood. Yanus kept an eye on the man to see if he was going to make a trip to the children's dormitory. Yanus usually turned in after the caretaker had gone to sleep or if Yanus knew that he would not be back that night.

Yanus continued staring in to the night like he always did since he was little. He wasn't afraid of the dark or the caretaker or even the sound of the constant barking of dogs like the other children were. He was perhaps the only boy there who had dared to venture outside the walls of the orphanage in the dead of the night. Yanus preferred to venture out alone and never let any other boy in on his secret way out. He made his little trips alone and walked without any specific destination fixed in his mind. He walked where his feet took him and let his imagination guide him. But the excitement wore off long ago and Yanus was now content to just sit at the open terrace and pass his time until he felt sleepy. The other children would panic and cry because of the sounds that came from beyond the walls of the orphanage when it got dark. But he had not felt that fear for a long time. He had heard a lot more. He had heard sounds that still haunted his nights.

But tonight sleep eluded him. There was an uneasy sensation of restlessness within him. Something was not the way it usually was. Yanus thought to spend the night on the stairs leading up to the terrace and settled down. He wondered what was bothering him unnecessarily. Somewhere within him, he could feel it: Something was coming.

Sohrab had a rough day. He was not expecting the entire affair to be bungled in this way. He had been unable to salvage anything out of it all. He had always known that there were going to be a few problems and had even been ready for the eventuality of a few losses, but this had been totally unexpected. All he wanted now was the day to end. He wanted to go home and lie down peacefully and not think about the day's events. He thought back to the way the day had started. It was full of promise and he been unable to think of any major flaw in his plan. He had thought that it would be easy for the most part. But it had not. In fact, Sohrab had never come across an individual as difficult as his new boss.

Boss! Sohrab thought ruefully, he was hardly in his twenties and was barely out of college. Sohrab knew he should have prepared himself a lot better for the meeting that took place every six months with the trustees to ascertain the expenses Sohrab had to meet as care taker of the orphanage. Sohrab didn't really care about the orphanage or the kids sheltered in it. But it was an important source of income for him. It was in fact, his only source of income and for the first time in twenty years he had been unable to get the trustees to hike his allowance. Sohrab had milked the trust fund for years on the pretext of providing the children in his orphanage a good life. He did provide them a life, Sohrab thought, not a good life, but a life nonetheless. Thanks to him they were alive and not begging on the streets. Sohrab thought of himself as a good man who was doing the society a service by keeping these children off the streets and deserved a lot more than what he was actually entitled to by the trustees. So he helped himself to a majority of the money that was allocated for the orphanage and let the children fend for themselves with a little help from the pittance that was left over after Sohrab's largesse was satisfied. Sohrab thought over it as he rode toward his house. This was a problem that had to be solved. It would be better to go to the orphanage and think over it tonight. He turned around and headed toward the orphanage. It was late and the children would be asleep. He could think of a solution without any disturbance.

Sohrab walked up to the gate and opened the lock with his set of keys. The watchman gave a loud snort, woke up, and ran up to the gate.

"What took you so long? Sleeping as usual?" Sohrab shouted

"Sorry, just dozed off! I'll get your bike." said the watchman apologetically.

"There is no need for that. Just get back and stay awake. I don't pay you to sleep."

The watchman hung his head as Sohrab stormed off toward his room. Sohrab did not look back as the watchman stared at his back for a long time before walking down to his chair and began snoring again.

Sohrab threw open his door and sat down on the bed. He was near to bursting with anger. There must be some way to solve his problem. Every year his increment had paved the way for an increasingly comfortable life. This year, he had not even managed to get what he had last year. He had his new boss to thank for that. He had decreased the amount on the grounds that a hostel warden wouldn't need this kind of money. Sohrab flung the keys at the door. It made a huge sound in the silence of the night. Sohrab got up and began pacing the room, trying to think of a way out. It would come to him. He was sure of it.

Yanus nearly gave a shout when he felt the keys hit the door. He was trying hard to listen to just what was happening inside the caretaker's room. He did not know what he was trying to listen to but he strained hard anyway. When there was no other sound, Yanus turned toward his bunk. There was nothing more to it. Sohrab had gone to sleep.

Yanus was sure that the caretaker was annoyed with something. Whatever it was, Yanus hoped he did not take it out on the kids. Yanus had felt a feral rage at times when the caretaker would hit the kids. They were young and could not help crying at times. The caretaker would come charging out of his room and grab hold of anyone within his reach and thrash the child. Yanus had learnt never to get within close range. But this was different. This was not annoyance at little children spoiling his sleep, this was frustration. Yanus crept inside his dormitory and lay down on his bunk. The kids were in deep sleep and even the older ones were now in bed. As he lay down and closed his eyes, Yanus wondered what or who could have angered the care taker so much.

Samar stared at the man seated at the opposite side of the table, and he stared in disbelief. Samar could not understand how this man could have been responsible for so much at FS Industries.

"So you see Mr Samar, we really cannot do anything about the factory in Mumbai. We had been paid up front for the consignment and we have been unable to deliver. After your father's death, nobody in the market wants to help us with credits or time. We have run out of options. If we sell the factory in Mumbai, we might be able to pay off some of our debts. It will also help us get rid of something we don't need."

The man waited for Samar to give his confirmation. Samar instead asked him a question.

"Tell me Mr Lok, since when have you been with FS Industries?

"Since before you were born." said Lok with a smug smile

"That sounds impressive. How many years would that be though?"

"At least 25 years." Said Lok not knowing where this was going.

"And before that...?" asked Samar staring in to Lok's eyes.

Lok was beginning to get uneasy. "What do you mean?"

"I mean where you were before my father employed you. I know you were on the board when you joined the company. I just wanted to know where and what position did you hold before?"

"And why is that necessary?"

"Just answer the question, Mr Lok."

"I don't think I will, Mr Samar. It's got nothing to do with you."

Samar got up and walked toward the window. "My father's been gone just a few weeks, and you start talking of selling assets to pay off debts. You do not talk of how to solve a problem, just how to run away from it." Samar continued quietly, "Makes me wonder why Dad hired you?"

Lok too got up from his seat and said angrily, "Samar, I will not be insulted in this way, not by you, not by anyone. Do you understand?"

Samar continued looking out the window and started to smile. He was dealing with either a very daft old man or a very crafty old man. Lok seemed very angry at the insult and didn't care that he was talking to his former employer's son.

"I am not going to sell the factory or anything else, Mr Lok. I suggest you get busy finding an alternative. You may leave."

Lok turned around and was nearly at the door when Samar called back. "Mr Lok, I too will look for that alternative. Pray though, that it's you who finds it. If it's me, then I will ensure you go back to sweeping the roads of Mumbai, just like you used to before my father met you."

Lok paled, started to say something but thought better of it and walked out quietly closing the door behind him.

Samar settled down behind his desk and put his head down. He felt tired. He could not understand how Dad did it. Most of the conversations he had with his father had been from the other side of this desk. Samar wished he had paid more attention when his father wanted to teach him, groom him, and prepare him. But it was too late. His father was gone. He would never get to hear his voice again. The pang of sorrow returned time and again to haunt Samar. Samar felt helpless...alone.

Samar lifted his head up and blinked his tears away. He admonished himself. He had to remain strong. Dad had always believed in him, now he had to prove that faith right.

First he had to win back all those people who had lost faith in the company after his father had died. He had to think of a way of getting to them, fast.

He had to ensure that he kept the company operational and profitable for all.

A strange pattern was beginning to emerge from all the files that he been through so far. He was not aware that his father's company was dealing with such a wide variety of businesses. What was puzzling was that there was no connectivity between any of Dad's businesses. People related to one company were not aware of the existence of the other, all thinking that they were the only one run by Mr Jabar Falak; Samar's father. Samar was no expert, but he found this odd, even illogical. Why would Dad keep everybody in the dark? There were huge sums of money that seemed to be missing in the accounts. Sums which mysteriously returned by the time the final yearly reports were published. Nobody seemed to know where the money went and how it came back. Dad had authorised most transactions, but again, in many instances there were no records to shed light on who was the beneficiary. Stranger still, Samar had found old files in his father's locker which had odd figures and diagrams on it. Samar had been to college and understood math and science. But these diagrams were too complex and detailed for him to make any sense of them. There were dated to all the way back in 1976. All the pages filled with those diagrams and calculations had one thing in common: the letters CLR written at the bottom. Samar had tried to find references to CLR in the balance sheet, in the files kept at various offices, and even in Dad's phone book, but he found nothing. Worse was the level of incompetence of most of Dad's staff, from that orphanage's caretaker to Lok. They were either dumb or corrupt or both. Samar was tired of dealing with them. One thing was certain: his father had left him quite an enigma.

With growing impatience Sohrab paced the reception area at the FS Industries Head Office. This was the limit. He couldn't believe Samar had kept him waiting for nearly 2 hours. He had been here since morning and had hoped to be the first one to meet the Boss. Sohrab wanted to be the first thing in Samar's mind but had watched helplessly as a steady stream of people went in and out of Samar's office. He had been asked to wait.

Finally the stern woman at the desk called out to Sohrab, "Mr. Samar will see you now, Mr. Sohrab."

"It's about time! I have been here for 3 hours!" said Sohrab.

"An hour and forty five minutes." said the woman without looking up.

Sohrab did not want to waste his time and gave the woman an angry look as he knocked and entered Samar's cabin.

The boss was standing by the window looking out and did not turn when Sohrab entered and wished him a good afternoon.

"It's still morning, Sohrab. Didn't the children teach you anything?" Samar chuckled at his own attempt at humour.

Sohrab smiled and took a seat, wondering if this was a good sign. He didn't mind being made fun of, if he could get what he wanted.

"So Mr Sohrab, what can I do for you?" Samar asked as he took a seat behind the large wooden desk.

"Mr Samar, I wanted to make the same request that I made the last time, only this time...."

"I already told you, Mr. Sohrab, I am not going to grant any more funds this month." Samar cut him short.

"Mr. Samar, our expenses have gone up. There are so many bills to pay, food to provide, not to mention my salary which is...."

Samar cut in again, "Your salary?"

"Yes, my salary. You see Mr. Samar my salary is...."

Samar did not let him finish, "....quite sufficient for the work you do. Maybe even more than what you should get. You see Sohrab; I have seen the records of the funds the orphanage has received. I do not believe that the orphanage has been maintained properly. The facilities that should have been provided to the children are not in place either." Sohrab tried to protest but Samar continued, "All that money and you have nothing to show for it. In fact I wonder where all that money went?"

"Mr. Samar, I assure you...."

Samar raised a hand and silenced Sohrab. "I do not need assurances, I need results. I want to see some accountability from you and an improvement in the facilities in that orphanage. If you can do it, the orphanage, and not you Mr. Sohrab, will get more funds. If you cannot do it, then you will be replaced, and soon. That will be all Mr. Sohrab."

Samar had once again walked up to the window and was staring out. The meeting was over in a few minutes. Sohrab had no choice but to leave.

Sohrab was shaking with anger and humiliation. He could not believe that this was happening. All his attempts at getting more money from Samar had failed. He barely had half of what he used to get and it would be required to pay the utility bills and food for the children. There would be hardly anything left. His salary would not cover all the instalments he had to pay. They were usually covered by the money Sohrab got at the pretext of price rises, paying for tutors, or maintenance. He thought of using the money he had now but that would mean he would have no money left for the orphanage. No, thought Sohrab. He could not get away with it for long. He could get away with not providing sufficient food, but he could not get away with starving them. There had to be another way. Sohrab made his way to his favourite restaurant and ordered his usual drink. Sohrab began to think of a way out of this dilemma.

With each drink, the desperation began to diminish and a reckless rage came over him. Samar was leaving him with no choice. Sohrab was not going to forsake his comfortable life just because his boss had noble ideals. Besides, Sohrab thought, with all his wealth like this city's other super rich folk, Samar could afford those ideals. But what about those who couldn't? Those poor unfortunate wretches who did not even have enough to pay for one morsel of food. Did they care or have time for ideals? Those who had to fight for space just to sleep. Those whose lives were filled with horrors from beginning to end had to fight just to survive another day. Noble ideals were not always compatible with the struggle for survival. Samar did not understand that those who went through this struggle could not afford nobility. But Sohrab was done trying to convince Samar. Sohrab was going to make Samar pay. Make him pay in a way he could not imagine. Samar did not realize that the most valuable asset in the orphanage was not his money or the building or the land it stood on.

The children were more valuable than all that. Children who were now going to help Sohrab get what he wanted. Silently, he cursed Samar for forcing him in to this.

But as the Devil took over his mind, Sohrab allowed himself a grim smile as he thought: Nature would take its own course now.

Sohrab took the final turn down the road which led to the evil which resided in the city's dark shadows: To the kingdom of Babur.

This time, Sohrab knew, there was no turning back.

Sunny was really tired of this game. But Babur was still talking to the man from the orphanage and had asked Sunny to wait till they were done. Sunny was not looking forward to the conversation he knew would take place as soon as the man left. He knew what that man, Sohrab, wanted. Sunny had been down this route too many times in the past. He picked up the stick again and threw it far and watched the dog run after it. This time something was wrong. He just could not figure out what it was. He could feel it in his bones that this whole thing was going to go wrong. He decided he would advise Babur not to deal with Sohrab. Babur did not need such people. Sunny just did not understand why Babur was dealing with scum like Sohrab. After all, Babur had enough businesses running in Mumbai and was both rich and influential. Sunny had been advising Babur for a long time and his opinion was respected. They had taken too many risks together. They had both endangered their lives for each other. They had fought wars against the law and even other mafia. And they had survived. They had won. Sunny remembered when people were being whipped up in to a frenzy to turn on each other. Those were the wars of religion. Sunny had been worried that Babur might end their friendship for such silly issues. That he might join the madness too but that had not happened. Babur had sent a message to the police and the administrators concerned about law and order that there would be no rioting in his part of the city. Those who dared to violate Babur's decree came face to face with the fury of Babur himself. Sunny had witnessed the man's capacity for violence and his rage many times. But Sunny had witnessed something else that day. Usually Babur sent his men to do such menial work. That time Babur himself had gone to those who had defied him. The man responsible for the disturbances in his area held a high designation in the city's political arena and was an arrogant man. Babur had dragged him out on the street outside his office and thrashed him to within an inch of his life. Babur had made an example out of the man. Babur did not take kindly upon those who crossed him. Perhaps the issue had touched a nerve. But that was a long time ago. Sunny stared at the stick he was about to throw again. Babur would listen to him. Sunny looked up at the pair of people descending from the first floor. The meeting was finished. Sunny threw the stick far away and watched the dog run after it. He would be gone by the time the dog returned.

The eyes expressed more than mere words. That was Babur, a lion of a man. Babur was a man who had built an empire with a combination of brains, sheer strength, and daring. Babur sat opposite Sunny and listened quietly as to why this venture with Sohrab was not correct. Babur listened patiently without interrupting. There was no more valuable asset in him than patience. These were men who controlled their own destinies. No law or regulation dictated terms to them. They had amassed this power by being aggressive and prudent in the right place and right time. And so Babur listened to Sunny's arguments against Sohrab. Finally Sunny came to an end and waited, like he always did for Babur's verdict.

A rare smile came to Babur, "Tell me Sunny, are those really the reasons why we should not work with Sohrab?"

"I have given you all the valid and reasonable points against this, Babur. There is nothing else." said Sunny.

"Reasonable? What does reason have to do with this? I want to know why you object to this particular deal."

Sunny gave a sigh but did not answer.

Babur's smile faded, "I know why you object Sunny, I know! If I have felt it, I am sure you have felt it too. Something about this thing is not right."

Sunny looked up, "So you agree with me."

"Yes, I can feel that there is something about this operation that is going to cause us a huge deal of trouble." said Babur simply.

"Then I don't understand, why go ahead with it? We are not struggling here, we don't need this. We were supposed to withdraw from such dirty work." said Sunny

"Because I must." said Babur.

Sunny did not understand, "Must? Why must? What is so special about this deal?"

"How many times have we done this, Sunny?" asked Babur ignoring the question.

"Done what?"

"You know what I am talking about."

"I don't remember. Why?"

"We have been in this dirty business for so long; we do not even remember how it all started."

Sunny wondered why Babur was being so philosophical.

"All these years we have done whatever we could for power and money and nobody could stop us. We were invincible." said Babur.

"We are invincible!" Sunny shot back emphasizing the 'are'

Babur went on "....and yet there is something that needs satisfying."

Sunny was getting seriously worried now. What needed satisfying?

"Repentance!" said Babur reading Sunny's thoughts.

"I do not know how that cockroach Sohrab is involved in this, but down this road I believe we will both be able to repent."

Sunny was shocked. He did not know how to react.

He wondered how much repentance a man would require to save his soul after using children to beg on the streets. Babur had been doing it for years. Disabling them and forcing them to beg for money. Babur had even used older children to sell contraband. That activity had lessened over the years but not completely stopped. There was still a lot of other work that was...evil. Sunny just could not think of any other word to describe what they did for a living.

Repentance indeed!

Babur knew his time was at an end. He had caused too much pain and suffering to be allowed to live a full life. It was a slow realisation that had crept up inside of him that had led to this conclusion. Babur knew that Sunny was right. This particular venture would bring a challenge that they would not be able to handle. This would be how it would end. This too he had realised as age was beginning to catch up with him. Age, it seemed, taught more than most people let on. Babur had faced many adversaries in his youth. But he was too cunning, too devious and today, with remorse he realised, too ruthless. Remorse! Today he felt remorse for all the wickedness he had perpetrated. But remorse was not punishment. His punishment was long overdue. Whether Sunny would suffer as he would, he did not know, but Babur knew full well that after defeating the most varied sycophants in the city, he would find his match down this road. He was sure of it. Babur wondered how and who it would be.

Sunny left Babur to his own thoughts. He realised that this was not the best time. Closing the door behind him, Sunny thought it was best not to waste any time and get to work.

Samar now knew that there was nothing to be found in his father's office. Samar had concluded that not everything his father had been involved in was connected with the office. The cupboards in the office held financial records, supplier details, and sales projections for restaurants and transport vehicles that were run in his father's name. The only exception was that one folder that contained those files which had so perplexed Samar. Samar had the odd feeling that those files belonged somewhere else. Samar had to know. He wanted to know. Suddenly he felt a profound sense of sorrow. How many times had his father asked him, "When will you learn? When will you want to know, Samar? When will you be ready to face the world, Samar?" Samar had never answered his questions. In truth, he had not bothered. Samar wiped his tears and spoke up to his father, "I will learn, and I will make you proud."

Yanus struggled to get a breath. He wanted to scream. He wanted to kick, punch, and then scream. But first he had to get a breath. He tightened his muscles and tried to lift the leg that was pinning him to the ground. He tried to free his other arm but the grip was like that of a vice. Yanus gave up and relaxed the tension in his body, and tried to slip out. Miraculously, the hand on his mouth lifted. The pressure on his back and legs eased and Yanus was able to struggle to his knees. A gruff voice came out of the darkness, "Be quiet!"

Yanus tried to make out who it was. But it was too dark. The figure was turned toward the commotion outside. Yanus wrestled himself out of the man's grip and got up. The man turned toward Yanus. It was the watchman that guarded the orphanage. Yanus thought as much. Yanus had been kicked out of the bed in the middle of the night and then dragged out of the little doorway at the back of the orphanage. Yanus was not weak and had brought down his fists at the man's head and back with as much strength as he could. But Yanus was too disoriented to think of something more innovative. His head was clearing now and he remembered the watchman yelling at Yanus to shut up. Yanus looked in to the man's eyes and took a step further toward him. Strangely, he was not at all afraid of the bigger, older man and was a twitch away from unleashing his right hand at his head. But before he did anything he wanted to know what was happening. The watchman however spoke first.

"Calm down. I was trying to get you away from those men. I didn't mean to hurt you."

"Hurt me? You nearly choked me to death, you idiot. And who are those men? What are they doing?" Yanus pointed outside the window.

"They work for Babur."

"Babur? Is that a person?"

"Most don't know his real name. But everybody calls him Babur. He forces young children to beg in the streets. That is what is happening to the children from the orphanage just now. That tall man is Sunny. He is Babur's trusted friend. He usually disables the children first before putting them out."

Yanus took one more step toward the watchman, "Not if I disable him first." There was a mad gleam in Yanus' eyes as he turned to step out of the darkness toward the captive children. But the old man grabbed his shoulders and pulled him back.

"What do you think you are going to accomplish against that many?"

"I won't hide here like a coward!"

"Fighting against impossible odds is not courage, it is foolishness. Or I would have fought them myself. Sohrab sold these children to Babur to make some money. He left earlier tonight after he told me his grand plan for revenge. It was important that I got to you before they did."

"Why?" Yanus was suspicious

"Now is not the time. We have to leave now."

"We are not leaving without the rest!"

"Yanus, listen to me. Those children are lost. We cannot do a thing, except get killed ourselves. They will kill you straightaway because you are too old for them. We must leave now and fight later on our terms. Trust me. That time will come. Now let's go find some shelter."

Yanus looked back one more time. They really were too many. The old man was right. What could two unarmed men do against that many armed men? It would be impossible. Reluctantly, Yanus turned away from the sight and followed the old man in to the night. The screams followed Yanus for a long time. Yanus quickened his pace and tried to shut them out.

The old man could not believe how careless he had been in his responsibility. He should have known that Sohrab was up to something nasty. He had been behaving strangely ever since his funding had been reduced. But the old man never thought it was going to be that soon, or this bad. He shuddered to think how close he had come to losing Yanus. The boy had been brought to him all those years ago when Yanus was still an infant: for safe keeping. He looked over at Yanus and smiled. The boy had handled himself well. He had not shown fear and had instead wanted to fight. He was enraged at what he had seen. His boss had been right. It was Yanus who he had chosen for his purpose. The old man never found out what that purpose was but Mr. Jabar was quite confident that Yanus was the one he needed. Yanus had never left the orphanage ever since he had been brought there and after he was chosen by Mr Jabar, he had never been made available for adoption. Some or the other excuse had been cooked up to prevent anyone from adopting him. The old man frowned in the dark as a worry went through him. How exactly had the boy been of any use if he never left the orphanage? All those visits by doctors and technicians could have been a farce. What did the boss want with Yanus? Had he got what he wanted? The boss had been very clear: Protect Yanus at all costs. But that had been many years ago. Even those strange men calling themselves doctors had come in many years ago. But the boss was still adamant: Yanus was not to leave the orphanage. Somehow the old man knew that Yanus's involvement in whatever that Mr. Jabar had planned for him was not over. Now that Mr. Jabar was dead, the old man did not know what to do with Yanus. May be he could just abandon him and leave. The boy could take care of himself.

Major Singh had never abandoned his men on the field nor ever entertained the thought of retreating or running away from battle. As he turned to look at the sleeping form of Yanus, he knew he couldn't do that now either.

Damn! Thought Major Singh! That was exactly why Falak had gotten him in to this.

It had been a while since Samar had taken his car out, but he needed this drive. His mind had gone through so many angles which could shed some light as to why his father had hid so much of his work. Not one of his businesses knew that the other existed. Not one of his businesses had ever defaulted on tax. In fact, Samar thought, the tax documents were a little too out in the open for everyone to see. On the outset, everything looked normal. Investments were transparent but there was no explanation for the missing sums of money which his father had personally withdrawn from the bank. A few days back Samar had come across transport consignments about which the accountant in the office had no information. All these thoughts kept swirling in Samar's head as he gunned his sports car through the steep incline of the Konkan Ghats. The one thing that his father had taught him: driving. Samar wanted to forget everything and just feel the adrenaline rush through his veins. The tyres screamed as the momentum of the car carried it in the opposite direction of the steer. Just before the car hit the edge, Samar once again hit the fuel pedal and cut the drift to accelerate out of the corner. Samar looked at his watch and smiled. He had got here 7 seconds quicker than the last time. Samar tried to recollect when was the last time he had been here when it suddenly got dark on his right side. Samar felt the impact before he saw it. A large vehicle crashed on to the side of his car and pushed it sideways. The uneven slide began to lift the car's wheels and threatened to overturn the small car. In the face of mortal threat, Samar's senses had become sharper. Samar tried to block the huge front grille of the SUV from crushing him in his car. The heat radiating from the bonnet bearing down on him was unbelievable and spurred him in to action. Samar had braked out of instinct and his car was skidding sideways toward the mountain wall. The SUV was too powerful and Samar knew he would never be able to break free if he hit the wall. Samar instead shifted in to reverse and accelerated. Samar broke free just seconds before he hit the wall. Samar braked again and spun 180 degrees in to the opposite direction. Samar completed the turn and drove for his life. He did not know who was in the other vehicle and he did not want to know. All he knew was that it was intentional. A dim part in his mind wanted to stop and fight but better sense prevailed and he began to put some distance between him and his attacker. Samar's hands and legs were still shaking. Samar almost breathed a sigh of relief when he spotted an identical SUV right in front of him. It had blocked the road and there was no way around it with the mountain side on one end and the drop on the other.

"So be it." Samar told himself

Samar calmly brought his trusted sports to a halt at the side and switched off the engine. He got out and walked toward the solitary figure standing in front of the SUV. Samar was surprised to realise that he was no longer afraid and no longer shaking. He walked towards the man without fear. The man did not move at all as Samar stopped at an arm's length from him.

"Who are you and what do you want?" Samar saw that the man was injured. He looked old and looked as if he had been in a war zone. His once immaculate suit was torn and burnt in places. He clearly needed medical help as some of his wounds looked deep. But there was no dearth of arrogance or menace and Samar still had to keep his tone in check. Also, the man did not answer his question but continued staring at Samar.

"What do you...?" Samar's words were cut out by the sound of the roaring engine of the other SUV as it came to a screeching halt. A man jumped out and ran towards Samar. Samar raised his fist and prepared to fight but his opponent was too fast and too strong. The punch went through Samar's fist and knocked him straight on to the ground. Samar cried out in the dirt as the huge man straddled him and started slapping him. He seemed to be shouting something, asking a question, but Samar could not make sense of it. Samar was getting giddy with his face being knocked about like a tennis ball. He tried to get up, but it was useless. The man on top of him was simply too heavy. Samar heard the other man say something and abruptly, the slapping stopped. Samar tasted salt in his mouth. He knew he was bleeding. But he had a feeling this was not over yet.

The big man caught hold of Samar's collar and pulled him close. "I will ask you one more time: how do you control it? How do you stop it? Answer Me!"

"Control what? Stop who? What are you...?" Samar felt his jaw creak as the man hit him once again. The man ground his teeth and spoke, "Don't you dare fool me boy. That thing is killing us all. I know you can control it. Just stop it and I will let you live."

Samar had gotten to his feet and looked at the older man who was still staring at Samar. Baring that time when he had mumbled something to the mad bull that was pulverising Samar, he had remained quiet. Samar realized that both men were running scared of something that they thought he could control. These men did not look dumb, but obviously, their adversary was stronger.

"Why do you think I can control it?" Samar's voice surprised not only the two men but Samar too.

The big man started to raise his fist but stopped when the other spoke. "You are Samar?"

"One in a million, of course, I am!" Samar could hardly believe his own guts.

Remarkably, the old man smiled, "You are the son of Jabar Falak."

Samar took a step forward and his tone surprised him further, "I am Samar Falak, son of Jabar Falak. I ask you again, what is it that you want from me?"

Finally, he stepped forward and came face to face with Samar, "This is really amazing! I cannot believe how devious that old man was!"

"Who the hell are you talking about? And what do you want?" Samar asked again

"You will find out soon. Too many have died already." Said the man who had beaten Samar

"Put him in the car and...." the old man started to say to his companion

Samar opened his mouth to protest that he was not going anywhere with them when he felt something brush past his head. Before losing consciousness, the last thing Samar saw was an intense blue light.

For the second time in less than a week, Samar was seated in front of Mr Jadhav who now looked more interested in him than before.

"So!" said Jadhav

Samar waited for the inspector to continue. But the inspector continued to stare.

"So what?" Samar asked

"How did you get hurt? What happened?"

"I told you, we were racing by the hill and I was winning. One of them got ahead of me after the race and blocked me. I thought they wanted to argue about the race but the big guy drove up from behind and beat me up." Samar looked at his feet as if ashamed of himself.

Jadhav looked at Samar and raised his eyebrows. Somehow, Samar knew that the inspector had seen through his lies. Even Yanus was amazed at how lame it sounded. One of the men was as old as his father had been. Old men usually don't race. Samar was sure that Jadhav would know this too, even if he was dumb.

"Don't you have any shame, Mr Samar?" asked Jadhav.

"What do you mean?" asked Samar, a little confused.

"Your father has just died and you are racing cars like school children. Don't you have any sense? Or is it just that your kind is too cold to feel what it is to lose a parent?"

Samar thought that he should be getting angry at someone, an outsider, speaking to him like that about what he felt for his father. But right now, that was not important. Samar kept quiet.

"How did they die, Samar?" Jadhav asked

"I do not know. As I told you, I lost consciousness when I was hit. I did not see what happened after that. I am sorry but I do not know how they died. I woke up in the hospital."

Samar wished he knew more. He knew that the two men had died. He did not know how. But he knew that the second he had woken up in the hospital. He knew, whoever had killed them had done so deliberately. Samar wondered why he had survived. Samar had heard that the two men had died due to severe burns. Samar wondered whether he was just lucky or it was by design. That he was supposed to live. Maybe the truth was somewhere in the middle. Maybe it was not worth killing him for no good reason.

Samar did not know what to believe.

"You can go now, Mr Samar, but you are not to leave the country. You may be called in for questioning at any time at any police station. Kindly cooperate with us till we find out who did this."

"Is there a danger to my life?" asked Samar.

"How would I know?" countered Jadhav.

"You are the police. I thought maybe you would."

"I don't have a crystal ball. Besides, those two are dead and you are not. So I would presume...."

"You are a fool!" said Samar quietly.

The men all around started to look at Samar and Jadhav, expecting something unpleasant. No one had ever spoken to Jadhav like that in the unit.

"What did you say?" Jadhav had got up and was bearing down on Samar.

"I said you are a fool. You have no clue what has happened. You have no idea who has done it. You have no idea who got killed. You know I nearly got beaten to death and instead of requesting me for help you drag me to the station and insult me and my family. You threaten me and even accuse me of being involved in a crime you know well I did not commit. Oh! I am sorry, I mean I could not commit." Samar too had gotten up and was nose to nose with the inspector.

"How dare you talk...?"

"Oh please shut up, will you? I got a measure of you when those children disappeared from my orphanage. You did nothing then and I am quite sure you will do nothing now. Please continue being stupid. Brains just don't suit you." Samar turned and stormed out.

Jadhav stood stunned at the sheer audacity of a teenager speaking to him like that. He could have arrested him on some false charge and teach him a lesson. But these rich kids were sure to have some back up. Or else they would not behave like that. They would fear him. Fear the police. Like all common people do. He would settle it with this brat later on. Right now he had to deal with the two dead men in his area. Now that was real trouble. And these were not the first ones either. Quite a few murders had taken place in city in the last few days. Ordinarily there would have been a huge furore over so much crime, but he had been lucky. The mayhem had gone unnoticed. Not one individual had come forward to claim the bodies of any of the dead people so far. Obviously, he was not going to try too hard to find their kin. He only had to worry if all those people had died because of the same reason or because of the same person. He would have to report to his seniors that a serial killer was on the loose. The media would have to be involved and that was never any good. It was never healthy to let those vultures anywhere near police work. More trouble than they were worth. No! It would be better to wait and see.

Besides all those kids that he had allowed Sunny to smuggle away would mean that a reward was sure to come his way soon. Yes, that would be best. It was time to meet the lion in his lair.

Samar was beginning to think that the 'devious old man' that the man had referred to was his father. He obviously did not know his father, thought Samar bitterly. There was nothing amazing about not knowing your own father. Samar had never really bothered to know. Then out of nowhere, those two had appeared demanding that he control and stop 'It', whatever 'It' was. And now they were dead too. Samar could not believe his incredibly bad luck. Once again Samar entertained the thought of just letting everything be the way it was. The company was making money. All the financial troubles could be taken care of by more senior people in the company. There were people to take care of any irregularities. He had done his job as the head of the company by pointing those irregularities out. Let those who get paid for it, deal with it. He could sit back and relax. Enjoy the comforts of life. After all, he was the C.E.O of his company. Samar clenched his fists. He was kidding himself. There was no going back to the old days. The responsibilities that had come to him had come for good, not for a few days. The picnic was over. All those irregularities had been caused by his father and there had to be a reason for it. Amidst great secrecy he had siphoned off funds to unknown locations and he had no idea where the money had gone. He was absolutely sure no one at the company office knew either. Not even his dumb board directors knew anything. They were nothing but props to show off. They knew less than his receptionist. Only his father was in a position to know what was happening with the money. A position that he had ensured would pass on to his son in his absence or death.

A fresh wave of tears threatened to overcome Samar and he had to fight to push them back. What was it that the man had said; "too many have died already...."

Including those two, thought Samar grimly.

Samar knew there was nothing to be found in the office. Samar was sure that there were more like those two. He had to find them before something happened to them. They were out there fighting someone or...something. Someone or something which he now knew he could stop or control. But first, he had to get out of the office. He had to visit each and every site that was remotely connected to his father's business. Samar corrected himself. It was his business now.

Samar looked at the watch. It was getting late. He had been in the office since evening after returning from the station. He could go home and start fresh in the morning.

Samar ran his hand over his chin. He wondered what kind of security was arranged for the factories outside the city. Better than the one he had for protecting the children in the orphanage, he hoped.

Samar started the engine and raced out of the exit of his office building. Samar looked in to the rear view mirror and did not see anything unusual. With little traffic on the roads, he reached the factory in quick time. Samar walked up to the gates and tried to see through them. Samar could see the guards on the other side of the gate huddled around each other. There were three of them wearing similar uniform and two wearing a different one.

Samar walked around the boundary wall which was the usual 8 feet high and spiked with broken glass and barbed wire on top. Nothing seemed out of the ordinary. The wall ran around the factory and the only gap was the gate at the front. This factory was outside the city limits and was involved in producing steel tools. It was nothing special. It was simple work that was done by simple people. Again, all was normal. Samar started to turn back when a flash of blue light to his right stopped him dead cold. Instinctively Samar jumped on to the ground with his head underneath his hands. Samar waited but nothing happened. All was dead quiet. There was no noise at all. No barking of dogs or the rustle of leaves. Samar slowly lifted his head up and looked to his sides. It was the same blue light that he had seen just before passing out when those two men had been killed.

After a few minutes Samar got up and looked around. Samar did not feel afraid. He wanted to confront whoever it was. But something made Samar remain quiet and not shout out. He was not afraid, but he didn't want to die either. The silence was deafening. Samar stood there for a few minutes trying to figure out if he had not imagined the light. He didn't think so. The flash of blue light had been real.

After a while, Samar got in to the car and drove off without looking back.

The light came on again, but did not follow. The light had followed from the mountain side to the big white building and then to a smaller brown one. Then the light had tailed and waited at the top of the tall building. It had wasted enough time. It was time to get back on the hunt.

Three floors underneath the ground, below the factory, and secure in their underground bunker, the men huddled around the tiny screen which was linked to the C.C.T.V. cameras in the factory above them. They watched with some amusement Samar's antics when he jumped to the ground and then drove off after a while. What was not amusing was what followed. A chill swept the room when it came in to view. The low resolution camera and the old monitor could not hide the awesome presence of the 8 feet tall body. The men noticed it as soon as the blue light came on to pierce the darkness and the black metallic body hovering above ground came in to focus. Not one soul took a breath as their eyes followed the blue light passing over their screen and disappearing over the side. All anticipated a screech of sirens and explosions any moment and continued holding their breath. All was still silent. The light had completely disappeared. It had been unable to detect their presence.

The men all sat down at their respective places, visibly shaken, and a little pale.

The man at the far right spoke first, "I think that settles the matter. We must…."

"No. It is still not time yet!" interrupted an old man seated at the centre.

"Sir, I think Mani is right. We cannot keep hiding till that aberration finds us." said another man.

The old man glared at Mani, "Why did I ever let you in this place? You have destroyed us all."

Mani put a hand on his shoulder, "We did not want this. Nevertheless, you saw it followed the boy here. There must be some connection. Besides, he is Jabar's son."

Suri Chetwal, Jabar Falak's best friend felt all his years catching up with him. He knew there was no escaping the punishment that was coming for them for their betrayal. This time he would not be party to what he thought was wrong. He also knew he was powerless to stop it. He turned to Mani, "Yes, he is Jabar's son. Danny thought the same and you all can see where it got him. None of you are to do anything. Other than the fact that he was followed here, it is evident that Mr Samar seems to be looking for answers himself."

Suri shut down the monitor and started to walk out of the office.

"So?" Mani stopped him.

"So? I think it would be better to let him find them." Suri shut the door behind him.

Every man in that steel enclosed room realised that sooner or later they were going to be confronted by Samar Falak, son of Jabar Falak, which might not be altogether healthier for them than what they had seen.

Scientists though they all were, Mani was sometimes astounded how naïve they could be at times. None of them had understood what Chetwal was trying to tell them. Chetwal had never been confident enough to come out with his convictions and in the end had gone along with the rest. But now he was making it obvious that he was contemplating his own path. Mani did not care. All that mattered now was stopping the machine that was hunting them. The fact that the machine had followed Samar but not attacked him could only mean that there was some link, however limited.

Samar may not have all the answers but he may have some and they had run out of options. Mani walked out of his office and made his way to the communications console. Once again, it was left to him. The operator at the console was a tall and thin man with a pencil thin moustache. He had been here since before Mani joined the team and always made it point to wish visitors a good day no matter what the crises. Perhaps it was his way to keep his sanity in this mad place.

Mani thought about it one last time and decided on his course of action. It was his decision to make.

"I have an urgent call." Said Mani curtly

"Of course, kindly fill in the details and sign the form please."

Mani, familiar with the protocols, was already pulling the pad toward him and quickly filled out the form. The operator tore out and looked at the slip.

Mani looked at the operator as alarm swept across his smiling face. The man wiped the sweat off his face with his hands and started to dial the number.

Yanus quietly crept up the incline and looked below. There was a wall that ran around the area and shielded the trough from view. The steep incline and the wall after it provided perfect protection and cover for activities that needed to be hidden. But a part of the wall was broken at the bottom and provided a view beyond. Yanus crept sideways and aligned himself with the gap to see better what was beyond the wall. Singh was correct in his estimate.

A series of tents had been slung and prepped up by rudimentary supports. Yanus could even see feet sticking out from under the little tents. Yanus tried to count everyone that he could see. Singh threw a small stone at Yanus to get his attention. Yanus looked back in annoyance and threw it back at Singh signalling him to be patient. Yanus climbed down and spoke angrily.

"There are at least 50 children down there and they seem to have been there for a while. How come no one notices them?"

"Welcome to Mumbai, Yanus. This is the dark underbelly of the city which is unseen, unheard, and for most, unknown." Singh turned away and sat down on the ground.

When Yanus did not say anything for a while, Singh asked him, "What do you plan to do?"

"I am going to lead those children out of there." Said Yanus

"Lead them where, may I ask?"

"I do not know, but I will think of something." Yanus replied quietly.

"That is not a good plan, Yanus. Besides we have to fend for ourselves too, you know."

"Better anywhere than here. I am going to get them out."

Singh got up and put his hand on Yanus' shoulder motioning him to stop.

"If you get them out of here, then they become your responsibility. You cannot just dump them anywhere you like. You realise that, don't you?" Singh asked.

Yanus looked in to the old man's face a while before replying confidently, "I do."

Chapter 2

The First Challenge

Yanus walked amidst the sleeping children waiting for someone to challenge him. He knew someone would. These children were a source of income and would not be left unguarded. That was Singh's theory and Singh had warned him to be prepared for a fight.

For now though, everyone seemed asleep. Yanus once again felt Singh's hand on his shoulder, but also saw his other arm pointing to something in the distance. There, in the dark, was the guard, sleeping peacefully.

"Do all guards sleep on duty? Wait here." Said Yanus to Singh

Yanus walked toward the man sleeping on the table and looked down upon him. The man was sleeping peacefully and seemed without any worry, oblivious of the threat now standing above him. Yanus reached down and grabbed his hair and started to pull him up to his feet. The man started to scream and shout, waking up the children.

Yanus did not let go of the man's hair and shook him from side to side causing the man to scream in pain. That's when Singh saw another man, slightly bigger, charging at Yanus from behind.

Singh yelled at Yanus to warn him but Yanus did not respond. Singh started to run toward Yanus to protect him.

Singh looked up to see that he was going to be late. He screamed Yanus' name but Yanus still did not turn. Singh knew he would not make it. He cursed out aloud at Yanus. At the last moment Yanus swung the man in his grip a full turn and slammed his body in to the man charging at him. Both went down in a heap. Neither man got up.

Singh came to a stop beside Yanus.

"Are you alright?" asked Singh.

Yanus seemed surprised, "Why, do I look hurt?"

"No you don't. Still, be careful next time. Also keep your ears open."

"I heard you. I knew what I was doing."

"These men were nothing compared to what you are going to face later, Yanus. It would be best if you do not get too confident."

"Oh yes, tough men who beat up children. That is really worrying."

"It's not men who beat children that I am asking you to worry about." Said Singh

"Who then?" asked Yanus

Singh said nothing. He was sure that Yanus would find out.

Singh turned toward the children and changed the subject, "So, are you going to share with me your grand plans?"

All the children were awake now and were looking at the two strangers with growing fear, wondering what new and strange turn their fate was taking, again!

"Yes! Mr Singh, given that I have never learned how to read and write, I am hoping you could write something for me."

"Write? Write what? What are you going to do?" asked Singh, bewildered.

"I need you to write a letter. Two letters actually!"

"Are you sure of this, Yanus? Putting them back in the orphanage! Sunny might just take them again." Said Singh

"If he has any sense in him, I don't think he will try that again. Not now. Anyway, he will have to figure out that the missing children have returned to the orphanage." Replied Yanus

Singh noticed a look of confusion on Yanus' face.

"You okay Yanus? Not sure about what you are up to, eh?" Said Singh smilingly

"More than fifty children are stolen from an orphanage and forced to beg. I steal them back and put them back in the orphanage. Yet, there is no one to question. No one notices. They might die here and nobody will ask any questions. What is the value of our lives Singh? What are we doing here?"

"Oh! Back to that are we?" Asked Singh

"Yes, we are." Yanus seemed angry.

"I told you Yanus. Most people do not even know such things exist. I have witnessed this for so long...I know it is a part of this city."

"But how can people let it happen?" asked Yanus

"How are they to stop it? You expect them to finish work at 5 p.m. and then go around the city solving problems at night before dinner? Every individual here struggles to survive. Survival is their primary responsibility. Every effort is spent in ensuring their survival. We call it a city, but we live by the law of the jungle: Survival of the fittest. Those who are weak do not survive. It is unfortunate, but true. The mad race for survival does not give decent people time to think about anything else."

Yanus thought about what Singh had said and began to understand people like Babur and Sunny. It was this indifference that people like Babur and Sunny exploited. There was no one to question them, let alone stop them.

"You sent the letter?" asked Yanus

"I did. Remember Yanus, Sunny will not keep quiet. It would be a matter of prestige to him and he will come after you, to avenge this insult."

"I think he has more than his prestige to think about. He has to worry about me. Tell me, Singh, would there be more places like the one we found tonight?" asked Yanus

Singh stopped in his tracks and turned around. "What?"

"I am sure you know of them. Help me find them."

"No. We have wasted enough time."

"Saving those children was not a waste of time, Singh. Besides, what else are you going to do? You are needed some place else?" asked Yanus

"Not me. But you are definitely needed elsewhere." Thought Singh

"Look Yanus, there is a reason why we are here. Rather, I should say, 'you' are here. Running after child traffickers is not part of my responsibility. Besides, you cannot get those children off the streets faster than they can put them back. Like I said, it is a waste of time and dangerous in the extreme."

I also need to take you to Mr Jabar's office. There has to be someone there who can help you. Take you off my hands. Thought Singh but realised Yanus was about to complicate the situation.

"Okay then, we both got our own separate ways. Thanks for your help. Good Bye." Yanus said abruptly and started to walk away, quickly picking up speed.

Surprised, Singh rushed after Yanus. "Hey! Stop! What are you doing?" Singh came to a stop in front of Yanus.

"What?" Yanus asked

"Where do you think you are going?" Asked Singh instead

"I think I made myself quite clear. I am going to find a way to get those children off the streets."

Singh was exasperated. How was he supposed to make Yanus understand that it was not that simple?

"There must be thousands of them all over the city. How will you find them all? You don't have any money. How are you even going to get from one place to another? What will you eat? This is not a game Yanus. There are no winners and losers here. There is only suffering. Think about it, kid. Don't waste your life. You do not have to do this." Singh was hoping Yanus would see sense. He needed Yanus to come with him.

"That is your problem, not mine. I do not owe you anything, Singh. I ended up in that orphanage because someone thought I was not needed and dumped me. I nearly ended up on the streets because someone wanted me to beg with a bowl in my hands. Now, I choose my own path. I will not go down to some other place just because someone else wants me to. It is just that simple." Yanus was quite calm and had said what was in his mind. There were no hidden motives. He was aware Singh still had to explain his actions, but to Yanus they were not important. Maybe later, but now he just did not care.

Singh thought about it for a while as Yanus searched Singh's eyes. "Why are those children so important to you?" asked Singh

"It's nothing in particular. I think I can help them and that's why I will. Can you understand that?" said Yanus

"No! I don't understand. But I will still help you." Said Singh

"Why? What about your little speech about winning and losing?" Yanus gave a little smile

Singh rolled his eyes and shrugged.

"It's nothing in particular. Let's go."

Yanus knew there was something here that he was missing but realised Singh would tell him when he was ready.

"How did this happen?" asked Sunny

"It was too dark. We never saw where those men came from. We tried to stop them, but there were too many of them. They had weapons too." Stuttered the first man

Sunny's gaze shifted to the other man. There was no response. The man just looked at his feet.

Sunny slapped the man...hard. He could not believe it. In all his years of operating businesses in the city, this was a problem that he had never faced. He had been attacked on many occasions in the past. Men had even attacked Babur in the early days. But this was different. This was an attack on the business. Fifty six children had been stolen from right under his nose. It was a failure that was going to be difficult to take to Babur.

No! That would be unwise. Babur had been acting strangely of late. Sunny would have to solve this himself. He would find those children. He would find who did this and then he would take them to Babur. Sunny went through everything in his mind. He decided he could not believe the two guards he had placed over the children, especially about the weapons. He had to know for sure. He had to know the nature of the enemy that he now faced.

"Rohan!" yelled Sunny.

A big man came out of the shadows and stood next to the two guards.

"Put some men out to keep watch over the children. Real guards, not amateurs like these clowns. Rohan looked sideways at the two men who were supposed to be guarding the children.

"What do you want done with these two?" asked Rohan

The men looked alarmed at the question and looked at Sunny.

"They are of no use to me. Throw them out." The men looked relieved and began to move toward the door.

"Oh! On the other hand, take them with you and put them to work." Said Sunny casually and walked out of the room.

The colour drained out of their faces, the men watched Rohan as he caught the back of their collars and began dragging them out behind Sunny.

Night was Sunny's favourite time. He stood under the old bridge and looked out at the small tents erected haphazardly. He could see Rohan's shadow as he talked to the men charged with the responsibility of guarding the children. There had been a time when these children were the primary source of their income. That was many years ago. Things had changed with tougher laws and more focus on beggars in the city, especially children. He and Babur had found other avenues for business and a lot more lucrative. But there were still those who were involved heavily in trafficking. It was impossible to totally rid the city of this menace.

Sunny shook his head. He himself had argued with Babur and advised him against this folly. But Babur was adamant. It was totally unnecessary; Sunny had told the old man. But he would not listen. Eventually Sunny had to divert some resources to keep this business running. Sunny himself was never interested in this and found it troublesome. But the attack had made it personal. The only worry was Sunny did not know who it was that could have done it. Once he found out, it would be a different matter. He had to find out. Sunny snapped out of his thoughts when he heard the screech of the tyres up above on the bridge.

"Rohan, it's time to go!" yelled Sunny and started to run up the way to get on the road above.

Rohan joined him as he got to the top. "All good?" asked Sunny

"Yes! I have told them to keep their eyes open. There is no need to worry, Sunny. They do this every day." Said Rohan

Sunny was looking at the man that had just stepped out of the car.

"I have a feeling Raj is going to change all that." Said Sunny looking at the hunched fellow walking towards him

Rohan gave Raj a dark look, "I don't like that man."

"That is nothing to worry about. He does not like you either." Laughed Sunny

Raj looked up when both Sunny and Rohan were close and lifted a warning finger toward Rohan. The big man paused.

"I think you better stay here, Rohan. I have to speak to him alone." Sunny placed a hand on Rohan's shoulder and kept walking toward Raj who turned the other way.

"You know you keep getting on everybody's nerves." Said Sunny

"By everybody, I think you mean Rohan, don't you?" asked Raj

"Him and most of everybody I know. Nobody likes you."

Raj just stood there and said nothing.

"Okay Raj, what is it?" asked Sunny

"Why the sudden interest in this ghastly business? I thought we were getting rid of...this?" asked Raj

Of all the people who worked for Sunny, Raj was the only one permitted to speak to him like that. They had been together for many years. They had fought beside each other many times. Raj was the best soldier Sunny had at his disposal and his question was more personal rather than business.

Sunny said only one word. "Babur"

"But why after all these years? I thought boss had his people letting go of the children. I thought this petty nonsense was behind us." Raj seemed to be a lot more worried than Sunny had thought.

"Is there a particular reason why you are here, Raj?" asked Sunny

"Do you have any idea where those children wound up?" asked Raj slowly

"Still looking, but I don't care where they went. I only want to find out who did it." Said Sunny

"Sunny, the children are at this moment back in the orphanage where you got them from. I just got it from my people. The owner of that orphanage got a letter from someone to ensure it does not happen again. I just checked it myself. There are more guards there now, private guards in uniform."

Sunny was stunned. "That is not possible. Why would they end up there? What use are they to anyone? And are they the same children or did the owners shift in new ones?"

"That I think is the problem. This was someone who was interested only in rescuing them. Obviously they had no place to go and given the competence of the local police; they went straight to the place where you got them from.

And yes, they are the same ones you kidnapped from that building and some more who were working for those two idiots you stationed there."

Sunny leaned against the railing. "Well that makes things a lot simple."

"How?" asked Raj

"There are more like those children, all over the city run by all sorts of people. From slums to chawls, there are hundreds of runners. This person will try his stunt again. I am sure. He is not after me or Babur." Sunny laughed an unnatural laugh.

"And this time I will be ready. Tell me Raj, you found out who runs the orphanage?"

"The orphanage is registered under the ownership of FS Industries. The man at the top is a man called Samar Falak. He just inherited the company from his father."

Raj got in to his car again and looked up at Sunny. "I am going to check the other camps."

The two men nodded at each other and Sunny turned back.

Sunny watched Raj drive off as his mind wandered off toward Babur once again. Rohan caught up with him just as Sunny got to his car.

"What did he want?" Rohan asked Sunny

"He wanted to know if I still needed you around. He wants to feed you to his dogs." Said Sunny dryly as he felt a vibration in his shirt pocket

"He thinks too much of himself. Just who does he think he is?" asked Rohan

"Take it up with him. Would love to see what happens. I am sure Raj will love it too." Laughed Sunny as he flipped open his cell phone

Rohan turned in the direction where Raj had driven off and said slowly. "Maybe I will. Maybe I will enjoy it even more."

Sunny's attention was elsewhere. His muscles grew taut as he pressed the cell phone to his ear to listen clearly.

Without a word Sunny flipped the piece close and yanked open the door. Rohan got in and asked, "Something?"

Sunny's silence was answer enough. Apparently, this was not the only place.

It had begun to rain. Settled on his haunches, Sunny shifted his weight from one leg to the other. He cupped the man's face and pulled him closer. One of his eyes was swollen shut and there was blood everywhere on his face. The man was struggling with his breath, but still trying to say something. Sunny could barely hear him. "Let me go, please. I didn't do anything."

Sunny turned to the two men and asked, "What was it that he was asking about?"

"He was asking about their parents. He wanted to know what they were doing here." said one of them

"We caught him snooping around the area and talking to the children. He bolted when he saw us." Said the other

Sunny looked again at the two men who had caught this man in his camp. Both had their shirt tails hanging out of their trousers. Both were flexing their muscles and had metal hanging around their necks and wrists. Sunny gave a sigh. He turned back to the face in front of him. The face was still trying to say something. Sunny leaned closer, "What were you doing here…?"

The man began whimpering, "I am sorry. Please. I made a mistake. I didn't know. I thought…."

Sunny's punch lifted the man off the ground and he fell back unconscious. The men who had been flexing their muscles were sobered by the power behind it. Sunny rose and addressed Rohan.

"What do you think, Rohan? Do you think this is our man? You think he is the one causing me trouble?"

Rohan shook his head, "No! He doesn't look like it! It looks more like these two clowns have wasted our time!" Rohan's voice carried a hint of amusement.

Both the men were looking concerned. This is not what they had envisioned would happen when they had excitedly made the call to Sunny.

Sunny turned to the first man and gestured him to come forward. "What is your name?" asked Sunny

The man reluctantly obeyed and replied, "Baseer."

"What do you think, Baseer? Do you think this man could have stolen from me?" Sunny asked

"I…"

Sunny kicked the man right between his legs with a force that sent him flying. His screams were louder than any his own victim had made.

Sunny turned to the other man and made a similar gesture. Knowing what was coming for him the second man stayed rooted to the spot.

Sunny reached out and put a hand on his shoulder and pulled him closer. The second man flinched but didn't say anything.

"Get them both out of here. If they talk, you will answer. Understand?" Sunny pointed to Baseer and the unfortunate snooper.

The man nodded and helped his former victim and his partner to their feet and led them away.

"What a waste of time!" Said Sunny

"You sure it could not have been him? For a second I thought…." Asked Rohan

"It was not a wimp who did it. It was someone with guts. Someone who knows what he is doing." Said Sunny as he pointed to the place where the man had lain and asked, "Did that waste of space satisfy that criteria?"

Sunny did not wait for an answer and walked out.

Rohan had seen the man angry before. He had seen him beat people senseless quite a few times. But this was not anger or frustration. This was something else that was causing Sunny to behave strangely. Rohan suddenly realised what it was that Sunny was going through. Rohan smiled to himself. It must have been the first time Rohan had ever known the man to betray it, Rohan was sure of it. It was fear.

Sunny climbed up the steps two at a time and reached the top in a few seconds. He paused to catch his breath. Frowning, he clutched at his heart. He felt a little tired. He was not as fit as he used to be. He opened the door to his flat and switched on the lights. Sunny promised himself to hit the gym more often and try to make it a habit. He could not afford to be slow or unfit.

Sunny froze. Pinned to the opposite wall on a nail was a note. Sunny ripped it out and read it. Sunny felt an uneasiness that had nothing to do with the stairs; he recognised it now: Fear

It was the next door. Singh was sure of it. What he wanted was on the other side of that door. Singh ran through it and saw another door. Singh went through it too and saw that there was an identical door again. Singh just kept running though doors feeling certain that his destination was beyond the next one. But the doors kept coming and

Singh ran through them with rising fear. The fear kept rising till Singh thought he would drown in it. Singh had to get there before he ran out on courage. Before he drowned, before his courage drowned, he needed to get through that one last door. Singh reached out for the lock with his hand and just then felt a tap on his shoulder.

"Wake up Singh, you want to sleep all day?" asked Yanus

"What time is it?" asked Singh groggily

"What does it matter what time it is?"

"You know Yanus, this is ridiculous!" said Singh getting up on to his feet

"What is?"

"Do you realise that you never answer a question and instead ask one of your own?"

"Isn't that what you always do?" replied Yanus

"There you go again!" Singh got up and grabbed his watch trying to make out the dial.

Singh groaned. It was just 5 a.m. That's why he couldn't see properly. It was still dark.

"Why are you up so early? Going somewhere?" asked Singh still trying to get his bearings

Yanus was looking at the faint glow coming from the east. The first rays of the rising sun.

"I never miss this time of the day." Said Yanus

Singh watched Yanus looking in to the distance. There was a sinister change creeping up in to Yanus' demeanour that Singh had been noticing in the last few days. Singh walked up beside Yanus and asked softly, "Why?"

"I don't know. I just feel it is the best time of the day. I feel...more alive."

Singh said nothing as Yanus took a few deep breaths.

"Time to go to work!" said Yanus

The air was stale and mouldy. The dim yellow light coming from the solitary bulb was barely sufficient to illuminate the small room. The one window had probably never been opened for decades. A low ceiling and a harsh stone floor gave the room an environment suited to a nightmare. Its walls were decaying and there were enormous webs hanging from every corner. Little kingdoms within empires, for here it was where it all started for Babur.

Babur sat on the floor without any cushion. He had asked Sunny to bring his friend here, of all places. Sunny didn't ask why. Perhaps, Sunny thought, the old man was getting nostalgic.

Sunny didn't like this place. It made him feel claustrophobic. He hoped this was over...soon!

The third person in the room, Sunny's friend, was Sohrab.

Sohrab looked up at Babur and looked away again. Babur was smiling. He turned back to look at Sunny who was standing just a few feet behind him. Sunny looked angry and ready to tear Sohrab apart. Sohrab was nearly in tears. They still hadn't told him what he had done wrong. The wait was killing him. He had no idea how Sunny had found him. But it didn't matter now.

"What happened? Why have you brought me here?" asked Sohrab gathering every bit of courage he had

Babur continued to look at him and smile. Sohrab had never imagined a smile could look so...evil.

Instead, Sunny spoke. "Those kids at the orphanage that you gave us, do you know where they are now?"

"I don't know. With you I thought…." Sohrab clearly was at a loss for words. He had no clue what was happening.

"They were smuggled out of my grounds and put back in the orphanage!" snarled Sunny

"But…but I don't know anything about that. Nothing… I didn't even know where you took them."

"Sohrab, was there someone who was interested in those children before you sold them?" asked Babur

Sohrab turned toward Babur who was no longer smiling.

"I don't know. You know why I sold them. I know nothing about them. Not even where they came from. I swear on my life. Please believe me." Sohrab's hands were pleading and he knew there was nothing else he could do. All he wanted was to get out of here. He would leave the city. Leave the state. Leave the country if he could. But first, he had to get out of this room.

"Leave." said Babur.

Sohrab was not sure that he heard right. But then Sunny lifted him and threw him out. Sohrab nearly cried out in relief. He was sure he was going to die or worse. He got up and ran out of the building. He kept running till he was out of the area. First, he was going to get out of the city. Away from orphanages and the long arm of Babur, he would run as far away as he could.

"This makes matters a little more complicated now." Babur seemed to be talking to himself. "Show me the paper again." Sunny handed over the note that had been nailed in his flat.

Babur looked closely at it.

"Ever seen anything like it before, Sunny? I know I haven't." Babur crumpled the paper and threw it away.

"The message is clear enough." Said Sunny

"The message was clear the first time this person hit us. But this…." he patted his pocket "…. this is different. This is a challenge." Sunny knew what Babur was thinking.

Sunny kept silent. He wished he could leave. He wanted to get some fresh air. This room had a way to make a person feel as if he were condemned to stay here forever.

"What do you want me to do?" asked Sunny

"Nothing."

"Nothing? What about this Samar? He may be the one responsible. I could make him talk."

"Maybe, but I do not think so. Rich boys like that don't go around slums looking for the dead and dying. Whoever it is, it is someone connected to the children on a personal level. It could be anyone.

Keep a close eye on all our assets. I am sure this person will come to us. Soon."

That is simple, thought Sunny. The unease began to grow in Sunny's mind. He had never been asked to sit back before by Babur. Babur may have his reasons but Sunny had to know who had done this. He could not wait to be found out by some upstart. He had to find them first.

Rohan slammed the glass on the table. The people around him ignored him and went about their conversations. Such emotional outbursts were a common phenomenon and nobody paid any attention. Rohan staggered to the door and walked up the path leading to his flat. He wanted to get back at Raj for insulting him, time and again. He was enraged that Sunny too had laughed at him. He had worked for Sunny for as long as he could remember. He had done whatever he had been asked to do, but still it was Raj whose judgement counted with Sunny, not his. That would change, thought Rohan savagely. He knew this city better than anyone. He will show Raj what he can do. And Sunny too! Rohan was unable to focus on the road and couldn't distinguish between the road and the pavement.

He fell a few times but struggled back on his feet. Rohan wished he hadn't had so much to drink. His body was out of his control. Rohan fell one more time and this time, went completely to the ground.

Rohan opened his eyes. He could taste blood in his mouth. He was still unable to see clearly. He realised one of his eyes was still closed. He couldn't remember what had happened. He tried to focus his eyes on the surface he was lying on. Rohan groaned and tried to get up. It seemed he was still outdoors and had tripped and fallen on the road. He must have fallen flat on his face. He knew he shouldn't have had that much to drink. He didn't even know what time it was. Rohan tried to get his bearings. It was still dark and not a soul on the street. Rohan threw up and fell back on his knees. Rohan got back on his feet and started to jog to get some fresh air. He felt a little better on his feet. But once again, Rohan felt his knees buckle and he collapsed on the road.

"Is he still conscious?" Rohan heard a voice ask. He tried to speak up but none of his senses were helping him.

"I think he is. It's the alcohol. He can't feel a thing. He's spent more time on the ground than on his feet all night. A sober man would have passed out by now. But the alcohol in his system has numbed his senses. He can't feel any pain. This is just one more reason why drinking is bad for your health." Rohan tried to make sense of who it was but still his body wouldn't respond.

"Shut up old man! It's not the alcohol. You hit like a girl. Help me lift him."

Rohan felt his body being dragged off the road and on to the pavement. He saw blood trailing in front of him as the two men lifted him and dropped him on to the side wall.

"Hello Rohan! We heard you were looking for us. Fortunately, we were looking for you too. Before we say what we have to say, is there anything you want to say? You might not get the chance later on."

Rohan fearfully looked at the two men, petrified. He wanted to ask something, but he couldn't remember what it was. He looked up again to see the man raise his hand. Thankfully, this time Rohan passed out.

Sunny raced the steps to his flat and stopped at the door to catch his breath and to look for any signs of a break in. There were none. But there were none even the last time. He opened the door and barged in. Everything was normal. He took a deep breath and settled down on the wooden chair. It had been a long time any problem had caused him this much stress. He knew he should not have gotten in to this dirty business. He had tried to warn Babur but he too wouldn't listen. Sometimes, he felt Babur actually wanted to be punished for his crimes. That in itself was maddening. If it hurt him, why do it again? There were lesser reasons to do it now than back then. Back when opportunities were limited to smuggling. He decided to sit with Babur and try and convince him to abandon the children and look after other interests that needed far more attention and his guidance. Sunny stroked his chin and wondered why he too wanted out of this muck? Somehow, within the last few days, he too had realised that something far darker and deadlier awaited them both down this road. But unlike Babur, he didn't want to see it. He wanted out. There were a lot of things that he wanted to do before anything happened to him. There was a lot more that he wanted to achieve. This particular adventure, Sunny thought, had run its course. It had to end as soon as possible. It would be difficult to convince Babur, but he would try. It was too much trouble looking out for something that they couldn't see. He had even detected uneasiness among his men. Sunny promised himself that he would go easy on them. They were after all, risking their lives. Sunny got to his feet, his mind made up. He would go to Babur first thing in the morning and explain the problem that he and his men were facing. He felt tired and worn out. He had spent the entire day looking at the security of the children and even when they were out. Far more men looked out over the slums than ever and he was sure he had closed every loop hole that could be exploited. With these thoughts in his head, he finally drifted off to sleep.

Even the tents were gone. There was nothing left. There was no trace of the children at all. Sunny stared at the open space with a passive expression. He had stationed extra men here yesterday. This was the last place he had visited as it had been the closest to his house. He looked over at the four who were supposed to be guarding it. They stood silently waiting for their punishment. Sunny wondered what he should do with them. He should have them whipped, he thought. But really, he thought again, would that solve anything? If there was one thing he had learned from Babur was that he had to respect his enemy's strength and not punish himself or his men for failing. And it did look that they had tried. There were bruises and cuts wherever he looked on them. Still he had to reprimand them. There had to be some consequences. Lest his men think he had gone soft.

"Only two men then?" asked Sunny

Three nodded but one, an older man, shook his head.

This was interesting, thought Sunny.

"Why are you shaking your head? Were there more? How many men did it take to beat you?"

The older man didn't look scared, but did look a little angry, Sunny was happy to note.

"One was an old man, no less than 60. But the other was a kid, no more than 20. It was the younger guy who...." The man looked angrier with every word he said

Sunny nodded and turned toward the empty ground. One thing was becoming clear. These two were targeting only children and putting them back in some or the other orphanage. Sunny remembered all those years ago when Babur explained the basic rules of this dirty business. No kidnapping was to be allowed. Babur was adamant about that rule. They could not use children whose parents might possibly be searching for them. In view of these events Sunny was glad he had listened to Babur.

"I wish I could get my hands on those two." Sunny spoke to himself

The answer came in the form of screeching tyres. Sunny looked up to see Raj getting out of his car. Something about the urgency in Raj's step told him that there was more to this day than disappearing children.

"Everything okay, Raj?" asked Sunny in mock casual tone

Raj walked right up to Sunny and spoke in a whisper so Sunny's men could not hear, "Rohan got in to a fight last night. He got seriously injured. I got a call from Jadhav's unit an hour ago. Somebody helped him in to a hospital. The doctors had to call the police because it looked like an attempt on his life." Raj paused for a breath and leaned back.

Sunny was stunned. It was impossible. Nearly everyone knew Rohan worked for him. That made Rohan an asset of Babur. Who in this city had the guts to stand up to the might of Babur? Sunny brushed his hair out of his face with his fingers. Attacking people guarding businesses was one thing. Attacking people unnecessarily quite another. Rohan was not as experienced as Raj or some other men that Sunny knew, but he was smart and wouldn't pick a fight to show off. He knew when to fight. Raj was wrong. Rohan had been attacked. Rohan wouldn't get it in to a fight. Someone had started it.

Sunny turned to one of his men, "Separate these four. Tell them not to repeat to anyone about their work here."

"Where should I put them up?" the man asked

"Send them to Costa. I owe him a few men anyway. That should shut him up for a while."

The four men followed the man away from the ground. Sunny hit the last man on the head as he passed him, "Use those muscles for something other than sleeping."

Sunny shook his head and turned to Raj, "They're not like us, Raj. Too soft and depend too much on things like gyms and empty trash-talk. They're not hard like us."

"Rohan was hard. He was tough. It must have taken something tougher to beat him." Said Raj

"I need to know who's doing this. Rohan will have the answers."

Raj pressed his lips together and looked away, unable to explain.

A look at Rohan was all that was needed. Raj was glad that Sunny had come down to the hospital to look at Rohan. Men had been injured before. Some had paid the ultimate price. But Sunny had never bothered before. Visits to the hospital were definitely out of the question. Raj obviously appreciated that Sunny for once thought that information was important. That this was a battle of wits as much as it was of power had been clear to Raj the first time those orphans had been smuggled from under their noses. The warning to Sunny had shaken the very core of the underworld. The warning was a veiled challenge. He had known that Sunny would not take the warning lightly but was also sure that Sunny had not fully understood the nature of the problem. Raj had spoken to the people who had been guarding the children at the sites from where the children had been taken. Whoever it was, they wanted the children and the guards had been in the way. Now it was Sunny's turn. Sunny had made the basic mistake of not understanding his priorities. For years Raj had advised Sunny against child labour. Though Raj could not have foreseen these events he had always known that this business would spawn a greater evil. Now Sunny's reputation was on the line. His mania of following Babur to whatever end had brought him in the direct line of fire of whomever it was that was behind this. Word too had gone around of the challenge to Sunny and indirectly to Babur.

Finally Sunny had grasped the magnitude of the problem. Every pair of ears and eyes that could be used had been pressed in to service. Finally Sunny was waking up. Every bit of information that could be used was being gathered. Every resource that could be summoned in the name of Babur had been summoned. Raj watched Sunny staring at Rohan and tried to understand what could be going on in his head. Whatever it was, hopefully, Sunny got his priorities right this time. Raj knew that priorities in this business, like in any other business had to be in the right order. Raj was not an uneducated fool who had been drawn in to this life for lack of choices. He had years of experience at corporations. He had once led a normal life. A life he had shared with his loved ones. Raj closed his eyes as a tear threatened to run down his cheek. That was another time, a different life... a different hospital. He shut the painful memories away before he was overwhelmed. Now was not the time. He had to focus. Hospitals always had this effect on him. The feel and the smell, the people lying on the beds...whispering

"Well, he's not talking." Said Sunny

Raj instantly came out of his reminiscing. "I know. I just wanted you to see." Said Raj

"I have seen enough. Come on. We're wasting our time." Sunny walked out of the room

Raj looked at Rohan one last time and followed Sunny out. Sunny was already in conversation with the unit inspector. Raj's brow tightened. His eyes were mere slits. How many times did he have to tell Sunny not to talk to the police in full view of the whole world? Raj came to a stop beside Sunny.

The inspector stopped talking and greeted Raj. Raj simply stared at the man. He mildly wondered how once upon a lifetime ago, he actually feared this witless worm.

Sunny snapped his fingers in front of the policeman's face to get his attention, "You were saying...Mr Jadhav."

"Ah...yes! This is how we found him. We're waiting for an eyewitness to come forward. But in the absence of a complaint I can't do much. I have also sent a notice to the owner of the orphanages where these children are ending up. He hasn't responded so far. Maybe he is the one..."

"Did you just say that you can't do much?" Sunny asked with a smile

"I know you want me to find out who did this, but I cannot...."

Raj abruptly patted Jadhav's shoulder and walked away. Jadhav turned to see him but Raj kept walking, apparently not interested.

"Err...what happened to him?"

"Jadhav, could you please explain your reasons to Babur? I am sure he will understand." Sunny too walked away.

"Sunny...please, listen to me." Jadhav wailed but Sunny too didn't want to listen and kept walking without looking back.

Jadhav bit his lip. This was a fine mess. Now he was supposed to look for gangsters! If only he could use his staff to do it. There was no way he could justify using police personnel to search for a person who had crossed a known mafia boss. It didn't even make sense. *Why do such things happen to me?* thought Jadhav. On the other hand he didn't fancy his chances in a meeting with Babur either. He was sure nothing good would come out of that.

Jadhav began to sweat. That would never happen. He would never get as far as Babur. Raj would make sure of that. Raj had been a proper Damocles' sword hanging on his head for many years. His usefulness to Sunny had prevented Raj from taking his revenge on him. Jadhav swallowed. He knew Raj would never forgive him for what he had done to him and his family. If only he had known what Raj was going to become. A common man, weak, and fearful had turned in to a monster. Raj had a deadly reputation for cunning as well as cruelty. He had to find a way around this.

He could lose his job. He could go to jail if it became known that he was helping Babur. But Raj would probably skin him if he didn't. Then there was Sunny. Then there was Babur. Jadhav was nearly in tears. It was his worst nightmare. It wasn't even his fault.

A light flickered in his brain. He thought again about prison. In one instant the plan came to him.

He quickly got in to his car and sped toward his station and called for the constable on duty. The burly man entered his cabin with a salute.

"Kamble, issue a circular to all the night patrolmen to be on the lookout and bring in for questioning any young man of medium height and build. He is accompanied by an older man. If they see anyone like that, detain them immediately."

"Is it anything serious? I have not received any complaints." The man asked

"No. There are no complaints. Nobody wants their name on record. But everybody wants to be safe. Nobody wants to come forward to testify. But everybody wants us to catch criminals and put them behind bars on the basis of what we think. I could go on and on."

"I know what you mean, Sir. It's always been like that. I wish citizens could understand the difficulties we face in fighting crime." The man looked a little annoyed himself

"Anyway, issue the circular and ask the men to report to me in case they find anything. The target is around twenty years old and has a dark complexion. The older man with him is above 60. But the focus is to be on the younger one. Any of the night patrol men see people like that moving about the streets at night, they must detain and bring here immediately." Jadhav repeated

The man wrote everything down and left, leaving Jadhav to his own thoughts.

He remembered the description Rohan had given before he had passed out in the hospital. He wondered why this man was after Sunny.

"Go home and get some sleep, Sunny." Raj kept his eyes on the road

"I can't sleep. Not with all this going on..." Sunny said

"That boy will not move in the day and we can't keep waking up to news in the morning. I am going to be out in case something happens."

"Raj, I am going to make this man pay for the trouble he is giving me. I swear I will."

"You need to find him first. Please Sunny, let's meet Babur and then go home. We need to be out tonight with clear heads."

"There is no need to go to Babur. Besides, there is nothing to report. And we're not going home either."

Raj was surprised and relieved to hear the ring of command in Sunny's voice. He was beginning to get worried.

"What do you want to do then?" asked Raj

"Remember Adi?" asked Sunny

"Yes. That's fine. We'll stop there for the day." Said Raj

Raj knew that soon they would face an adversary that was unlike any challenge that had ever faced. Contrary to popular belief, a man fighting selflessly for someone else usually had higher levels of motivation than those who fought for themselves.

Sunny watched as Raj made the usual enquiries with the guards at the camp. It had been two nights but there had been no incident at all. Raj had gone about his business during the day and the two had spent the last two nights moving between different locations. But there was still no sign of the two men.

This was a big camp and there were quite a few guards here. It was probably the safest and Sunny wanted to move away to the next one. There had been no news from Jadhav either. He didn't expect anything from him. Raj too had made it clear that there was no use expecting anything from Jadhav.

"Everything is normal. Kuni there has a few boys missing since afternoon. They didn't show up." Raj had walked up to Sunny

"Hmm. Forget that. You know some usually figure a way out to disappear after a while. But nothing else?" asked Sunny

"There is nothing else." confirmed Raj

Yanus watched as the two men talked to each other in the beam of the car's headlights. Yanus could not listen to them clearly and just caught a few words here and there.

"Have they left?" Singh looked a lot more tired than usual

Yanus saw the men get in to the car and drive away. He waited a few minutes and jumped down from the wall.

Singh understood and settled down on to the ground. Yanus leaned on the wall and counted the minutes in his head until a random thought came to him.

"Why did Samar not come to visit the orphanages?"

"We wouldn't know if he did. It does not matter, anyway. The children are well looked after now. His presence is not required. He has put the right people in the right places..." Answered Singh *"...just like his father used to."* Thought Singh to himself

Yanus let go of the matter and started to walk out toward the camp. Singh followed.

The guards at the front were the first to notice the two men walking toward them. They were seasoned men and not prone to panicking. The first one raised his arm to block the approaching man's advance.

"Stop! You're not allowed here."

Yanus held the outstretched arm in his left hand and said, "....own this place, do you?" and smashed his other hand to the side of the man's head. The blow took the man to his knees and he fell to the ground. The second man was already on Yanus with a punch aimed for his belly. Yanus's kick got him first. The second man doubled up with pain screaming abuses. Singh pointed toward the rushing figures.

"Wake the children, I'll deal with them." Said Yanus calmly

"They're already awake. Watch out!" screamed Singh as men poured in from a gap behind the wall.

Yanus caught the fist of the man, who got to Yanus first and pulled him closer to whisper in his ear,

"That's not good enough."

Yanus brought down his punch on the man's head and dropped him.

Singh ran through the camp herding the dazed children toward the other end of the camp, away from the fight.

Singh reached the edge of the ground and looked back. It was not a fight. It was a mockery.

Yanus fought like the devil himself. The men tried their best. They attacked him with sticks and belts. But Yanus was simply too quick. He didn't duck or dodge the way Singh had been trained to when he was younger. Yanus fought with ease, sometimes not even looking at his opponent. He blocked and punched back. He caught their silly weapons and turned it on them. He moved between them like a ghost. What struck Singh was the power of his blows. Yanus didn't simply stop or block. He annihilated them. It took five minutes. Seven men were lying injured on the ground as Yanus silently walked through the camp to join Singh.

"The children are good?" asked Yanus

"Yeah, they're okay. What about you?" Singh knew the answer but asked anyway

Yanus looked at the children. They were quite young. Younger than the ones he had lived with at his orphanage.

"Let's go. We have a long way to go. Can they walk that far?"

"That's what they do all day. They will be fine. It's you I am worried about. Try and keep up."

Raj didn't even bother to answer the phone. He watched as the screen lit up from the dash and he saw the number flashing. Sunny screamed and Raj spun the car around and raced toward the camp.

They were back in less than ten minutes and less than thirty minutes after they had left it. Their guards were huddled around each other.

Both got out of the car and ran toward them.

"What happened?" screamed Sunny

"They came and...took the children." Stuttered one of them

Sunny could see that they were hurt badly. In a fit of rage, Sunny slapped the man closest to him and then punched another.

Raj wiped the sweat of his brow and waited for Sunny to finish.

"I don't believe this. This is...this is not possible." Screamed Sunny

He picked up a stick lying on the ground and started hitting the already injured men. Sunny flailed them until the stick broke. Sunny looked around for something else and went for something on the ground.

But Raj stopped him and said quietly.

"They have to succeed every time. We need to succeed only once. We will find them."

"They have no idea who they are messing with!" screamed Sunny and stamped his feet on the ground

"They will." Said Raj

Raj grabbed the collar of the nearest man, "Get yourself and these men to Old Mill camp. Stay there."

The men hurried in to a van and moved away.

"Raj, these two are striking us at will. We need to do something. If word of this gets out…."

"Word will get out. We can't stop that. But we will make examples of these two. I have a plan."

Singh was twisting and turning again in his sleep. Yanus knew he was having bad dreams again. It was happening a lot these days. Ever since Singh had agreed to help him, there seemed to be something going on with him. All those veiled questions; remarks about his character, Yanus knew they meant something. Singh wanted to take him some place but wouldn't say where until Yanus agreed to come… and not ask any questions. Even now Yanus did not care what Singh had on his mind, but sometimes he wondered if there was more to his life. Singh had agreed to help him and largely due to his help he had been able to free children from seven different locations. It was three days since the last attack. Singh was adamant that they should plan their attacks on different days and keep their frequency random. More difficult had been locating Samar's orphanages. It had to be orphanages under his name. The letter he had sent made it absolutely clear that there were to be no questions asked when children were brought to the orphanages. So far it had worked. Singh had even told him that he had seen more security guards around the buildings with proper staff. The security guards were competent and were expecting children to be brought in. No questions were asked. At least Samar had learned his lesson and was taking the security of his assets seriously. It was time to wake the old man. It was time to catch bigger fish.

Raj looked on with an impassive face. Sunny was clearly stunned. This boy was unlike anything they had ever seen. He had gone through the guards with ridiculous ease. Sunny saw his best men chasing a wind as it cut through them. Within a few minutes, the men had been injured enough to lie on the ground and not make the mistake of getting up. Yanus now stood among the children like a statue while the older man spoke to them. Raj patted Sunny's shoulder.

"It's time to go."

Raj and Sunny had got the call from one of their guards who had been keeping an eye on the camp from outside. One such guard had been put up at every camp with the sole duty of relaying any incident to Sunny and not to engage the enemy. The call had come to Sunny just twenty minutes ago and Raj had belted through the streets to get there as soon as possible. The man had been instructed to follow the two and not lose them. But Raj wanted to get there before they left and so they had; to witness a mauling. Yanus had demolished every guard stationed there with ridiculous ease.

Raj and Sunny ran back to the car. Raj got in and waited for the group of children to come out on to the street. Sunny waited outside on the other side of the street in the shadows close to the street lamp. But there was nothing to worry. The children emerged on to the road and were being led in the other direction. It was so easy. After days of frustration, their target was walking down the road surrounded by children. Raj frowned. He looked closely. There was only one adult with the children. Where was the other? Raj turned to warn Sunny who was also looking at the crowd from less than 12 feet away from him. That's when he saw him. Sunny's attention was on the children and he never heard Yanus creeping up behind him. The boy had crossed the street from behind them and crept up to where they were hiding. Raj shouted but it was too late. Yanus caught hold of Sunny's collar and swung him around. Sunny, however, was no slouch. He had not survived the streets of the toughest city in the world by being weak. Quickly realising what was happening, he used the momentum to swing a punch on Yanus' head. Yanus rocked back and looked up to see Sunny swinging another punch at him. Yanus took the punch on his face and fell to the ground.

Raj had jumped out of the car and ran across the road to join Sunny.

"This is it? This is it? That's what you got? You think you could steal from me, you little dog?" screamed Sunny as he aimed a kick at Yanus.

Yanus rolled over and tried to get up. Sunny got down on his haunches and spoke lightly, "You will not be able to do anything after a while. But before you lose your memory, the use of your limbs, and your speech I need to know why you did this?"

Yanus looked up from under his brow. There was strange smile on his face that sent a shiver up Sunny's spine.

"Sunny...get back." Said Raj softly

Raj realised something was wrong. But Sunny raised a hand to silence him and leaned closer to Yanus to hear what he had to say.

"You know I was getting tired of doing this. I thought you would never show up." Yanus was positively smiling now. Yanus was up on his feet and had risen to his full height. Raj noticed that the boy was nearly as tall as Sunny who had also gotten up to face Yanus.

"What do you mean?" asked Sunny

But Raj had understood. They had not tracked him down. The boy had drawn them out in the open. They were not the hunters. They were the hunted.

Sunny watched as Yanus came close to him and whispered, "Got you."

Sunny erupted with rage and lunged forward to punch the boy, "Why you...."

Raj saw Sunny lift off his feet and sail past him as Yanus kicked him squarely in the chest. Raj turned back to see Yanus raise his hand to strike him. Raj tried to block the punch to enable him to land one of his own. But Yanus was too strong for Raj. Raj took the punch in his chest and it drove the air out of him, pushing him back a few steps. Yanus advanced toward Raj and caught his throat. Raj put his arms around Yanus and tried to smother him. But Yanus did the same and lifted Raj clear off the ground and threw him away. Raj landed with a thud next to Sunny who was just getting on his feet. Yanus advanced toward both of them. Raj noticed that Yanus was not concerned about the fact that there were two much bigger men who were fighting him. There was only anger and Raj realised that he intended to kill them.

Sunny screamed and rushed to meet him. Sunny tried everything he knew. But he couldn't get past Yanus's defences. Yanus blocked Sunny easily and kept slipping in blows that began to take the steam out of Sunny. Raj had no idea how this boy could fight like this at this age. He had to try something different. The boy fought ferociously but Raj understood that there were tricks that he had yet to learn. Raj got up and dropped a kick to Yanus's side. Yanus struck Sunny's throat that send him reeling to the ground and turned to Raj. This time Raj stayed outside the reach of Yanus's arms and punished him from the sides. Yanus took a few hits before side stepping Raj's kick. Yanus caught hold of Raj and swung him around and crashed him in to Sunny who was just getting back up. This hit hurt Sunny badly and he crumpled to the ground again. Sunny was barely conscious. Raj got back on his feet but was hurt too. This little dog had proven more troublesome than they had thought. Raj gritted his teeth and landed a quick punch on Yanus's face. Surprised, Yanus blocked the second punch and gave Raj a shove. Raj, already a little dizzy, lost his balance. Yanus had him right where he wanted. Before Raj could complete his fall Yanus aimed a kick at his head. Raj sensed the kick and turned to his side and took it on his shoulder instead. It was a bad idea as the shoulder took the kick as badly as the head would have. Raj stumbled to the ground clutching his shoulder with his other hand. Raj turned around to see Yanus advancing toward him. Yanus tried to grab his collar and smash Raj's head on the ground but Raj used all his strength to block Yanus's hands. Raj was strong but Yanus was stronger and brought down his weight on Raj who was nearly on the ground. Raj tried to bring his leg up between him and Yanus to break contact. Raj finally managed to throw Yanus off him. Yanus was on his feet in a flash and once again lunged at Raj. Raj saw Yanus come toward him and prepared once more to fight him off. But Yanus stopped midway with a frown on his face. Yanus went to his knees and reached for his back. Raj couldn't see clearly because of the blood in his eyes. But he saw Yanus collapse and fall on his face. Raj slowly got up to his feet. He rushed to Sunny and felt a large bump in his head. Sunny was still unconscious. Raj looked up and saw Jadhav walk toward him.

"Why didn't you shoot him?" asked Jadhav

"Just shut your mouth." Said Raj

Jadhav clenched his fist. "I just saved your life...."

"No, you didn't. You saved your own. What did you do? Shoot him?"

"No. Hit him on the head with my gun." Said Jadhav

"Take him to your station. I will call." Raj had carried Sunny to his car

"Shall I call an ambulance? Sunny is hurt badly."

"I will worry about Sunny." Said Raj

"Tell him it was me who got him, huh. Don't forget!" cried Jadhav as Raj started the car

"Cuff him before he wakes up, you moron." Shouted Raj as he drove off

Jadhav looked at Yanus's inert form and thought *"....now how much trouble could a young boy cause?"*

Singh realised something was wrong when he reached the orphanage and Yanus had still not caught up with him. He was not sure if Sunny would show up, but Yanus wanted to double check around the camps. He had been doing that since the last few raids. The guard at the gate simply opened the gate and let the children in. In addition, there was a huge woman; the biggest woman Singh had ever seen standing behind the guard. She eyed Singh as the children gingerly walked up past her in to the entrance of the two storey building. Singh avoided her gaze as worry filled him about Yanus's delay. As the last of the children filed past the gate, Singh turned to leave. It was best not to linger. Singh saw the woman give him a tight smile. Singh couldn't bring himself to smile. If anything had happened to Yanus, it would all be his fault. For now, all he could do was wait.

Jadhav cupped Yanus's face in his hand.

"What is your name?"

"Yanus."

"Yaa-nus? What? What did you say?"

"Yanus"

"That is your name? Yanus? What does it mean? Where are you from? Are you from the North?"

Yanus felt the wire cutting in to his wrists and tried to take the weight off them by trying to ground his feet. But all his feet could do was to lightly skim the floor. It was not enough to take his weight.

Jadhav punched Yanus in the stomach, "Answer my question, you little dog."

Yanus's scream startled Jadhav so much he nearly tripped while backing away, forgetting that Yanus was in chains.

Getting back his composure, Jadhav smiled a little, "You think you are tough. Do you even know why you are here? You are going to see Babur soon. Know who that is? A while back, you were nobody. Now I have made sure that the world thinks you are a murderer. Once Babur is through with you, you will come back to rot here forever. You see, serial killers are never allowed to go free...ever. Of course that is if you are lucky, you will have to survive Sunny. And there seem to be some other people who are interested in you as well...the kind of people I don't want to get in to trouble with. But Babur gets first priority. So, your prospects are not looking good, 'Yaa-nus'. Be as tough as you like. But this is the end for you."

Jadhav let a small chuckle and left the room.

A constable came up and wiped the sweat off Yanus's face.

"Please let me down. It hurts." Yanus pleaded.

He looked at Yanus for a while and left shaking his head.

Yanus balled his fists and tried to find courage within him.

Singh looked at the pavement where he had last seen Yanus. The blood lying around told him that there had been a fight. He couldn't find any tell tale sign of gun fire, so that was good news. But there was no sign of Yanus. It had to be Sunny. Sunny had been his major worry since the beginning. Singh wished they hadn't separated. It must have been him. Yanus would not have been prepared for Sunny. Sunny must have overpowered him and taken him to Babur. Singh swallowed. That must be it. Had he been killed, Yanus would have been left here to rot. He had been taken alive. There was only one thing to do. It was time to pay his old friend Babur a visit.

It was near morning. It had been more than four hours since Yanus had been half hanging to the ceiling. Yanus could no longer feel his arms. He could no longer feel himself. The door opened and Jadhav walked in with a constable in tow looking fresh. Yanus saw the constable from last night looking inside the cell but he didn't join Jadhav.

"This is one of my good friends, Mr Yanus. He will take good care of you. Better than I did last night. Until you are released or die of old age here, you and he are going to be spending a lot of time together. Have fun." Jadhav turned to leave when he heard a voice.

"Ja...dhav"

Jadhav turned to look at Yanus. But Yanus was staring at the floor and didn't seem to have moved at all. Jadhav smirked at the constable and left.

Yanus looked up to see the man unbuckling his belt. Yanus looked straight in his eyes and said, "Let's begin."

The man laughed and launched himself at Yanus.

Every part in his body was aching. Raj wished he had used his gun. He dimly wondered why he hadn't. He had plenty of chances last night. But it had been an awesome night. And it had been an awesome fight too. Sunny too had been badly injured but he had recovered and woken up with a stream of abuses. He couldn't believe he had been knocked unconscious by a boy and he wanted to go to Jadhav's unit and kill Yanus. Babur had expressly forbidden any such antics as exposing links with the police was out of the question. Sunny was to stay with Babur and the boy would be brought before them. Raj had given specific instructions to Jadhav to bring the boy here so that he could take him to Babur. This time Raj would take no chances. As he leaned on his car, he felt his gun under his jacket. Besides, Jadhav must have been working on him all night. Raj checked his watch. It was past the time Jadhav had to be here. Raj wondered if he should have gone to the unit but Babur had specifically told him not to meet with the police where people could see. Raj slammed his fist on the hood of his car. Something was wrong! Where were they?

Yanus had been dragged out of his cell and bundled in to the jeep. He was thirsty and hungry. He was sleepy and he was tired. But above all else, he realised his feet were no longer tied. Sure, his hands were tied but at least he could rest his feet. Jadhav got in to the front of the jeep with a driver and the constable who had given him his special treatment got in the back with him. Yanus felt his ribs, his legs, and his face. Every part he could see and feel was either cut or swollen. Yanus swallowed and looked out from the open end at the back of the jeep. Yanus smiled to himself; *there was nothing official about it.*

"So Mr Yanus; fun time ends for now. Time to go see Babur and I am sure you will have a great time there too." Jadhav seemed to think he was funny and laughed at his own joke

Yanus ignored Jadhav and kept a watch on the driver. He wanted to time it perfectly. He wanted a perfect spot or it would be of no use. There will only be that one chance and he didn't want to waste it.

He had nearly given up hope when after an hour of driving and another half a dozen bad jokes he saw what he wanted: A small bridge over a dried up river. That was as good a place as any to crash a car.

Without warning, Yanus leapt forward and yanked the steering from the driver's grip and turned it as much as he could. The powered steering immediately threw the vehicle off the road and crashed on the railing. The driver braked as hard as he could and send the vehicle in to a spin. Jadhav was thrown forward and he went through the windshield and landed on the hood. The man in the back had held on to Yanus's body and pulled him back. Yanus used the momentum and brought down the heavy manacle on his head, knocking him out. Yanus saw the driver get out of the vehicle and jumped out to meet him. His hands were still tied but his adversary was too slow to react. He clumsily tried to punch Yanus which he easily side stepped. The driver took the manacle on the side of his head and he dropped like a stone. Yanus ran back to the back of the vehicle to check on the constable who had beaten him up. He was conscious but dazed and not alert. Yanus went to the front to check on Jadhav. The windshield had cut him before giving way and Jadhav was writhing in pain. Yanus took the keys from Jadhav's belt and set himself free. Yanus wanted to punish the two men for what they had done to him. But he was still too weak. He could barely stand and this little adventure too had taken its toll. Yanus could feel blood trickling down from behind his ear. This was not the time. He had to run and save himself while he could. Yanus leaned down to Jadhav's face and whispered, "See you soon, little man."

Sunny kept quiet as he listened to Babur. Babur was in one of his moods. Sunny knew a reprimand was due. He had not kept more guards or he had communicated too much to the police or just something that Babur had to get off his mind. Sunny sincerely hoped that Babur was now beginning to realise how risky and unnecessarily complicated this business of child labour was getting. It was too much to handle with very little resources at hand and where were the profits? Not to mention the whole sordid affair put everyone on an edge. Not one of his men was ever excited when he stationed them at the camps. No one was comfortable with forcing children and he was getting sick of this ancient nonsense. It put him on an edge too. He just wished Babur could see what he could. Mildly, he wondered if Babur knew it. He remembered the conversation that had taken place just after that little rat Sohrab had left. Babur had spoken of repentance.

"This boy will go to prison and stay there, Sunny. You will not touch him and there will be no further discussion." Babur finished

"How long do you think Jadhav will be able to hold him? This mess has gone public. People are already asking questions. If we don't do something now, somebody else will. He might go to work for someone too..."

"Killing this boy will solve nothing, Sunny. There is something afoot that I still cannot understand. That a mere boy has caused such trouble is disturbing. Do you not see that none of the other bosses have moved an inch? They too sense something far serious than just a troublemaker." Babur seemed a little worried and kept staring at something that Sunny could not see. That apparently was not the only thing they were not seeing together.

"Okay, so if you think this is more serious than what it seems, why allow it to linger? Why allow it to survive? Isn't that what you did? Eliminating all possible threats before they grew was your specialty, why hesitate now?"

Babur finally took in Sunny and marvelled how the young man had grown over the last few years. But he was also disappointed at the lack of depth in understanding.

"You do not become master of anything until you understand the nature of what you face, Sunny. I will say no more as these are lessons you must understand yourself, just as I once did. You will not touch the boy when he comes here. I need answers which are important. Is that understood?"

Sunny smiled. It was his way to reprimand him since the first day they had met. Not once had he regretted following Babur's orders. Without a word Sunny turned and began to leave when the door crashed open nearly hitting Sunny. Babur was on his feet in a flash as one of his men came rushing in to the room.

"There is someone down there shouting your name."

"Who is it?" Sunny asked

The man looked at Babur and cast his eyes downward, too scared to say anything.

Sunny made for the door but Babur stopped him and addressed the man. "Let him in." The man rushed out again.

"What's this all about?" Sunny was agitated

"This is about the other end of the threat. You've met the muscle. Now prepare to meet the mind behind it. I believe there were two men who were hitting our camps?" asked Babur

Sunny remained silent and nodded. Understanding came over him.

Babur led the way out in to the room where the man was being brought. Sunny followed, idly feeling his gun in his jacket.

The man was standing in the middle of the room and didn't seem too bothered by the two armed guards flanking him. Babur entered first and said simply, "Singh."

"Still rolling in the dirt off people's shoes, Babur? Not tired yet?" asked the man

Sunny could not believe what he had heard. The man obviously knew Babur and had dared to insult him...in his home, no less.

"Let's see you roll in your crap, old man...." Sunny advanced towards Singh

"Stay where you are sonny boy. I didn't come here to trade insults with you. Where is the boy, Babur?"

"Hold it Sunny. He is your son?" asked Babur addressing Singh

"Babur, where is the boy?"

"Wherever he is, is my business, not yours, Singh. Take my advice and leave. Our friendship will only allow me to spare you. The boy has caused me too much trouble. He will pay."

"You were never my friend, Babur. And the boy will leave with me now. You hand him over or it will be you who will pay."

Sunny could stand it no longer. The man's disrespectful tone and his arrogance had ignited his rage and he lunged forward to grab his throat.

Sunny opened his eyes to find himself lying on the ground with a sharp pain in the side of his head. He could see the two guards lying on top of each other a few feet away from him. In panic he tried to get up but felt a hand on his shoulder to keep him on the ground. Sunny heard the man speak again.

"That is really surprising, Babur. The boy is loyal to you."

"Just as you once were." Said Babur

"I was loyal to a man who was my friend and brother. You are not him. The boy...Babur, I will not ask again."

"He is not here. Judging by what I have seen, I have no idea where he is. You must leave Singh."

Singh leaned toward Sunny who froze instantly in his prone position.

"He will turn on you, just as he did on me." Sunny heard Singh whisper in his ear, but loud enough for Babur to hear him.

Singh reached the door when Babur called him one last time, "Singh."

Singh stopped and looked back to stare in to the eyes of the deadliest man he had ever known in his life.

"You are right, Singh, we could never be friends. Don't cross my path again."

Singh turned and left.

"You okay, Sunny...boys?" Babur nodded towards the guards and Sunny

It had been many years since he had seen Singh. The old man was still agile. Babur was proud to see that Singh was still the same. Sunny obviously could not face up to someone like Singh. But this changed everything. If it was Singh who had anything to do with Yanus, then things were a lot simpler than he had thought.

Sunny got up holding his head. The pain came and went in droves.

"Who was that?" asked Sunny

"Someone I thought I knew. It does not matter."

"So this guy walks in, throws his weight around and walks out. And you say it does not matter." Sunny was a little annoyed

"I say it does not matter because those two will not trouble us again. Like you said, Sunny, eliminate trouble before it grows on you. This man was driving that boy against us. Not anymore."

"This will not look good on us Babur...."

"It will not look at all. Nobody will know. Pursuing these two will get us nothing other than ridicule for getting involved with nobodies. No news will settle the matter. And Singh knows the score."

"That's what I am interested to know. The score, I mean."

"Like I said, someone I thought I knew."

Before Sunny could say something, his phone buzzed. Sunny answered the call and spoke for a few moments.

"Was it Raj?" asked Babur

Sunny nodded. "He found Jadhav's jeep in a ditch a few kilometres away from where they were supposed to meet. The boy is gone."

As Sunny had expected, Babur was not surprised. He merely nodded.

"Tell Raj to drop the matter and get back to work. Enough time has been wasted already."

Babur's mind seemed to have made up. Sunny asked a question to which he already knew the answer.

"Of course, the camps will remain. Maintain the security and be alert."

Sunny knew there was nothing more to say on the matter and left. He was still not convinced and wanted to argue. His ego had taken a beating and he wanted to get back at that old man and that boy. A lot of effort had gone in to trapping the boy and nothing had come out of it.

Patience, Sunny told himself. An opportunity will arise. If there was one thing Sunny had learned from this business was that there was a positive in every action. Sunny's mood lifted. Now he knew who the two were.

Looking at the stars and the moon always calmed Yanus. Now, more than ever he had to remain calm. He was hurting everywhere and Yanus wondered if any of his injuries were serious. It was a good thing he had Singh with him. Singh had taught him how to find his way back to a designated spot in case they got separated. Yanus had somehow managed to reach where they had slept the night before. It was always an abandoned warehouse, a park or some other place which was locked from the outside. Singh avoided open spaces as much as he could. Yanus wondered where Singh had picked up so much about surviving outdoors. Singh had once said that surviving in a city was far easier than surviving elsewhere. Yanus did not want to ask where 'elsewhere' was and had focussed on learning as much as he could. Sometimes Yanus thought that Singh was hiding something from him that concerned him. He had known that the day he had rescued Yanus when Sunny had arrived. Then Yanus had not bothered, but once in a while Yanus' curiosity got the better of him and he drifted in his imagination about a family and having a home. That was perhaps what Singh knew. May be he knew his parents or somebody who was close to him. Yanus shook his head. He was 18 years old and had there been a family, they would have come to get him. More obvious, he would never have ended up in that infernal place. Yanus felt like throwing up. Where was Singh? He should have been here long back. In fact he should have been here waiting for Yanus as it was he who was late. A worry crept up in Yanus. Had Singh been caught too? That policeman had not mentioned anything about Singh nor asked any questions about him. They must have known about Singh. Or did they?

"Yanus!"

Yanus smiled. Obviously, they didn't.

Yanus looked around the warehouse with its stock of scrap metal. It was a perfect hideout. They could stay here for days and no one would know.

Singh turned around a corner and appeared before him.

"You're late, old man." Said Yanus

"And you're hurt. Your plan did not really work out, did it? Had to run for your life, after all?" Singh got down and started to check his injuries.

"I didn't count on that policeman showing up. He works for Sunny too?"

"None of your injuries are serious. You are lucky your bones didn't break. In war Yanus, it's the things that you don't count that hit you..."

"Okay, I got it. Spare me the lecture. I will get back at Jadhav later..."

"Jadhav?"

"The policeman who arrested me called himself Jadhav. I thought his jokes would kill me."

"You are not going to get Jadhav or anyone else, Yanus." Yanus stared at Singh.

"Don't look at me like that. This is over. You understand? We are not wasting time over this anymore."

"Singh, what's got in to you? You know why we were doing this? Those children..."

"Listen to me, Yanus." roared Singh

Yanus was startled to see Singh shout like that. He usually expressed his displeasure with silence.

"You nearly got yourself killed today. Had you not escaped Jadhav, you would have been at the mercy of Babur. That man would have skinned you alive. There would have been no escaping from there."

"So that's got you concerned. One minor setback and you want to run away. What did you think? It was going to be easy? I have started this war and I will finish it, with or without your help."

"No you will not." Said Singh

"Who will stop me?" asked Yanus getting to his feet

The fire seemed to have gone out of Singh. He seemed to be fighting an internal battle.

"Do you know who owned the orphanage where you grew up?" asked Singh out of the blue

"I know it was Samar Falak. What's he got to do with this?"

Singh shook his head, "Samar is the only son of Jabar Falak. It was Jabar Falak who owned the orphanage."

"Good for him. What should I do about it?"

"17 Years ago you were adopted by Jabar Falak." Said Singh simply

"What are you saying, old man? I have never met this man." Yanus knew something was coming

"Of course you haven't. He did not adopt you because he wanted you for a son. There was something else he wanted. I had known Jabar Falak for many years. But he was very secretive about his work and did not have many associates. Obviously none of his associates were his friends. Around 25 years ago Jabar started visiting orphanages around the country. His businesses were spread around the country and he donated generously to every orphanage he visited. Nobody noticed that he was not only visiting orphanages but was actually bringing a lot of them under his management. Are you still with me?"

"Of course I am. Where do you think I would go in the middle of such a gripping story? Go on."

Singh wasn't sure if Yanus was mocking him but decided to go on and keep it concise. He had decided that he would tell Yanus everything he knew...if he got the chance.

"In reality, he was looking for something...or someone. That someone was you."

Singh let it sink in for a while. Apparently this bit of news had not impressed Yanus as he had thought. Yanus was looking at Singh without any expression of surprise. Singh went on.

"You were found in an orphanage in the northern most reaches of the country. Whatever it was that Jabar was looking for, he found it in you. When he did, you were immediately brought to Mumbai and placed in the orphanage where you grew up. Jabar Falak forced me to retire and I was placed to protect you until you grew up."

"You have been at the orphanage all these years to protect me?" Finally Singh had Yanus' attention

"Not just protect, you were never to be adopted or sent out for any education or for any of the social activities that the other children went for. You were to be kept isolated. All records of your birth were destroyed by Jabar Falak soon after you were brought here. I do not have all the details, but I know Jabar went to great lengths to erase any record of your existence. Of course, as you have seen, these days there are too many of that sort on the streets without anybody's help."

"But why did he do it?" Yanus' voice was weak

"I am sorry Yanus. I do not know. I had a career that I was pursuing. It was my dream. But Jabar Falak saw to it that I sacrificed it to protect you."

Yanus said nothing as he sank to the ground. Singh too lowered himself and spoke softly.

"I cannot understand what you are going through. I won't pretend that I do. All I know is that somebody went through a lot of trouble to protect you and perhaps prepare you. Running after gangsters might jeopardise your safety. I do not even know what might be at risk."

"You have no idea why Jabar did this? Then let's go ask him." Yanus' voice hardened

"Jabar Falak is dead."

Yanus just stared at Singh waiting for more.

"What does that mean?" asked Yanus

"It means we have to be very lucky if there is someone who knows what to do with you. I think it is time to meet Samar Falak. However, we must not get our hopes up too high. Like I said, Falak was extremely secretive."

"Why not?"

Singh smiled a little.

"Now I wish you had met Babur. You would have had a measure of how devious people can be."

"Have you met Babur?"

Singh remembered that he had neglected to mention today's episode to Yanus. But he decided to be truthful to Yanus. It was the least he could do.

"Babur and I grew up together and were best friends. We both chose different lives and eventually our lives drew us apart so far that now we do not even recognise each other. Of course for many years we had worked together and I know well the capacity of Babur. There is not one person living I know of who could take on Babur and win. He is too powerful and no one can cross him. He is not a paper tiger, Yanus."

"Surely you could..." began Yanus

"No I could not, not a chance. Like I said, there is not one living soul that could go against Babur and survive and I am talking about influential and powerful people here. I am talking about mafia, high ranking ministers, and even influential businessmen."

"Not one living soul..." said Yanus very slowly

Singh smiled again and clapped Yanus on the back, "Catching on, are you?"

Yanus looked at Singh for an explanation.

"I told you. You should have met Babur and you would have got a measure of how people can be. I would not be surprised if Samar Falak knows nothing about you."

"If he doesn't, then who will?"

Singh was relieved to see that Yanus was intrigued and wanted to know more.

"At the moment Samar is our only hope and that is who we have to meet. Get some rest Yanus. I am sure you will want some time alone with your thoughts. I have told you all that I knew."

Yanus nodded

"I just hope Samar has answers."

"Yeah I hope he does. For now, forget about Jadhav and Sunny and focus on something that is going to be more important in your life." Singh got up and threw a small bag at Yanus.

"Put that on your wounds. It will help. See you tomorrow."

Yanus caught the bag and turned back in his bunk. He took out a tube and applied it on his arms and legs. The burning sensation started to fade and in its place came a soft cooling one. Yanus felt a tear roll down his eye. He wondered what could have been so important that one man had done so much to protect one child and that same man may not have shared his biggest secret with his own child. Singh was right. The world was not as simple as it seemed. It was full of people with secrets and lies. Nobody seemed to do anything for what it seemed. All had hidden agendas and ulterior motives.

Yanus knew one thing as clearly as he had ever known. Whatever it was that this Jabar had wanted was not going to prevent him from destroying Babur. Singh knew a lot. But he was wrong there.

People were not machines. The strengths and weaknesses of people could change from time to time. All men were fallible. Nobody was invincible. Babur was no different. Yanus now knew what his strengths were. Somehow Yanus also knew that his strengths were also his greatest weakness. What he needed, Yanus thought, was a plan.

In all his years at the orphanage, there was not one time he had ever felt out of place. Looking around at the grand statues of unknown people, the indoor fountains, and the large photos on the walls, Yanus felt that this was a place to wake up every morning. Yanus smiled to himself thinking about his little bed back at the orphanage. One wrong step and you would step on someone's face. There was enough space here for a thousand people, and yet just a few people walked about talking in hushed tones. The people were a little odd. Everybody you looked at smiled, but quickly averted their gaze. Except the annoying woman Singh had spoken to when they got here. She had not moved her eyes away from either of them ever since she had asked Singh to wait. The silence of the place was unnerving. It was the woman, Yanus was sure of it. It was as if the woman was sucking all the noise away from the room. Yanus looked right back at the woman. To his surprise, the woman continued to stare at him. Yanus thought to himself, *"What are you looking at?"*, but kept his thoughts to himself. Maybe it was because he looked like a tramp. All the people here were dressed in immaculate clothes and polished shoes. Yanus looked down at his feet, his 1 size too small canvas shoes were threatening to fall apart at any moment.

"How long is it going to take? I thought this Samar would want to meet us.'"

"Why did you think that? I told you, he might not know anything. Anyway, he is not here. So that is good." Said Singh

"How is that good?" asked Yanus

"No news is good news." Said Singh and looked at the receptionist and raised his head as if to ask, *"What's up?"*

In his opinion, Yanus thought, no news was bad news.

"Does that old lady know when he will be back?" asked Yanus

"She said he is not here, but might be back soon. So we have to wait."

"She doesn't know when?" Yanus persisted

"No! Have some patience, Yanus." Singh sighed.

Yanus walked around and took in some more of this new environment. But the novelty was wearing off. He imagined that people must be getting used to this place; even become part of it. He looked at some of the pictures hanging on the walls. Some he recognized and some he didn't. The largest picture hung at eye level rather than high up. It had a gold encrusted frame and the man in the picture seemed a lot different than the other pictures. For one, there was no smile and he had obviously not posed willingly for this picture. Yanus was no expert but it seemed to him that the picture was probably taken when the man was busy with something. There was an intensity in his eyes that Yanus had never seen anywhere before. He looked full of purpose and energy. Suddenly it came to him. Yanus turned to Singh who was watching him as intently as he was watching the photo.

"That's Jabar Falak, isn't it?" asked Yanus

Instead of Singh, it was the receptionist who answered.

"Yes, it is. Could you take a seat? Mr Falak will be here shortly."

Yanus walked toward her and put his hands on the desk.

"You mean, Mr Samar Falak?"

The woman nodded, "Yes, now do you mind…?"

"You have been very kind to us. But could you tell us when he was here the last time?" asked Yanus in a voice that made Singh raise his eyebrows. This was interesting. The boy seemed to be up to something.

The woman stuttered and Yanus detected a lack of sincerity.

"He is here most of the time. He has… just stepped out of the office. If you could wait…"

Yanus continued to stare at the woman with a smile that promised murder.

The woman stopped talking and returned the stare.

Finally Yanus turned away and sat down next to Singh.

Singh looked at Yanus with a questioning look.

"Samar hasn't been here for a while." Said Yanus

"I don't get you. How do you know that? You heard the woman..." Said Singh

"She has no idea where Samar is. If I am guessing right, nobody here knows where he is."

Singh thought about it for a minute and then asked an obvious question, "How does that help us?"

"I didn't say it did. I would bet he hasn't been here for a long time. Something is wrong and this woman knows it and she is just as confused as we are. I thought she looked worried even."

"What do you think we do?" asked Singh

"For a start, get out of here. I am feeling all closed in. I need some air."

Yanus could feel eyes on his back as he walked out of the office in to the corridor. Well, he thought, it wasn't a complete waste of time.

Singh walked out of the building with a feeling of dread. His one hope had eluded him. What was he going to do now? He looked at Yanus and felt irritated with his confidence. Yanus didn't seem to care that Samar was missing. Maybe he left for a holiday. Singh seriously began to contemplate the option of leaving Yanus alone and moving on. With the death of Jabar Falak, whatever it was that Yanus was involved in could have become irrelevant. The boy should live a normal life too. May be he could try and trace his family. May be it was all for the best. Yanus was safe and he had done his duty. There was no reason to continue looking for needles in a haystack. Singh wasn't even sure if there was a needle to look for. Singh felt a little better and looked at Yanus. The boy was still injured. A few days rest and medication would have him back to normal in no time. Without any pressing matters at hand, Yanus could perhaps pick up his life.

"What are you thinking?" asked Yanus

"Not much." Lied Singh aware that everything depended upon what was going in the mind of Yanus.

Chapter 3

The Path of The Cyclone

Samar stood silent in front of the black suited men. Not one looked up in to his eyes and spoke to him directly. Mani had been speaking for over an hour, but he too had avoided looking in to his eyes. Samar wished he looked up. But not once did Mani lift his head. They all looked like confident men; sure of themselves. Yet, they had made a mistake that had cost many of them their lives. And they were fully aware that it would be a miracle if any of them survived the monster they had created. The purpose of which, Samar still was not sure of. That their petty politics had derailed this ambitious project was obvious, that their betraying his father had sealed their fates but it was the purpose that Samar wanted to know. Why build something like this?

"Get up. All of you." Said Samar in a commanding voice

They all rose obediently and waited.

"Mani, could you please see these silent lambs out of the room? I want to speak to you alone."

Mani smiled and motioned with his head to the others. Yanus got the feeling that Mani was enjoying himself.

Mani waited till he was alone with Samar. Then he sat down motioning Samar to do the same. But Samar remained as he was.

"Who outranks you in this office, Mani?" asked Samar

"A few do. But they are no longer here. I don't know whether they are still alive. So I am assuming…"

"After all the trouble you have brought down on our heads, you still have the guts to… assume. You have some nerve, Mani."

Mani noticed the continued absence of a title before his name and it was annoying him.

"You have questions for me, Samar?"

"Of course I do!"

"Then I think you should sit down. None of your questions can be answered without giving details. Remember, tonight might be the only night when you can seek answers. So make it count. Tomorrow is another story."

Samar thought of saying something but thought better of it. Mani was right.

"Why did my father want these machines built?" Samar asked the first logical question.

"I have no idea. There is absolutely no one who knows why your father wanted them. The whole thing began in the seventies. Back then our technology was primitive. Our economical resources were too restrictive. Even then your father put in a lot of money to identify the correct material, power source, and design for what became the Cyclone. Even the name was thought up by Mr Jabar. Later on, as the project neared completion, certain authorities supported and some were against this project. But still, even they did not know why these machines were built."

"What authorities are you talking about?"

"The first technicians that were recruited to build the machines were engineers employed in various technical fields nearly 40 years ago. These were ordinary working class people who had become part of something incredible. No technology came close to what they were developing.

Ordinary people with ordinary lives had kept the greatest technological innovation a secret for nearly 25 years. Some of whom just left this room a few minutes ago. The late eighties saw a different type of development in the machines: The development of software that would be the soul of the Cyclone. But the later generation of engineers were hot heads who thought too much of themselves. But Jabar preferred to overlook these shortcomings in view of the contribution they were making. I tried to shut them out of the system by denying them unnecessary access to the Cyclone. I feared if they figured out too much of the machine for which they were developing the software they could sell the information or use it themselves. Jabar never allowed any paper work but the location could not be kept hidden."

Samar sensed bitterness in his voice but he kept quiet and allowed Mani to go on.

"I still do not know who did it. But what should have been a matter between your father and the government became a tussle between him and civilians. Someone from within Falak's team had been in touch with a small time minister who I think passed the information on to his seniors. The information snowballed until the highest authority in the country got in touch with Falak. Thank fully this contact went unnoticed by the media. The machines were still not ready and Falak convinced them to stay away till they were. Falak managed to convince them that their untimely intervention could put the project at risk. But the long chain of people in that organisation could not guard the secret either. The armed forces do keep an eye on activities which...might impact the security of the country. That's when the army got involved. Falak obviously felt that decades of secrecy had been blown to pieces."

"I can understand the army, what's with the politicians?" asked Samar

"It's all about control." Said Mani simply

"You don't look like a scientist or a technician to me. What are you doing here?"

For the first time Mani looked a little uncomfortable. Finally Mani looked up and sought out the eyes of Samar.

"I think it is more logical to ask why you are here, Mr. Samar."

Samar stared back at the man's face. The eyes were rimmed red and there were dark circles beneath the eyes.

"No! It would be more logical to ask why you betrayed my father."

Mani looked even more uncomfortable but his voice was strong and even.

"I respected your father, Samar. Nobody here would think otherwise."

"That is your answer?" asked Samar

"No. My answer is that it is too soon for you to come to terms with your father's loss. Thirty years of research and hard work is difficult to explain to someone who has not even lived that long. Even more difficult is to explain the emotions and sacrifices of people who put their lives behind this work."

"I do not understand you."

"Of course you don't. But you will, when you are ready. For now you must trust that your father and I had nothing but respect for each other. We need your help. Hopefully down this road, you will understand."

Samar was having a hard time trying to understand Mani. Mani was giving the same information he had given when all those men were in the room. Philosophies! Hah! Samar decided he had no time for this. It had been a long time since his father had died. Yet it was only now that these people had approached him. For now he had two questions that needed answering. One was simple and Mani had guessed it. Why was he here?

"Let's follow your logic now, Mr Mani. Why am I here?"

"The first Cyclone was completed a few years back. Since then there have only been upgrades in the software. The problems began soon after the software began to be upgraded at rapid speed. Your father had disagreements with some people over the control of these machines. These people in turn had trouble with the top army brass over the same problem. Frankly, I think your father made the mistake of not caring enough about this matter. However, Falak's indifference with matters of security caused us a huge problem. He did not plug the leak that caused this information to get out. But the work continued and details were being leaked to that minister on a regular basis. His party was not in power but they were not far from it. Their interest in our project had been consistent from the beginning. But Falak outsmarted them all. I had always thought that the machines would be controlled by people. But Falak had been working on something else. I learned that Jabar had somehow managed to link all the Cyclones to one master Cyclone. The first one built. The one we named Cyclone R. The control of this Cyclone was linked to your father. I found out about this much later and could not do anything about it. Two days after your father died, we had our first encounter with the Cyclone that has so far killed nearly a hundred of our people. We had no information about this machine."

Samar saw too many gaps in the story. Mani had carefully guarded his own role. He had not named anybody and stayed safe behind terms like 'politicians' and 'army official'. Mani still did not explain what had caused the fall out between his father and the people here. Samar laughed inwardly. This Mani was good. His father must have liked him too. Both liked to play with secrets.

"Dad was gone. Who was controlling this Cyclone?"

"Ah! Mr Samar. That is an intelligent question!"

Samar made a face. What was intelligent about it? But as Samar thought this, he instantly knew why he was here. Samar slapped his hand on the table.

"You think I control this machine? You think that thing is going to listen to me?"

"Not listen! Recognise your command."

"You are nuts. I never knew anything about this till you told me. Dad never told me anything about it."

"I believe you have come across the Cyclone, haven't you Mr Samar?" Mani asked abruptly

Samar didn't know how Mani knew this but he played along.

"I think I have. All your people wear suits like that?"

"Yes! They do. They have been wearing that as a uniform since the beginning."

"Two of your people cornered me some time back and…" Samar was too angry to continue.

"We know about that incident. As time went on after the first few…encounters with the Cyclone, some of us began to toy with the idea that you might have the key to this Cyclone. A few, of course, were getting more desperate and took drastic action. Believe me, we did not approve of it. I am sorry that I could do nothing to prevent it."

"How are you any different than those two clowns?" said Samar angrily

"You noticed that I did not try to drive you off a cliff. Secondly, I told you some of us were getting desperate. Our friends and colleagues were dying and we could do nothing to save them. The idea that you could somehow stop it grew wilder until someone imagined that you knew how to stop it and were taking revenge on us." Mani looked a little worried

"Revenge?" asked Samar

"Mr Samar, every man in this building thinks that we were all responsible for this mess. But of course nobody wants to die."

"That is not a very clear answer, Mr Mani. But your friends were so sure that I knew about the Cyclone."

"Danny was one of the people who were designing software for the Cyclone. Nothing he ever designed was eventually used, but he had been on the team long enough to know what was happening. The other gentleman who was with him was Amar. Amar was one of the first people who joined us and he was one of those responsible for weaponry. Amar was not a highly educated man and I have no idea where Falak found him. I heard that he and Romi had been rusticated for experimenting with illegal compounds when in college. The weaponry used on board the Cyclone is not anything like the conventional weapons that you see on television. Of course at that time we did not know. After the first few kills though, it became too obvious. Anyway Danny and Amar were convinced that you could stop the Cyclone. I had forbidden anyone from leaving this facility. But they disobeyed me. They took matters in to their own hands."

Mani looked sad for the loss of his friends.

Samar however did not find any sympathy for the two. Little pricks!!

"Who's Romi?" asked Samar

"Romi was the one who helped Falak design some of the weapons systems on board the Cyclone. He too is no longer with us." Said Mani before looking away

"Anyway, the Cyclone tracked Danny and Amar down before they could track you down. And you can hide from a Cyclone, but you cannot run. The machine sucked the life out of them in an instant and then took off again. That I think was the first time you came in contact with the Cyclone. Thankfully you survived."

"The strange thing happened after it killed Danny. The machine followed you. It must have followed you all the time until you arrived outside the factory above this facility. When you left, it did not follow. That was the first time we saw it. The Cyclone disappeared from view and we did not see it again."

"Mr Mani, did you know why it did not attack me that day?" asked Samar

"I really do not know." It was Mani's turn to frown. "You were brought to the hospital in an unconscious state, were you not?" asked Mani

"Yes, I was." Samar said

"How did that happen? Did Danny...?" Jabar's voice trailed off at seeing Samar's smile.

"That monster of yours makes a sound when it moves. My back was turned so I could not see it. Danny did but before he could react, I felt something hit me in the back of my head. Before I hit the ground, I saw a light pass over my head toward where Danny would have been standing. I am estimating that the Cyclone knew that I was in the way and it took me out. Amar probably went the same way. At the hospital, I found out that there was no wound where I had been hit."

Mani took in what Samar had said. This was strange in the extreme. Cyclones could not do that. Mani had known that the machine had attacked Danny and Amar, ignoring Samar. But the machine had actually acted to take Samar out of the equation.

"Samar, I really think you should try and control this machine. It did not attack you and in fact it even went out of the way to protect you. There has to be…" Jabar looked excited but Samar cut him short

"No. I do not think so, Mr Mani. I am sorry but that door is now closed."

"What do you mean?" asked Mani completely bewildered.

"Can you tell me anything you know about this link business? I am afraid I am still not clear how that works?"

"All I know is that the main machine's control board has a voice recognition system. The main machine then directs the other Cyclones through a language developed specially for this purpose. The only problem is that the main machine also has a system that was developed for one other purpose. That was to read DNA. This was to be done right at the end when we were to decide whose voice the machine was going to recognize. Apparently, Falak had already decided."

"Can't it be changed? Usually…."

"No! It cannot be changed. That knowledge resided in Falak's brain. He had said that he would eventually show us how to link a machine to its human controller on a permanent basis, but given what happened later he may have regretted his promise. He never did reveal it anyway. Once it is done, it is final. The machine is now live and the only one who controls it can allow any changes to be made. Why do you think it is not you?" Mani asked

"I think this machine has not been made according to your usual specifications." Said Samar

Mani once again looked worried, "What do you mean?"

"You are right. It did follow me. But it did not come in contact. If it was exactly as you say, then it would have, but it didn't. Obviously, my dad didn't think I was the right person."

Mani detected a hint of bitterness in Samar's voice. "What is your problem in life, Samar?"

Samar looked up to see Mani boring in to his eyes. "What problem?"

"You sound like you have a problem with your father."

Samar nearly shouted, "No! No problems. You pricks build machines and then let them loose. You put in a Start button but forgot to put in a Stop button. Now you expect me to stop it. Dad never told me anything Mani, nothing at all. Apart from that, everything is just fine. No problems."

Mani sighed. "Samar, your father loved you. He did not tell you anything because he wanted to protect you. No good has come out of this. Please understand that your father made a lot of sacrifices and a lot of enemies because of this. He nearly went mad trying to develop a machine whose purpose he could never fully explain to anyone. He lost his wife when she was just beginning to understand all this." Mani gestured towards the room.

"My mum?"

"Look, any solid reason why you think that this machine will not recognize you?" asked Mani instead

"Yes! The last time we came in to contact, the machine came to the conclusion that I was not connected to it in any way. My estimate is that the DNA link in that machine could only be recognized by Dad. It may have got confused as I have the same genes as my father. But obviously, that was not enough. A limited connection through blood, but it is not on the level which the machine reads. I think the machine made the same mistake that you are making, thinking I am my Dad. I am not. I know it. The machine knows it too. You should accept it."

Mani had no answer to Samar's logic. It did sound like Samar was right. That meant that they were back to square one. Mani suddenly felt tired.

"Mr Mani, this particular Cyclone was built without your knowledge?"

"Yes! I did not know about it till after your father died."

Samar had waited till now to ask this question.

"How come my father built a machine just to hunt you down? What did you do?"

Mani too had feared this question. It was a question that had been feared by everybody who worked here. That was why nobody had wanted to meet Samar. He had a right to ask. He had a right to know.

Mani rubbed his head and took in a deep breath.

"Your father thought we betrayed him." Said Mani simply

"Why did he think that?" Samar asked

"I told you Samar. Things are not as simple as they seem to you. There is no black or white here. There was too much animosity and years of frustration that took its toll on people."

"Yeah, it killed my Dad." Samar shouted on the top of his voice

Mani paid no heed to the raised voice and answered calmly

"Do you know how your Dad died?"

"He was found dead in his office. The autopsy report said that it was a heart attack."

"For years your dad fought for his right to control the machine that he built. Yet eventually the stress got to him. I have no doubt that your dad had got in the way of too many important people and he knew that his life was in danger. Yet he persisted with his beliefs. It came to a point that sometimes I felt that your father was losing touch with reality. Yeah, he had a heart attack. But his indifference to issues surrounding the Cyclone was the reason why he had it."

Samar stood up angrily and shouted, "Don't talk about my dad like that you…you traitor."

"That my boy is a matter of perception. We genuinely believed we were acting for a greater good."

Samar was breathing heavily and wanted to hit Mani.

Mani on the other hand was cool. "Sit down Samar. I believe we can still help each other."

"What could you help me with? And what use am I to you now?" Samar's voice was still hard.

"You were asking about the Cyclone that was built by your Dad. What's your reasoning?"

Samar sat down again and put forth his theory, albeit a little rudely.

"The Cyclone that was built to attack you has no connection with the other Cyclones. That much is obvious. Did you try to control the Cyclone that was actually built to do that?"

Mani had an answer for that.

"Good point. The Cyclone that we have in our possession is the one we always thought was the one to control them all. It was this machine that we were supposed to link with a person. That's where the focus was. We thought that it was controlled by your father and it went dead after your father passed away. We have tried everything we know. But it will not respond. We do not understand the technology that your father came up with."

Mani ran his hands through his hair.

"All the while that is what we thought. And Falak went ahead and built that abomination without us knowing. I have no idea how it is functioning without anyone directing it. Obviously your dad knew about software a little more than he let on. He probably understood the machines better than he understood himself." Mani looked frustrated

Samar felt a gush of pride surging through him. He wished he had valued his time with his father. Samar blinked his tears away.

"The machine here, Cyclone R, would respond only to Dad and we do not know anything about this other machine which probably was also controlled by Dad. Things are not looking good, Mr Mani."

Mani was looking a little more frustrated and said with some difficulty,

"Would you give it a try?"

"Okay Mr Mani. I will try but do remember that further decisions regarding the Cyclone will be taken by me alone. I want every man here quarantined. Nobody leaves without my permission. I want a list of every call made and received since my father was last here. I want a list of every person who works here and what they do. Do you accept?"

Mani was already smiling. "Will there be anything else, Mr Samar?"

"Oh yes, Mr Mani. I want to see the machine that my father built."

Mani's smile widened. "Welcome to the home of the Cyclones. Follow me."

Ordinarily Samar would have laughed out loud. The whole idea had seemed unreal to him from the start. But he knew people had died. He had seen the desperation of Danny before he too had been killed. Still, when Mani explained the shape of the Cyclone, Samar began to have second thoughts. He got the image of an electricity pole floating in the air, or an elongated egg. Samar suppressed an urge to laugh as he walked toward what Mani had simply called storage room. An odd name for a place, Samar thought, used to house a killing machine. But up close there was nothing funny about Cyclone R. Samar's blood ran cold seeing the tall body resting on a grooved pedestal. It was standing up right at a height that Samar guessed could be at around 15 feet. It was leaning slightly on one end. No part of the body protruded out. Its diameter was at least a metre. Samar's eyes travelled all the way from its base to its head. It was completely white. There were no markings on it, no lights, and no way to tell which end was up and which end was at the front.

"Err… Mr Mani, why does the machine have no features?" asked Samar

"What features are you talking about?"

"Where are its arms? Where is its face? It looks weird."

"Samar, Cyclone R has been designed and built for a single purpose. I think you know what I am talking about. A face and limbs have nothing to do with it. The machine will not be any more deadly with human features. I think you have in your head an image that you have seen in movies. This is not a movie, Samar. This is the real thing. No dramatics and nothing that is not needed. The entire body is a projection of power…."

Samar looked at the place where there would have been a face on a human being. Samar realised that this was the scariest thing he had ever seen.

"Okay I got it. Can we leave? I have seen enough." Said Samar

"No you haven't Samar. Come with me."

Now what? Thought Samar

Mani walked through a metal door followed by Samar and then a long passageway. The entire area was deserted. It did look by all the signs on the wall that at some time, this place must have seen a lot of activity. Now it looked abandoned.

Mani went through a massive doorway and came to a stop. Samar had slowed down to read some of the signs.

'No Flames', 'Time limit: 120 minutes', 'No Sound', 'Entry Without Communicator Not Allowed'

Not your average signs, thought Samar as he sped up toward Mani.

Samar came to a sudden stop at the edge of the doorway. His words wouldn't come out of his mouth. Samar stepped back with dread. Mani's words had not been able to describe this scene. It was beyond imagination. The most obvious question had come to Samar. He just had to know.

"Why in the world did you make so many of these? How many are there?"

Mani said nothing. He too simply stared at the row upon row of Cyclones standing erect in the storage facility.

Samar went closer to one of them. It looked exactly like Cyclone R. There was not a stitch different in design except the size. Around 8 feet tall and half the width of the Cyclone R, these looked sinister because of their multitude. Samar realized that its eerie appearance was largely due to its size and…its simplicity. Like Mani had said, it was a machine designed with a purpose, not for display. What could be the purpose to make so many of them?

"Mr Mani…"

"Falak had been asked this question too many times before I got the opportunity to ask him. I think by the time I got around to ask him, his answer had been well rehearsed."

"Which is…?" Samar wished Mani got on with it. Somehow, Samar also thought that perhaps Mani was deciding whether to say anything at all.

"Our economic resources did not allow us to maintain a huge and sophisticated army. Falak's idea was to build a robot army that would eventually replace the soldier on the battlefield."

"Why did dad have to think up of something like this?"

"I have no idea about that. All I know is that he wanted to give the country a more sophisticated and more powerful army. He realized that it would take time to design and develop such a force. That would mean starting with a design in the seventies that would outclass all rival technologies in the new millennium. That was going to require a deadly commitment and an extraordinary level of intelligence. It was not lightly that your father embarked on such an ambitious project."

"It doesn't feel right." Said Samar

"What doesn't feel right?"

"Let me put it to you in another way. Why did dad feel he had to do this?"

"I think you are weighing the current crises against the viability of this project. Obviously, given the nature of your generation to search for worth, it is understandable."

"Don't jump to your conclusions, Mr Mani. I want to understand this problem. Part of that has to do with why dad built it. You are telling me the advantages of an army of killers."

"Samar, it is difficult for your generation to understand the difficulties that this country faced post independence. We saw our country being dragged in to wars it did not want. We saw our country fall prey to doubt and suspicion from within. We, as nation never got the breathing space we needed to blossom. Year after year, our difficulties with our neighbours and internal issues eroded the strength of our economy. What could have been was lost before it could fully grow. Falak belonged to a generation that saw these problems from the beginning. It was natural for him to want to do something about it. Of course at the time it may have been the succession of wars that may have forced his hand. Maybe he felt that the army needed better weaponry or it could have been any other reason. But the purpose of the machines was simple. There were meant to…"

"…replace soldiers in battle." Samar finished for Mani.

Samar touched the machine and tried to understand what Mani was saying. Samar tried to feel the frustration that his father must have felt. Did he think his creation would make a difference? Mani did say that his father had not liked dealing with the army when it came to deciding who would control the Cyclone. Did his father think that the presence of a robot army would give the country, a better sense of security? Samar knew the answers to these questions as they came to him. The answer was no. Samar may not have known his father too well, but he knew him well enough. Jabar Falak was a realistic man. He did not believe in fairy tales. No machine, no matter how proficient could guarantee the safety of borders. That required human judgement. Mani had either misunderstood his father or his father had not been entirely truthful to Mani. Or maybe Mani was not telling the truth or all the truth.

Either way, Samar felt that this was not the right time to delve deeper in to the subject. He had the information he needed. Now he had to think of a way to solve this problem. At the moment, there did not seem much hope of stopping the machine that was hunting the people here. Samar walked back to the holding area of Cyclone R and looked at it again. This one was his trump card. But Samar knew that the answer to his problem was not here. Something flickered in Samar's memory. Samar turned to a silently waiting Mani who still seemed to be considering his own words.

Samar snapped him out his reverie, "Do you have a fast car? Your friends busted my previous one."

For the first time Samar felt, Mani's smile was genuine, "I think we do owe you a car. You can have Danny's Evo."

Samar nodded and put his hands out for the keys.

The huge glass panel did little to block out the night. Suri Chetwal got that feeling more frequently these days; that the night was chasing him. Suri watched from the factory above the facility as Samar drove away in to the night. He had been here a long time. He hoped Mani had done what he was supposed to have done. Suri heard the door open behind him and close again. Mani came around the desk and stood beside Suri.

"Did you tell him everything?" asked Suri

"He asks good questions, just like his father." Replied Mani

Suri nodded his head a little and said more to himself than Mani, "Its' your head, anyway."

"Any news on Romi?" asked Mani ignoring the comment

"There might have been." Replied Suri

Mani understood the significance behind the statement. Like Danny, they too had tried to do something different. Romi had proposed trying to destroy the Cyclone and Mani had shot the idea down. It was too risky. Romi had disappeared three days back and there was no sign of either him or the 14 men who Mani presumed had left with him. Suri had forbidden any contact with those who left the facility. Mani probably would do the same. Suri was right. There was no point risking their safety.

Romi pressed the cell phone to his ear as hard as he could. He had been trying to make this call since morning. It was near midnight now and nobody was answering. Romi threw the phone away in disgust. That bloody Suri Chetwal! He must have figured out what he was up to and cut him off from the facility.

Romi walked up to the SUV and got in.

"No news?" asked the young man at the wheel

Romi shook his head and gestured to the other SUVs parked in the front and behind their own, "Signal the others. Let's get out of here."

The young man flicked his head lights a few times and waited for a response. Each SUV in turn flicked their lights once in reply: *understood.*

"What next, Romi?" asked the young man

"I don't know. I am sure the rest would vote to return to the facility. What do you think?"

"Now you care what I think? All these years I advised you against dealing with that snake Kasid and you never listened. Now that this mess is flying everywhere around us, you are asking my opinion?"

Romi closed his weary eyes and thought about what to do. The boy was right. It had been a mistake to leak the information. It had brought about more harm than good. It was probably his fault that Jabar had died too. Even Amir here had warned him against meddling with politicians. But his ambitions and greed had overcome his sense. Romi wished he could come up with some way of getting around this problem. His idea to track the machine and destroy it had failed too. It had been nearly 4 days since they had been hunting the machine. But there was no sign of it. Romi knew it moved only during the night. That was when it was most effective. Now, they had run out of options. The only way was to return to the facility and plan ahead. Romi tapped Amir on the shoulder, "Signal them to return to base."

"You don't think we should try and locate the machine?"

"I am worried that the machine might locate us first. I am not even sure how to kill that thing. We need to get back and analyze the information we have."

Amir pressed his lips tight and got out of the car.

Romi watched Amir speaking to the people in the car in the front. Romi regretted dragging all these people with him. He should have listened to Mani. The idea was foolhardy. But he regretted even more for Amir. A brilliant engineer whose career he had groomed from the start. But he had led him astray. This was not the future Amir or even he had envisioned. Amir walked to each car in turn and conveyed his message. A few short words and Amir moved on. It was dangerous to be out like this. Amir returned to the car and got in.

"Be prepared for a severe round of arguments when we get back. People are pissed, Mr Romi.

"I don't think…" Romi's words were cut short by the blast of a horn from the car parked behind him.

Romi jerked his head upward and saw a streak of blue fly past through the roof visor.

Amir screamed as the Cyclone came to a stop in front of the SUV parked ahead of them. The driver of that car tried to ram the machine. Before it could move an inch the Cyclone fired its weapon through the windscreen. The car and its occupants instantly blew up. Amir didn't waste any more time. He reversed as far as he could and then swerved around the car behind him. Romi yelled at the people sitting inside to get out. Even Amir took his hands of the steering and hit them on their window as he shot past them. But every person in there was paralysed. The stationary jeep was a perfect target and the Cyclone fired at it. The car blew as Amir drove just past it. Amir braked and turned the car around to move forward. The other 2 vehicles had already sped away and Amir was trailing behind them.

Amir couldn't see the vehicles up ahead. He tried to locate the machine in his mirror but couldn't see anything. Amir drove as fast as he could to put as much distance as possible between him and the machine.

"Can you see it?" roared Amir

Romi had turned in his seat and was waiting for the Cyclone to follow. He could not see it anywhere.

"No! Keep going as fast as you can!"

Something was wrong.

"I don't think so." Said Amir as he braked as hard as he could and completed a 180 degree spin and brought the car to a stop to face the direction they had come from

"What are you doing? It is right behind us!" shouted Romi

Amir didn't say a word and got out of the car. Romi followed suit. "Amir! What are…?"

Amir was watching the road in the direction they had been travelling. Romi was looking the other way; where they had come from, fully expecting the Cyclone to catch up to them.

Then they heard a huge explosion that shook the earth. Romi turned around to see a ball of fire coming from where they would have been. The machine had by passed them and got one of the SUVs that had been ahead of them.

"Let's go!" said Amir

Amir shifted in to gear and sped away from the sound of the explosion.

Amir wiped tears from his eyes and said a silent goodbye to his friends. He slammed his hands on the steering in frustration and anger.

"You have doomed us all! You have doomed us all, Romi! I hope that Cyclone finds us. I hope we are the ones who burn next." Amir shouted and kept hitting the steering wheel.

All Romi could do was put his hands over his head and try to hide his tears.

Dhir had been driving the last SUV in a line of five looking for the Cyclone. As soon as Dhir had seen the Cyclone sail past above him and the lead car blowing up he had reversed and got out of the area. He had seen the third car standing still and Amir reversing past it in a bid to escape the Cyclone. Only the last 3 SUVs had gotten away. The third explosion had occurred just minutes ago. Amir, who was the last to get out was closest to the Cyclone and was probably dead. That meant that only he and those in Tej's car were left. His fear had pushed out the momentary grief he had felt for Amir. The machine was probably bearing down on him. Dhir was alone in his car and knew he would not survive in a race with the Cyclone. He had to hide. Dhir kept his eyes open for a large gap in the trees that would accommodate the SUV.

He kept his speed up in case the machine got closer. It could not be too far away. Dhir finally saw what he wanted. Dhir slowed the vehicle down as much as he could to prevent the tyres from burning rubber on the ground and eased his vehicle off the road and entered the thick of the trees. He went in as far as he could before the SUV finally could go no further. He had deliberately avoided revving the engine to prevent any noise. He silently opened the door and made his way through the trees without closing the door. Thankfully they had always insisted to wear black. It served as perfect camouflage in this environment. All he had to do was survive the night. He had definitely heard only three explosions. The fourth car must have escaped too. They could link up in the morning and reach the facility. He wished he could have killed Romi himself. Amir had told him many years ago that it was Romi who had leaked the information. Romi wanted a better life. That politician had lost no time in getting his party bigwigs involved and there had been a power struggle for the Cyclones ever since. He wished Sir Jabar were still alive. Dhir hugged himself as he sank down on to the ground. How were they going to get out of this? Had Romi never gone to that man, Jabar would never have…? It was too late to think about that now. Dhir had told Amir to go to Jabar and tell him about Romi. But Amir was loyal to Romi. And Dhir could never bring himself to do it either. Dhir put his hands on his head. They had brought this upon themselves. There was nothing to it. Sooner or later, the machine would find them and kill them all. He had been developing software for it since he had been out of college. Jabar had recruited him and Amir from the same place. He remembered well that day when the big black SUV had brought Suri Chetwal and Jabar to his college. The campus had been abuzz with excitement. There was a sense of mystery about the whole recruitment process as the principle had not given them the name of the company or any other details. The day had ended in disappointment as there had been no interviews at all. Everybody forgot about the incident the next day. Until, a month later, he and Amir were asked to report to the principle. The two men were there waiting for them. He remembered the first words of Jabar Falak, *"Welcome aboard, son."* Suri Chetwal had not so much as looked at him. Jabar had trusted him with some of the more critical software that the Cyclone was to be equipped with. One of them was its ability to track and to hunt. Dhir knew what the machine was capable of. It was not going to quit that easy. Even he was surprised when Jabar had spent hours trying to explain what it was that he wanted. Dhir had been daunted by the task and wasn't sure he could do it. But Jabar had faith in him. Jabar had said so. He had betrayed that trust. Dhir rubbed his eyes and looked up from the ground. His breathing stopped.

In front of him, floating a few inches above the ground was the Cyclone. The moonlight gleamed off its jet black body. Dhir stood up. He had stopped crying. He took a deep breath and held his head high. The Cyclone drifted a little further toward Dhir. Dhir could hear a small hum as it approached him. Dhir swallowed and wondered mildly how it had found him? The Cyclone should not be able to do that.

They had never designed it in that way. But it didn't matter now. He would not die like a coward. The machine rose a few inches in the air and recorded the image in front of it. The image matched its record of targets. Immediately, it fired on the target. The body disintegrated and fell on to the ground. The Cyclone came close to the body and scanned for evidence of life as it had done with all the others. The target named Dhir was dead.

The Cyclone rose up in to the air and proceeded toward the next target.

Amir and Romi had left the car on the road and were following a small trail than ran parallel to the paved road, but through the trees. Romi had always known that the chances of stopping the machine were remote. He thought he could contain it with his own weapons. Romi smirked to himself. He hadn't even been able to get close to it. He still had a chance though. But Romi knew it would be no good to use conventional weapons against the Cyclone. The machine's exterior was built with a material that had been forged in the facility. Only Jabar knew how the raw material had been sourced. Romi knew that Jabar had spent many years trying to identify the metal that would eventually make the Cyclone. Small arms fire wouldn't even tickle it. Large bore ammunition might have some success. Romi idly fingered the gun that was now strapped to his back.

"You think that will stop it?" asked Amir eyeing the weapon strapped to Romi's back

"That is my plan." Said Romi looking at Amir

"I mean no disrespect Romi, but would you stop talking about plans? You are not good with them." Said Amir with a hint on annoyance in his tone

"It's a rocket launcher. It can stop anything. I just need a clear shot." Said Romi

Amir had look on his face that suggested that he didn't believe a word of it.

"It's all we got." Said Romi in response to the look

"Then we are dead. You think Jabar didn't think of rocket launchers?" asked Amir

"I am sure he did. But I have made some modifications here that I am sure Jabar wouldn't think of."

Amir shrugged his shoulders. Romi did sound very confident.

"Let's stop here for the night." Romi settled down next to a large tree and put his gun beside him.

"Let's not and keep moving." Said Amir as he continued walking

"You cannot walk all night, Amir. Listen to me, stop." Romi had blocked Amir's way

"I am done listening to you, Romi."

Romi had known this was coming. He was just wondering when it would really happen.

"Come on Amir. We need to stick together." Said Romi

"It's too late for that, Romi. We should have stuck with Falak too. My best friend has probably been killed and everyone I worked with for that infernal machine has probably been..." Amir couldn't finish

"I understand how you feel..." Romi put a consoling hand on Amir but Amir brushed it away

"How can you understand anything, Romi? All you care about is yourself. What were you thinking? You thought Kasid was going to make you part of something bigger than this. What exactly did he promise you in return?" Amir asked angrily

"I have no time to discuss this with you. I am going to keep walking. I don't think that toy of yours is going to bother the Cyclone anyway." Amir stepped aside and walked away

Romi sank down on to the ground. He could not deny that Amir was wrong. But he was trying to rectify what he had corrupted. If only he got a chance.

"Romi... Romi, look out!" Romi looked up to see Amir jumping toward him. Romi had no clue what was happening until he saw the blue light flickering behind him. Amir's momentum pushed him out of the way of the Cyclone's fire, but it hit Amir squarely in the face. Amir was dead before his torso was ripped apart from the rest of his body by the intensity of the fire. Romi was still rolling in the dirt when he saw Amir fall a few feet away. His fingers found the gun and in an instant Romi fired the weapon at the machine. Romi had needed a clear shot as he had only one round in it. One was all he would need, or it would not work anyway, Romi had said to himself. The one projectile that would be launched would also create a pulse when it would crash on to the Cyclone. The pulse would disable the machine's main control board. Romi had worked on that one round for days increasing its destructive power ten-fold using the rarest compounds.

The impact of the launch threw Romi off his feet and he fell on his back fifteen feet away. Romi let the launcher drop out his hands. It had done its job. So had he. He felt a pang of sorrow for Amir. He had saved his life. Romi tried to get up but his leg wouldn't move. He felt a sharp pain in his right ankle that suggested it had broken. He propped himself against the flat side of a rock to balance himself. He massaged his leg to relieve his pain when he heard a small hum.

Romi looked up to see the Cyclone hovering inches above him. There wasn't a scratch on its body.

Romi's last thought was an apology. He apologised to Amir for wasting his sacrifice. That he couldn't stop the

Cyclone. Romi looked up one last time at the Cyclone, the machine that he had helped built.

The Cyclone fired its weapon. The intensity of the blast shredded Romi and the rock to smithereens.

The machine hovered at the scene for a few more moments to complete its check and began to drift away.

Suddenly the machine stopped. The machine recognized a new program running. There was a change in priorities. There was a new hunt.

Chapter 4

First Blood

Singh woke with a start. It was the slightest sound that he had heard, a sound that was not made by nature. Singh did not move an inch. He took stock of his surroundings from his prone position. He wasn't sure if it was a voice that he had heard or something else. It was silent again. He couldn't see Yanus anywhere but he was sure that he was still asleep. He couldn't sense anyone else in the tiny room that must have served as quarters for the security guarding the derelict building in front. Yanus had wanted to sleep in there but Singh had put his foot down. It was enough that they had nearly become vagabonds in the city but there was no reason to stoop to the level of scavengers. Singh was already making plans to go home. There was no reason to stay here any longer.

It was nearly five minutes since Singh had heard the sound. Singh took a chance and shifted himself to check at least their immediate surroundings. To his shock, the door was opened and Yanus was gone. Singh bolted out of the room and ran toward the building.

Idiot boy, thought Singh. Why did he have to explore all the time? And why did he have to do it at night?

Singh made as little sound as possible as he sprinted barefoot on the loosely paved ground. It was still dark and

Singh kept blinking his eyes to adjust them to the diffused illumination provided by the moon.

Something about the light made Singh come to a stop. Moonlight was not blue! Singh realized that there was a bluish glow in the night that seemed to be emanating from behind the building. Singh's heart beat faster. He tried to place the light as he approached it, somehow sure that Yanus was already there. Nothing Singh knew threw off that kind of glow. Singh hid behind the pillar that was shielding him from the exact spot he guessed where the source of the light was. Ever so slowly, without making a sound, Singh took a peek.

At first Singh couldn't make out the scene. Yanus was standing in front of a black electricity pole. Singh looked again. This time the reality of the scene hit him. It was not an electricity pole. It was something floating in the middle of the air and its top end was giving off the light. Singh stepped out from behind the pillar and approached Yanus. Yanus was rooted to the spot. Singh stood beside Yanus and faced the tall metallic body. Singh had never seen anything like this in his life. It had an intimidating presence and Singh got goose bumps by just looking at it.

"What is it?" whispered Singh

Yanus continued staring at it and did not say a word.

"Yanus!" Singh whispered urgently

Instead of Yanus answering, the blue light came a little closer. Singh started and stepped back. Yanus stood where he was.

"It will not harm us." Said Yanus

"It would have, if it wanted to. But I think it came to say hello." Said Yanus

"Hello…?" stuttered Singh

"Watch this." Said Yanus as he walked around the machine and the blue light followed Yanus as he came to a stop a few feet away from Singh.

"Why is it following you?" asked Singh

Yanus ignored Singh and began to walk backward while facing the blue light.

The machine followed Yanus ignoring Singh completely. Singh was completely confused.

Yanus now turned his back and started to walk quickly, occasionally looking over his shoulder. The machine followed him without trouble. It hovered over the ground and did not seem to be bothered about anything except to follow Yanus.

"Yanus. Wait!" shouted Singh

Yanus slowed down and allowed Singh to catch up.

Singh threw the machine a dirty look as he passed it, but cut a wide path around it nonetheless.

"What is going on, Yanus? Where did that thing come from?" asked Singh

"Around thirty minutes ago. I was awake and saw the blue light. It came to me before I could get to it. It just floated there as I stood watching it. When I tried to back up, it followed me. I heard you running but I was not sure whether it was safe shouting. I don't know what it wants though." Said Yanus

"Do you think it is safe to…?"

Yanus abruptly turned around to face Singh, "What do you want me do?"

"Nothing at all. I just want you to be safe." Singh knew Yanus enough not to test him right now. But this was testing him too.

"Look Singh. I don't think there is anything we can do right now. I need to find out why the damn thing is following me like a shadow."

"And then?" asked Singh

Yanus took a deep breath and looked at the machine floating a little away from him. Yanus noticed that this time the distance was lesser than before.

"Let's take it step by step. I don't think it's going to be possible to get rid of it. So please don't ask me to try."

Yanus led the machine all the way to the little room where he and Singh had put themselves up.

"Stay here." Said Yanus realizing perhaps for the first time how tall the machine was and that it couldn't possible fit in. Yanus entered the room and looked back hopefully. The machine had stayed back. It had followed Yanus' command. Singh stood outside and watched the machine with some trepidation.

Yanus stared at the machine in deep thought. He stepped outside once again and walked around the machine towards Singh. The machine rotated itself to keep Yanus in its line of vision. Yanus wondered how it could see. There didn't seem to be any sign of a pair of eyes.

"I want you to stay here. Don't follow me." Said Yanus to Singh

"What are you going to do?" asked Singh suspiciously

"I need to know something."

"What…?" Singh started but Yanus suddenly launched himself in to a sprint. Singh dove to the side as the machine drifted in Yanus's direction picking up speed.

Yanus looked back to see the machine easily keeping up pace with him.

Now to see if you can keep up! Thought Yanus

Yanus headed toward the building and went through one of the tiny entrances. He took the steps three at a time and kept climbing till he came to a stop on the fifth floor of the deserted building. Yanus held his side as he ran out of breath. He walked toward the open stair well and looked down to see if the machine had followed him. Before he could take two steps, the darkness behind him turned blue. Yanus stood still as the machine rose up from outside the building.

"You really are something, aren't you?" asked Yanus with a little laugh

Yanus walked toward the opening. An entire wall was missing and from this height and he could see the entire area in which the building was constructed. Yanus took a deep breath. This is what he wanted to check.

Yanus looked back and said, "Come closer."

Yanus was surprised it could understand such commands as if they were given to a person.

The machine stood beside Yanus also facing the world outside.

"Do you see that tree?" Yanus pointed. The machine did not respond.

"Destroy it." Said Yanus very slowly

For one instant Yanus thought that the machine had not understood and was about to rephrase his command, but the next instant the machine's top end let loose an intense blue light that sped away toward the ground. Yanus did not see where the blue light had gone but stared intently at the machine.

Yanus finally looked toward the ball of fire that had been a tree a few moments ago.

Yanus nodded to himself and turned toward the stairs.

Singh was standing at the bottom of the stairs with his arms akimbo.

"Had your fun?" asked Singh

"I told you, I wanted to see what it could do." Said Yanus

"You wanted to know whether it could burn a tree?" asked Singh incredulously

"Don't act funny, Singh! I wanted to know if it was armed. I wanted to know if it had firepower."

Singh had a pained expression on his face.

"Yanus! I know what you are thinking and I do not think…"

"I think we have been down this road before Singh. You want to go there again…?" cut in Yanus

"What are you trying to do?" roared Singh

"I want Babur." Yanus said in the calmest tone he could muster

Singh was speechless momentarily, "But…but…." Singh could not think up of a counter argument, He had used up all his resources to convince Yanus and now he was back where he had started.

"You were right at the beginning, Singh. This whole city is a mess. There is no point trying to sweep the mess. It comes right back. There is not a system in the city that could protect those children from being forced in to labour and who knows what else? My little soiree with Jadhav convinced me of the futility of it. People like Babur are above the law. The law does not even exist in their world. Those children would continue to die every day until they run out of breath. How many children did we rescue from those monsters? I lost count at around five hundred. And yet, do we see any difference? They put the mess back on the streets faster than we can clean it."

Singh watched Yanus and wondered if every child that had suffered like this had the same thoughts. For now, he did not have any answers for Yanus. Everything seemed to be going to pot anyways, thought Singh wryly.

"The best way to end this is to get rid of those who make the mess. Finish them and there will be no mess to clean up."

"You think it is that simple?" asked Singh

"Maybe not, but I think it is a better idea than doing nothing. Who have those children got to fight for them? You think the police will one day wake up and decide not to fear vermin like Babur? Why don't you think how to get things done rather than tell me why we shouldn't?"

Singh was surprised that Yanus had not lost his temper or said anything irrationally. There was a calm about him that impressed Singh, even if the issue itself was annoying. Singh thought for a minute and explained something to Yanus.

"The last time I met Babur; there was an unspoken agreement between us."

"What agreement are you talking about?" asked Yanus with a frown

"You see, Yanus, when Babur found out that it was me who was helping you, he knew that Jadhav would not be able to hold you and that you will escape. He guessed that you would know how to. But it also told him about our limits. We agreed that there would be no further trouble from each other, but if we persisted, he would act. This time he will know how to find us and kill us. Believe me, there will be no stopping him."

"Yes, I know that Babur can kill and get away. Like I said, who will notice if an orphan disappears from the streets?" asked Yanus in anger

Singh decided not to rise to the bait and answered in a manner that he now thought was appropriate, "Absolutely! There are plenty more. One would hardly matter."

Yanus looked at Singh in disgust.

Singh ignored the look and went on, "They will not bother protecting their assets like the last time. This time, they will know it is you and all their resources will be directed at finding you, which, I may add, will not be difficult at all."

"I don't see any problem. It's not like I am hiding. And I am not interested in their assets now either."

"You think this machine will protect you, don't you?" asked Singh

"I do not need protection, Singh. But this machine would even the odds against me. Sunny was not much trouble. I don't think he has faced anyone like me. But I understand that there are too many of them. That is what this thing will help with me with."

"Yanus, we do not know anything about this machine. It came to you of its own accord. What if it leaves? How will you defend yourself then?" asked Singh

Yanus looked at the machine. It was silently hovering between him and Singh, as if it could understand their words. Yanus wondered whether it could. Yanus turned to Singh, "This fight with Babur is personal, Singh. One way or another, I am going to end this. I know it will not be easy, but I will still do it."

"Remember one thing, Yanus. Babur is an incredibly resourceful person. He has not survived for so long by being stupid. Once he realizes what he is up against, he will unleash all his weapons. There will be others who will come after you. Are you ready for that too?"

"Ready? Who says I am ready? I might never be ready to fight people who control so much power. I might not last the week against them. But if I don't, at least I will give them a bloody nose."

As realistic as Singh usually was, he could not see reason in Yanus's arguments other than the fact that he wanted to finish Babur. In Singh's experience, sometimes not having a more concrete reason other than desire sometimes worked better, but this was two people with a floating tin can against a vast and organized man power. Babur will not care about a machine; he had people who fought like machines. Not to forget the fact that he could use his contacts in the police and other agencies to hunt for Yanus. Singh had put in some thought in to what the machine could do since it had turned up a few hours ago. It looked like it needed directions to perform a task. This thought gave rise to a new worry in Singh's mind. A weapon like this would be highly effective in a battle field, but not in a fight that Yanus was looking for. Somehow, Singh knew that the army had something to do with this machine. In all his years in the army, Singh had never encountered anything like this. They, without fail, had obsolete weapons. This thing was straight out of a nightmare land of the future. Singh racked his brains to think how Yanus would direct this machine. All Babur would need is a sharp shooter in the right place and the machine would be hovering over their dead bodies.

"Do you have a plan?" asked Yanus

"What?"

"You have been silent for a while. Hopefully you have thought up of something." Said Yanus

"Your fight is with Babur and him alone, right?" asked Singh

"Yes! And anyone who gets in the way."

"I will help you but there are some conditions."

Yanus started laughing.

"What is funny?" asked Singh

"And why do you think I should agree to your conditions? Why do I need to?" finished Yanus

"Because, without me, this machine will not be able to help you and you will not survive."

Yanus thought about it for a minute and then said, "Let's hear them."

"After we finish Babur, I will leave the city. You are free to come with me, but I will no longer help you. During this fight, we shall remain hidden and press our attack only when it is to our advantage. There will be no reckless running to people's houses and acting like fools. We shall focus only on Babur and deal with anyone who gets in the way accordingly. Do you agree?"

"I guessed as much. I agree. Tell me though; after this is over, what will I do with you? Where will you go?"

"I am going home. You could come with me and perhaps start a better life."

"A better life…?" asked Yanus

"I am sorry, Yanus. All I know is that this city has not been good to you. I thought maybe you would want to…." Singh left his thought unfinished

Yanus had a strange look in his eyes. He nodded and turned to the machine, "Could you switch off that blue light. You look like an ambulance."

The light went off and Yanus stared at it, "I was only joking. How much do you understand? And what do I call you?"

The machine was silent. Yanus shook his head and asked Singh, "When do we begin?"

"After I have had my rest, then we will talk. I am not a machine, you know. I need sleep and so do you. Get some rest now. Who knows, we may not get the chance tomorrow." Singh walked away leaving Yanus alone with the machine.

"Don't mind Singh, he gets like that." Yanus said to the machine

Yanus walked to the end of the boundary and sat down. This was it. All the years at the orphanage, he had wondered if there was something more to his life, that whether he was more than a discard. He wished he knew about his parents. No matter what he said to Singh, he would prefer to be with a family. But Yanus knew this was his reality. There was no changing it. The arrival of this machine too had put questions in his mind. Where did it come from? Who made it? Why had they made it? Above all, the question that troubled him was why had it come to him? Yanus knew the answers were there somewhere. He had to find them out. That was the real reason why he wanted to fight Babur. Somehow he realized that this fight would lead him to where he was supposed to be. Yanus tried to stay awake by watching and marvelling at the machine that had become his shadow.

His shadow… Yanus knew this shadow would become the lightening in his fight against Babur. Lightening… Yanus realized that all his childhood, he had dreamed about lightening in the sky. His vision blurred as he drifted away once more in to the unlimited world of dreams.

Singh sat on his bed thinking about the machine. It was not here by coincidence. It had come here by design. It had something to do with Yanus. That was the only reason why he had agreed to stay back and fight with him. The machine would follow Yanus wherever he went. Until Singh got to the bottom of this mystery, there was no abandoning Yanus. He still remembered the duty that was given to him all those years ago. Singh frowned in the dark. Did Jabar Falak have something to do with this machine? What if Jabar built it specifically for Yanus? Falak was capable of such things. But why build a machine for Yanus when Falak had many capable men at his command? Something was not adding up. It could be Jabar who was responsible. It was perfectly possible that Samar knew nothing about this even if it was his father. Then who would? Who would Jabar trust with this secret?

Singh lay down and tried to make sense of everything. As sleep took him everything turned to mush in his mind except one last thought: Babur.

Singh would break his agreement with Babur. Singh's last thought was that Babur probably deserved what he had coming.

Rohan still felt a little woozy. The doctor had warned him that his injuries were still not completely healed and that he should take it easy. But Rohan was not worried about his wounds. He had been injured before. What he was worried about was the humiliation that he had suffered because of Yanus. Rohan had tried to remember if he had ever heard this name before. But Jadhav had been sure that he was a 'nobody'. Rohan scoffed at the idea. A 'nobody' could not have done this to him. Rohan clenched his fist and felt an intense anger built up inside him. After all the trouble that the man had given them, Babur had let him go. Even Sunny had done nothing. All the time he had been in the hospital, he had taken solace in the fact that Sunny was hunting Yanus. And now he knew that the matter had been dusted under the carpet. No one was to do anything about it. Rohan had men who were still hurt and some had suffered seriously because of Yanus. How could Babur do this? How could Sunny do this? He had no hopes with Raj. Raj had no loyalties. Rohan was sure that Raj must have had something do with this. He never cared about anyone but himself. Rohan always felt that Raj was an outsider in their world. What did he care if Rohan or people who put themselves in the line of fire for Babur got hurt...or got killed?

Rohan stepped out of the hospital and was relieved to see his friends waiting for him. Rohan tried to walk as fast as he could and got in to the car.

"Where can we find him?" asked Rohan without any formalities

The man at the wheel did not look at Rohan but answered, "He is in the city and we know where he is. Are sure you want to do this Rohan? Babur's orders are to...."

"I don't care. By my account, this Yanus has to pay for what he did. I will apologize later if I have to. I am sure he won't mind though. Why did he let Yanus go, anyway?" asked Rohan

"Yanus never came to us. He escaped from Jadhav's jeep when he was being brought to Babur. Then this guy showed up at our place and I think Babur made a deal with him."

"What deal?" asked Rohan wondering since when did Babur make deals

"Babur knew the man that was with Yanus. You remember that old guy?"

Rohan understood. So that's why that little squirt got away. Well, Babur knew the old man, he did not.

"What did Sunny have to say?"

"I don't know."

Rohan thought for a minute and took a decision.

"Call everyone we know and put them on Yanus's tail. I want them in sight at all times."

"For how long, Rohan, Sunny will find out. You know he will not help you in this."

Rohan turned to see his friend. He too had shared his hatred of Raj and the general way things were being done.

"Only till tonight." Said Rohan

"Tonight... Rohan, are you sure?" asked the man

"Yes! I can't wait any longer. I wanted Yanus dead yesterday."

The man looked at Rohan and saw the steel in his eyes. He had his doubts but this was a wonderful opportunity to prove their mettle to Babur and get one over Raj.

Yanus and Singh had spent the day trying to communicate with the machine. As far as Singh was concerned, he simply did not exist in the machine's agenda. It followed Yanus' commands to every detail. It registered Singh's presence only when Yanus asked it to. Even then, names were of no importance to it. A command like "Go to Singh." had no effect on it at all. Yanus had to point out Singh in general for the machine to understand. Yanus complained loudly all morning that the dumb machine had to learn a lot until Singh pointed out that it had probably searched him out in a city like Mumbai. It had learned enough, Singh thought but he was sure that they were not going to be able to fully understand the machine. The machine didn't bring its manual, thought Singh to himself. There had to be a way to get the machine to perform tasks other than through oral commands. The machine after all, was not sentient no matter how intelligent. It was a machine and detailed tasks would have to be given it in a different manner. Yanus would have none of it. All day, Yanus spoke to it in different ways to get it to obey his command. Yanus was beginning to get the hang of it when he noticed Singh was staring intently at a building outside their building's field.

"Hey Singh, thinking about your wife?" asked Yanus playfully

When Singh did not respond, Yanus walked over to him and looked at what he was seeing.

"See something you don't like." Asked Yanus

Singh spoke with a slight smile on his face.

"I have a feeling we are being watched."

Yanus made a show of looking around, "Watched by who?"

"How would I know? I have been feeling like that since last night." Said Singh

"Wow! You must be psychic!" said Yanus completely amazed

Singh turned to look at Yanus, "Where did you pick that word up?"

Yanus gave a little laugh and walked back to where he had been.

"Don't worry Singh. It's just your imagination."

In light of what they were about to do, Singh thought that Yanus should learn a few things. Singh wondered if he would have the time. It was time to relocate to the wild, thought Singh.

Singh looked at Yanus and marvelled at how confident he was. He had training and experience in combat and even he still didn't feel sure. Perhaps that was exactly why he felt that way. Singh turned to Yanus to ask him whether he would like to learn how to look for people following or spying on him and even how to do it himself when, all of a sudden, two things happened.

Before he had taken a step, the machine suddenly turned its direction away from Yanus and sped toward Singh. Singh gave a start and fell backward as the huge machine bore down on him. Singh had not heard Yanus say anything to it and the machine had acted on its own accord. Even Yanus screamed and ran after it. Singh was sure he would be dead the next instant when he heard a small ping. Singh screamed at the top of his voice.

"Yanus! Get down!" Singh had understood

Singh realized that Yanus too had heard the shot and dove to the ground rolling behind a wall. Singh looked up to see the machine facing the other way. It had taken the bullet on its body and had saved his life.

Damn! Thought Singh

"Singh, what is going on?" screamed Yanus from behind the wall

"Just stay there, Yanus. Don't peek out. Keep your body behind the wall." Singh said quietly

Yanus stared at the machine. It had not followed him behind the wall. It had detected the bullet and deflected it. It had not been asked to do any of it, but it had. Yanus smiled inwardly. This is not a machine, he thought, this is a beast. This was a monster. It was time for pay back.

Rohan signalled to the man holding the rifle. He put the rifle down and in turn signalled the rest of the men. As one, they advanced toward the area where they had seen their targets. They had been keeping watch over the building's area for more than a day and had occasionally spotted the old man. Yanus had stayed out of sight at all times. Rohan finally decided to kill the old man and then attack Yanus. He would be alone…and without protection.

"Did you get him?" asked Rohan

"I am not sure. I think he got hit, but he survived. I didn't see him after I fired."

That was good enough. As long as the old man didn't get in the way, Rohan had no business with him. He wanted Yanus. But if he did, well, like he said earlier, he would apologize to Babur. He was sure Babur would not complain.

Rohan followed his men through the gate and proceeded toward where the old man had been shot.

"Hey!" Rohan turned to the side to see Yanus standing a few feet away.

Rohan signalled his men to stand down. They were too many and he was alone. The old man must have died.

"You must be Yanus." Said Rohan as he advanced toward Yanus

"Yes, I must be." Yanus stood his ground. Rohan stood toe to toe with Yanus and put his gun to Yanus's head. Yanus looked up calmly at Rohan's face and said, "How's your head?"

Rohan ignored the question and spoke quietly with gritted teeth, "Any last words?"

"Oh! Come on Rohan, not mad are you?"

Rohan lifted his arm and was about to pull the trigger when Yanus spoke again.

"Don't you want to fight me? I would, if I were you. I broke your head and put you in a hospital. And you come here with a small army with guns. Don't you want to prove you can beat me with your bare hands? I mean, what will your men think of you?" Yanus was smiling

Rohan lowered the gun, "You know, I think you are right! I'd rather shoot you when you are already bleeding to death on the ground. Leave this to me." said Rohan to his people.

"That's the spirit!" said Yanus clapping his hands and waving at Rohan's men to applaud Rohan

The men lowered their weapons, a little unsure. Things like this didn't happen in their world. The winner was who shot first, not who punched harder. That happened in movies. But every man there knew that things had become personal. All silently backed away a little, guns lowered but ready at hand.

Rohan suddenly swung his arm at Yanus's face. Yanus blocked it with his left arm and hammered his right on Rohan's head. Rohan's already injured head was unbalanced and he fell to the ground. The men lifted their weapons at Yanus who stood over Rohan, waiting for him to get up.

"I knew you were a softie, Rohan. All your bravado was nothing but hot air. Now get up and fight. Get up Rohan, look, your men are laughing at you. Once they shoot me, you are going to be laughed at…"

Rohan took advantage of Yanus's inattention and swung his leg. It caught Yanus at the back of the knees and he toppled backward. Rohan was instantly on top of Yanus. Rohan was significantly bigger than Yanus and he used his weight to pin Yanus down. The men breathed a sigh of relief as Rohan's longer arms pummelled every inch of Yanus he could get. What Rohan didn't understand was why Yanus was laughing? Rohan finally ran out of steam as the power behind his punches waned. He was already weak and his body had not had the time to heal. He ran out of breath and grabbed Yanus' throat to suffocate him. Finally Yanus stopped laughing.

"Is that it?" asked Yanus

Rohan increased the pressure on Yanus but felt Yanus free his leg from under him. Rohan knew it was coming but didn't have the energy to block it. The kick sent Rohan flying through the air. Yanus walked to Rohan with an eye on Rohan's men. They looked ready to fire and were waiting for a command. They still hoped Rohan could beat him. Yanus grabbed his hair and pulled him up.

"You wanted to know my last words? Here they are: Look at your men." Said Yanus savagely

Confused and dazed, Rohan involuntarily jerked his head toward his men. Men who had chosen to come with him and disobey Sunny and Babur so that he could have his revenge.

For a moment Rohan didn't believe what he saw. His men were waiting for an order from him. A gesture or a look that would send murderous fire raining down on Yanus from their guns, but while their attention was at Rohan, a tall shadow had grown behind them. An eerie blue light shone from the top of the shadow as it approached his men. Rohan could not make sense of it and tried to warn the nearest man who had already cocked his gun and was about to take aim.

Rohan was blinded by the intense discharge of power from the shadow. In less than three seconds, the shadow had vaporized every man that was advancing toward Rohan. Rohan choked on his vomit as he tried to comprehend what had happened. Not a trace remained of any of them. They were all gone.

Yanus caught hold of Rohan's collar and swung him around to face him.

Singh appeared from behind the machine and saw Yanus swing his arm back to strike Rohan.

"Yanus! No!"

Singh saw Rohan fall to the ground as Yanus struck his temple with as much power as he could. Singh reached Rohan and fell to his knees beside Rohan.

"What have you done?" roared Singh

"What he had come here to do to me! I have killed him." Said Yanus

Singh checked Rohan's pulse. Singh groaned and got up to face Yanus.

"He was no threat to you after his men had been killed. Why did you kill him?" asked Singh through gritted teeth

"He was not a threat at the time. Do you think he wouldn't have tried tomorrow, or the day after that, or some other time in the future?"

"Yanus, you should not have done that."

"I did exactly what I should have." Said Yanus with a finality in his tone

Singh looked at Rohan as a tear ran down his eye. It looked like death was catching up to him again.

"We better get out of here, Singh. He will begin to stink soon."

Singh watched Yanus calmly walk away. Singh noticed that Yanus had not shown even the slightest remorse or hesitation in ordering those deaths. Neither had he baulked at taking a life. Singh caught hold of his head and grieved for an innocence lost. What had he done?

"Where are the rest of the men?" asked Sunny slowly

"There was no one else there except Rohan. But I am sure he went there with at least 10 men from the west. Daya was with him too. By the time I got to know of this, it was too late. That is when I called you. I thought I could…." The young man broke off

Sunny stared at Rohan's bloodied form lying on the table. It had been a while since anyone working for him had been killed. But every time it did, Sunny had taken it personally. This time was no different. Rohan was a fool who had thought too much of himself, but he was loyal and he didn't deserve to die. At least, not like this. There was no doubt in his mind as to who had done this. Sunny vowed that Yanus will suffer for this. There was no way he was getting away with this.

But first…the door opened and Babur walked in.

"How did this happen?" asked Babur

"Yanus!" said Sunny

Babur was genuinely surprised. He came to Rohan and stroked his head.

"This is your fault." Said Sunny with a lot of venom

Babur did not look Sunny's way and neither did he respond.

"I warned at the start not to get in to this crap. You and your mania have cost me the lives of my men, men, who run risks daily, so that you can sit pretty on your throne. Look at me!!" shouted Sunny when Babur wouldn't look at him

Raj walked in to the room and shut the door behind him. Sunny looked at him and was about to shout some more when Raj spoke.

"There were 12 men with Rohan. They are all missing. But I think they are dead."

Sunny threw his mobile on the floor smashing it to pieces.

Raj looked at Rohan one last time and then left the room, not wanting to witness this.

"Do you realize that this cannot end here? It will go on until Yanus is dead. How many of us will he kill before we succeed?"

"Are you scared Sunny? You know our business. There is no…."

"I remember everything you taught me, Babur. Perhaps you need to remember your own lessons. I could sacrifice a hundred Rohans and not care a damn. But sacrifices need to have a purpose. What good came out of this Babur? You…."

"I am aware of what I taught you, Sunny. Perhaps you should have controlled your men a little better."

Sunny was too angry to give a civil response. There was nothing more to be said anyway. Whether Babur realized it or not, a war was on.

"I will come to you with his head." Said Sunny and slammed the door on his way out.

Babur did not feel any remorse for sending people to their deaths, but somewhere deep within him, a voice told him that Sunny was right. Rohan's death was unnecessary. Babur looked out of the window and took in the view. Just as he had thought; the end was near.

Once again, darkness fell over the city. The streets which were bustling with people and activity during the day were silent. Men and women who slogged during the day to earn a living had fallen asleep. Those who had a roof over their heads had locked their doors to feel safe and those who didn't fell asleep where they had fallen in exhaustion from the struggles of the day. But the city's harsh life relented at night. It allowed a place to rest, albeit for a price. You had to pay what they asked for, or you would lose what they wanted. It was a compromise thousands made in a city that had many faces.

A more sinister face now moved through the shadows. It was the night, whose darkness allowed faces to hide…. to conceal.

Chapter 5

In To The Shadows

Negi rolled down the window to let out the smoke. He looked at the watch and tapped the partition separating him from the driver. The driver did not respond. Instead he got out of the car and walked away leaving Negi alone. Negi heard footsteps coming from behind the car but Negi did not turn to look. Negi did feel fear sometimes but these days he had become immune to threats. There was nothing to guarantee any measure of safety. It was a curse that people of his kind had earned for themselves. In fact, the higher his position, the higher would be the threat, not to mention the hatred. Negi had been saddened at first by all the negativity around him but had quickly learned to ignore it. There were too many of his kind waiting to pull him down and bury him for a variety of reasons. Such was the life of a politician who had given a significant portion of his life to serve the community he once thought would thank him for his work. It was a fool's dream. People feared his reputation and rank, but the respect Negi had set out to earn didn't seem to exist in his world. Negi did not expect anything for the work that he was now about to begin. The enormity of this task didn't frazzle him. He just worried about the free will of those he could not control and had a far bigger role to play than he did. Yet, tonight was another attempt to gain some of that control.

The door opened and another man settled himself slowly in the opposite seat to face Negi.

"I hope you have learned your lesson, Jadhav." Said Negi

Jadhav looked at the floor and said nothing. He was having difficulty in breathing and his discomfort was apparent. His body ached all over and he wished he was at home sleeping rather than here.

"So what happened?" asked Negi

"He got away." Said Jadhav

"I know he did. What happened after that?"

"I think he killed some of Babur's men. I still don't know why he is doing it. There is no apparent connection between the two."

"Did you try to find him?" asked Negi thinking that the connection was quite obvious.

"No!"

"I specifically told you to keep him in your station till I could come and speak with him. Yet, you took him to Babur."

"I...I...." Jadhav didn't have an answer and he continued his study of the floor.

"Did you think I was making a joke? Or do you think my work is not important?"

"It's not that. Babur...."

"I could destroy your career for dealing with that scum. I could charge you with corruption and put you in your own jail. Do you want that?" asked Negi cutting off Jadhav

"You are lucky I need your help in finding this boy, Jadhav. Otherwise, you would be in a lot of trouble. I want you to understand that if you fail to find this boy, you will have no further use to me. Do not forget, you are not the only one who can reach Babur. You remember Raj, don't you?

The colour drained from Jadhav's face.

"How do you…?"

"It is not your concern. Now get out of my sight. Ten minutes in my car, and its already smelling like a garbage bin."

Jadhav quickly got out of the car and walked back in to the shadows from where he came, leaving Negi alone.

Negi wished he had a better way to find the boy. He wished he had secured the boy at the correct time when he had the opportunity. But that opportunity was lost. But in a way, Negi thought that this was going according to plan. It was just not his plan.

Yanus was proving to be a handful for Babur and that was saying something. Not many would have stood up to him. Negi knew too many instances when Babur had resolved problems in his own way. Brutality and violence were not Babur's only strong points. Babur's strong points were also his intelligence and cunning. Negi wondered when Yanus would finally get to Babur and who would win. Negi wondered if this too was part of the great plan. Negi didn't think so. This was a problem, Negi reminded himself. Too much was at stake for the boy to be playing on the streets. He had to be found. Negi winced. He was kidding himself. If Babur decided to kill him, Yanus would not stand a chance. So far, Yanus was dealing with his minions and not Babur himself. He was yet to come face to face with that monster. Yanus would need a miracle to survive. Negi decided he could not depend on Jadhav to search for the boy. He needed more help. It was time to leak some more direct information to his opponent, who Negi was sure, had better ways of finding people than he did.

The driver finally returned and got in to the car. Negi heard his voice on the intercom.

"Home, Sir?"

Negi thought about it for a minute. He was in no mood to go home. His wife would be asleep and so would the children. It would be best to utilize the rest of the night.

"Karim, do you know any more places like the one you took me the other night?"

"Of course, shall we....?" Asked the driver

"Let's not waste the night, Karim." Said Negi as he lit a cigarette

Karim couldn't help but smile as he shifted his gears and drove off in to the night.

The men did not speak to each other as they patiently awaited the arrival of their boss. Any conversation could betray information that could be used against them. All looked at any place other than each other. They would have preferred a private meeting with the boss but the boss had called all of them at the same time. The choice of location had a significance that was not lost on any of them. This was where they had discussed work which was not on the legal agenda of their boss. Everyone wondered what could possibly be bothering him that all of them had been summoned in haste. It had to be something important. Someone was obviously in trouble.

The door banged open and Kasid stormed in with his black robes billowing behind him. His dark eyes had a hard look. He looked tired but there was an energy about him that put everyone around him on an edge. He had a folder in his hands that he put on the table.

"Take a copy." Said Kasid in his gravelly voice

The men passed the folder and each took a picture from it. All had a picture of the same person.

Each man took a look at the picture and put it away and waited for instructions.

"His name is Yanus. Find him and bring him to me. He is heavily armed and is not alone." Kasid looked at each man in turn.

After 5 seconds, they all got up and left. Kasid remained seated as he watched them leave. Kasid too got up and sat on the sofa that he rarely used. He looked stonily at his hands and tried to clear his mind of all thought.

His poor attempt at meditation was interrupted by the sound of the door opening.

Kasid kept looking at his hands as a much older man entered the room, supported by a stick. He sat down next to Kasid and spoke.

"Your information is correct?"

Kasid finally looked up and answered, "It is. Negi has started looking for this boy. He has not explained anything to the local police. He is counting on his people in the police to find him."

"There are many reasons why Negi could be looking for a boy…."

"Not many reasons why he would be looking for a specific boy." Kasid responded

The old man seemed to be lost in his thoughts when Kasid broke the silence.

"This is it."

"If it is, make sure that this boy is under your control." The old man got up and walked to the door when a thought came to him. He looked at Kasid and asked, "Is he an orphan?"

Kasid turned to look at the man, but said nothing. The old man understood the meaning of the silence and left.

Kasid settled down in the sofa and waited for his phone to ring.

Singh was too sullen to have a conversation with. Yanus ate his food silently without looking at Singh. Singh had not spoken to Yanus since the night Yanus had killed Rohan. Yanus didn't care. Yanus knew Singh didn't agree with what he was doing. But Singh had promised to help him get to Babur. Yanus smiled to himself. That was not the reason for which Singh had hung back with him. Singh was intrigued by the idea of the machine that was now hovering beside Yanus. Yanus knew that Singh wanted to know more about the machine. Yanus was sure that Singh had his theories. Again, Yanus found it difficult to care. As long as Singh helped him, he could stay. His other motives were of no importance to him. With the machine at his side, Yanus knew it was a matter of time, before he got to Babur. Babur probably knew who had killed Rohan. He would be planning his revenge. Yanus looked at the machine. He wished Babur would hurry up and find him. As much as he was beginning to find Singh a hindrance, he knew he still needed him. His idea that he should wait for Babur to come to him was sound and apart from the waiting, Yanus could not find any fault in it.

Yanus was sure that Babur would come to him. But before Babur, it would be Sunny. Yanus smiled again. Sunny would not have forgotten him. He was sure that Sunny had wanted him right from the beginning. Now, more than ever, Sunny would be looking for him. Yanus would wait.

Yanus instructed the machine to stay. He wanted some time alone and walked toward the door of the warehouse. Yanus marvelled how Singh came up with such places. They were all over the city. This one had some kind of cloth laid in stacks. There was so much cloth here that Yanus wondered if it would be enough for an entire city. He had seen some interesting stuff every time they camped in a warehouse. He had seen toys, clothes, grains, and even books. More than the toys, which Yanus had never seen in his childhood, Yanus had been interested in the books. He wanted to ask Singh what the books were about. There were no pictures on it either to suggest what they contained. But Singh's mood had killed his curiosity. At night, Yanus had taken a book and looked at it from every angle he could and tried to match it with his memory of letters he had seen elsewhere. It was a silly process and got him nowhere. Yanus lost interest in the books too. His mind had been consumed with Babur. All he could hear were the screams of the children at night. He remembered Sohrab. Yanus used to be too scared to approach the children after Sohrab had beaten them for reasons known only to him. He wondered how the children had offended him. What was the purpose in abusing children? He would hold his head and cry himself and try to block out the cries of the children. As he grew older, he would try to console the little ones. But he was never good at it. The worst was when he had to see the little girls crying. Yanus found that far more disturbing than when the boys cried. The girls would begin to panic whenever Sohrab entered their dormitory which was opposite to the boy's dormitory. Yanus remembered Tara. She was around his age when she was brought to the orphanage. Tara had been the closest thing to a friend that Yanus had ever had. They had been the oldest kids in the orphanage. Yanus had fallen from the stairs during one of his usual forays outside the orphanage. Yanus looked at his knee and remembered sadly Tara stealing something from Sohrab's room to put on his wound. The wound had never healed properly and had left a permanent mark. Yanus would always keep an eye on Sohrab to see if he was coming up to the dormitories. He would hide children if he thought Sohrab was looking for them. But he could never hide them all. Sometimes, he used to hide Tara in one of the cabinets in the common rooms. Tara hated hiding but Yanus would insist. Yanus knew that every time Sohrab walked up to the children's floor, somebody was going to get hurt. There were plenty of children and Sohrab picked any one that suited him. He didn't always waste time looking for anyone. A few times, Yanus even made himself plainly visible and wished Sohrab would pick him. But he never did. He always grabbed whoever was nearest and hit the unfortunate child. Sometimes, he would take the children to his room and beat them there with his belt. The children returned in the middle of the night dragging their bruised bodies to their beds. With no medical care, their wounds would fester and hurt more. At that time, it never occurred to him to fight. It never occurred to him that he didn't have to suffer and that he could protect those who had no defences against such mindless evil. He now realized that he could have broken Sohrab's neck in an instant if he had just shown the courage. If only he had….

Yanus wiped the tears from his eyes as he remembered Tara. Her memory had been banished to the back of his mind for 3 years.

One late night Sohrab had entered the girl's dormitory and tried to drag out a little girl. Yanus remembered standing outside the girl's dormitory and watching Sohrab's wild behaviour. He remembered wondering what the little girl had done to deserve this. But Tara had shielded the girl with her body to protect her. Yanus watched in a stunned state as Sohrab kicked Tara repeatedly to push her off. Finally, Sohrab grabbed Tara's hair and pulled her up. Sohrab sneered at Tara and pushed her roughly to the floor. Yanus had not liked the look in Sohrab's eyes staring down at her as she tried to get up again. Sohrab grabbed the little girl and stormed out of the dormitory. It was the first time Sohrab's eyes met Yanus as he passed him. Yanus remembered Tara crying inconsolably. She had not been able to protect the little girl. Yanus had no words of comfort to give her.

A few nights later, Sohrab came up to their floor in a highly intoxicated state. Yanus had seen him coming and had run in to the girl's dormitory. Yanus had a bad feeling about this night. Somehow, Yanus knew Sohrab was coming for Tara. His heart beating faster than ever, Yanus took Tara in to the common room and hid her there. Tara had whispered a soft 'thank you' to Yanus. He had hid her there plenty of times, just like the other children. But it was the first time she had thanked him. Yanus remembered looking at Tara's face that night. Without a word, Yanus had shut the cupboard and run back to his dormitory. Yanus hoped Sohrab would turn toward the boys' dormitory and leave the girls alone.

Yanus groaned as a few moments later, Sohrab turned towards the girl's quarters. Yanus held his breath as he waited for Sohrab to emerge from the room with someone. Sohrab did emerge, but alone. Then Sohrab did something he had never done before. After stepping out of the room, Sohrab locked the door to the girls' dormitory. Yanus stood at the entrance of the boy's dormitory as Sohrab proceeded to lock the boys in too. As Sohrab closed the door, he looked at Yanus and gave him a smile. Yanus remembered that look in his eyes when he had pushed Tara.

Yanus realized that Sohrab knew where Tara was. He had known all along that he was hiding children there. Yanus slumped to the floor and began to cry. His body wouldn't stop shaking as he wished for a miracle that would save Tara. Then he heard the screams. Yanus rushed to the window and saw Sohrab dragging Tara out of the gate. Yanus jumped out of the window and climbed down through the pipes to follow them. By the time he got down, Sohrab had led Tara a fair distance away. Yanus ran like he had never run before. After a while, Yanus realized that he had lost them. Yanus hit himself in frustration as he tried to look for Tara. Once again, Tara screamed. Yanus guessed the direction from where the scream had come from and sprinted that way. Yanus was running in panic and in his haste, Yanus tripped and fell, skinning his arms and legs. Yanus got up and looked around. Once again he had lost them. Yanus cried harder trying to figure out where they had gone. Yanus held his bruised arm and winced in pain when once again, he heard Tara's voice. It had come from a small house just a few metres away. Yanus silently approached the door.

It was the last time Yanus felt fear. It was the last time he would fail to act. But his fear extracted a heavy price before it finally left him. It paralyzed Yanus. He could not even bring himself to knock on the door. Yanus could hear Tara inside the hut. She was crying in pain. He wanted to help but didn't know how. Yanus bit his knuckle and cried harder. He wished Tara would stop crying. He wished Tara would stop hurting. For fifteen years of his life, Yanus had never prayed for anything. He had never known what to pray for. That night Yanus prayed for the first and last time.

He prayed to God to stop Tara from hurting anymore and that she would not cry again.

Yanus just stood outside the door listening to Tara's cries and he prayed harder. Then the cries began to fade. Yanus realized that it was silent again. God had granted him his wish. A few moments later, Yanus heard footsteps. Finally Yanus was able to move and he quickly ran behind the hut to avoid being seen. Yanus peeked a little and saw Sohrab walk away toward the orphanage. Not knowing what to do, Yanus stood in front of the door, still too afraid to enter and waited for Tara to come out. It was completely dark inside and Yanus could not see anything beyond the door. He heard nothing either. He wondered why Tara was not coming out. Yanus waited till morning for Tara to step out. But she didn't. Yanus cried all his tears that night. He stood like a rock without moving, staring at the door. Yanus felt the first rays hit the earth. But even the sun did not enter the hut where Tara was. Yanus knew that Tara was never coming out. Tara would never come back. Yanus had failed.

Yanus had felt something inside of him die that night when Tara had gone. He had not acted to protect her. His inability to act had cost him a lot. It had been three years since that night, but it was only now that he fully understood what he had lost. He didn't care what Singh said. Nobody could understand the suffering of abandoned children. Nobody could understand the horrors that such children faced. Yanus wiped a tear with his finger and looked at it in surprise. It had been some time since he had remembered Tara. It was as if she was never been there. Nobody had missed her. Nobody came to look for her. She was just…gone. Yanus gritted his teeth. He would never be afraid to act again. Nobody could save Babur. Not even the devil himself.

Yanus stepped outside the door and instinctively ducked. But ducking was no help at all as the impact of the explosion lifted him off his feet and threw him back through the door. Yanus felt the hinges break and he landed on the ground with the door under him. Yanus struggled to his feet and checked the source of the explosion. He heard Singh shouting his name.

"Singh, get back!" shouted Yanus as he saw a man standing far back taking aim with something on his shoulder. It was too late. Something streaked through the air and hit the ware house. The second explosion tore through the wall and caused the roof to cave in. Yanus dove through the falling debris hoping that Singh had gotten away. Yanus screamed Singh's name but there was no answer. Yanus cursed himself and ran out of the burning ware house.

Ten men stood in a line in front of him. The man with the weapon had put it down and was watching him silently.

"Will you come with us willingly or do we have to take back your dead body?" asked one of them

Yanus responded by turning back and walking back inside the ware house. The fires were burning fiercely. Yanus guessed that the men would have to follow him in if they wanted him alive. Yanus hid behind a burning stack and scanned the area for Singh. He had to get as far back as possible to reach the machine. But he had to do it carefully. Yanus saw one of the men pass him looking the other way. Yanus put his hand on his mouth and hit him hard in the neck. The man slumped down. Yanus wondered if he should take his gun, but it didn't look like anything he could figure out how to use and left it. Yanus stepped carefully avoiding the heat of the fire and tried to locate the others. Suddenly, Yanus felt a kick on his back that dropped him to the floor. Yanus tried to get up but another kick to his ribs put him down again. Yanus cried out in pain and anger. Yanus blocked the third kick and pulled the leg toward him. The man lost his balance and Yanus drove his arm in to his jaw, shattering it. The man fell to the ground in pain. The others laughed at their fallen comrade. Yanus tried to grab the nearest man, but felt a punch to his head. Yanus punched back as hard and as rapidly as he could. Every punch sent a man down, but they were too many. Yanus screamed at the top of his voice so that the machine could hear him. He didn't know whether the machine could understand that there had been an explosion and that he was hurt. Yanus fought with everything he had and dropped at least 5 more men before the others realized that Yanus was not going down easily. One of the men finally withdrew a gun from his pocket and put it on Yanus' head.

"Stop or you will die."

The other men stood a little further, probably agreeing that this was the best way to control this guy.

"Not tonight! Tonight it is your turn." Said Yanus as he struggled to get on his feet

"You are outnumbered and we are armed, Yanus. Don't be stupid. Now put your hands over your head and follow me."

Yanus swallowed the blood in his mouth and said simply, "Kill them."

The man holding the gun wondered who Yanus was talking to when the men to his right disintegrated in to blood and flesh. The man screamed in terror and fell to the ground looking for what had caused it. He saw it a second before he died: A tall shadow drifting in through the fire. The last thing he saw was an intense blue light that blinded him. A third discharge killed the remaining men as they tried to escape. They had seen what had happened to their fellows. It was over in less than 5 seconds. Yanus looked around him and saw the carnage. The man who Yanus had hit was on his feet and groggily tried to get his bearings. Yanus mustered all his energy and hit him again in the neck. This time he dropped for good.

"Singh, where are you?" shouted Yanus but there was no response

Yanus looked everywhere but couldn't find Singh. The smoke was suffocating him. Yanus wished the machine could help him find Singh instead of just floating there.

In frustration, Yanus yelled at it, "Where is Singh?"

To Yanus's surprise, the blue light on its top stopped shining and concentrated a beam toward one of the stacks at the far end of the ware house. Yanus stared at it in amazement for only a second. Then Yanus ran as fast as he could, following the beam.

The beam shone exactly where Singh was trapped.

"Singh, wake up! Talk to me!"

"I am not sleeping, you fool. I am trapped." Said Singh weakly

Yanus cried out in relief. Yanus lifted the fallen stack off Singh and helped him to his feet. They both walked out of the burning ware house and quickly moved out of the area before the fire attracted anyone. Singh noticed that Yanus was limping.

"Did you get hurt?" asked Singh

"I am all right." Said Yanus

"Then why are you limping?"

"Those men were tough."

"I am sorry I could not help you. It won't happen again. Here, get some rest."

Yanus settled down at the pavement and asked,

"Did we get anyone close to Babur?"

Singh took a moment to answer, "I don't know. I was expecting Sunny."

Somehow Yanus had been disappointed about that too. He too had been expecting Sunny. He didn't care about these dogs. It was their master that controlled them. Yanus was sure that Rohan's death would anger Sunny enough to force him to hunt Yanus himself. It appeared that he was wrong.

"Sunny will not risk himself." Said Yanus

"Sunny is the only way we can get to Babur. The fact they are sending others means that they are not taking us seriously. Or there is the other possibility." Said Singh

Yanus knew what Singh was going to say.

"These men might not have come from Sunny. But I cannot imagine who else would go to this trouble to kidnap you."

"It doesn't matter where they came from. I want to know what we should do in case Sunny does not show up. We can't stay here forever...I want to finish this."

Singh frowned at Yanus, "What's the hurry?"

Yanus limped back on his feet and said, "We cannot go on like this forever. Sunny may have an unlimited supply of men who would be willing to die for him. The machine cannot protect us at all times. We have to succeed every time. They have to succeed only once. Not to mention the trouble we will have to face if this machine was seen by anyone."

"Then what do you propose we do?" asked Singh

"What would you propose we do, when we are still looking for places to hide, say two months from now or three or even a year? How will we survive that long? How much money have you spent so far? Did they pay you that well at the orphanage? Sunny can afford to draw this out. We can't."

Singh thought about what Yanus was saying. He did have a point. They couldn't do this for too long. And Sunny was sure to understand this as well. To survive was a big deal in Mumbai. But to survive while staying hidden was impossible. No one could do it. Singh knew what Yanus was going to say.

"You think we should go to him?" asked Singh

"I think we should kill him before he kills us. This machine is incredibly powerful, but it cannot be at two places at the same time."

"Hmm, I think you are right. We need to make plan to draw Sunny out. It would be foolhardy to go where he lives. Besides, someone like him might be on the move at all times."

"Let's plan later. I don't think I can walk very far. Let's find some shelter and we will decide what to do."

Singh got up and followed Yanus. Somehow, Singh thought, despite his best efforts, things were rapidly spinning out of control.

A knock on the door brought Kasid out of his meditation. It was very rare for him to succeed in meditation. There were too many things going on his head and he just could not relax. His appearance though, was dead calm. The knock came again. Kasid looked at his watch: it was nearly night time.

"Enter."

The door opened slowly and a small man entered. He kept his eyes down as he approached Kasid and stopped a little further than was necessary.

"One of the men was found dead at the ware house. There is no news about the rest."

Kasid merely nodded.

"No matter, send more men. If it is too much trouble, kill him."

The man bowed a little and left.

Kasid knew this was not going to be easy. Kasid had known all along that Yanus was going to be a lot of trouble. If only he had got to him before, when he was vulnerable, things would have been a lot easier. But Jabar Falak had covered his trail well. Kasid remembered the presence of the man in this room, so many years ago. Kasid was a force to reckon with even then. Even then, as now, the mere mention of Kasid's name made men tremble at their knees. He had the ability to make people nervous. But Kasid remembered that day in the presence of Jabar Falak. It was Kasid who had been sweating. Kasid had never known a man with more force than Jabar Falak. No matter how much Kasid had tried, Jabar had remained unmoved. It had been impossible to bully or frighten Jabar Falak. Kasid's party seniors had been most unhappy that he had failed at his task. Kasid had suggested that they should try it themselves. Kasid would have loved to see those fools try their luck with Jabar Falak. Jabar Falak had not cooperated and Kasid had thought that the idea had failed. For fifteen years there was no information about Falak's work. The trail had died completely. But five years ago, everything had changed. Kasid's source informed him that the machines were nearing completion, but Falak had given control of the machines to someone else. Kasid was stunned. Why did Falak have to build such machines only to have someone else control them? Kasid immediately changed tack and pressurized his source to find out who that person was. Kasid did not care what Falak's plan was but thought personally that it was a dangerous game that Falak was playing. But for five years, there was no information other than the news that the machines were ready. Kasid waited for the bomb to explode in the media. But Falak once again, threw a surprise at him. Kasid knew from his source that the military had people in Falak's team and they too were after the same thing he was. But it was apparent then, that Falak was not going to relinquish control to anyone. Kasid knew he had to bide his time. One day that person would emerge and then Kasid would have what he wanted. Kasid had thanked his luck, when he heard that Falak had died. Whoever it was, had no reason to keep the machines a secret. Kasid dreamed of glory as he would reach the pinnacle of power. But days stretched in weeks and there was no information. Instead there was a hurried call from his source: They were being hunted. A new machine was hunting the entire team and nobody knew who was controlling it, while the lead machine lay dormant in its hangar. Their chances of survival were slim. Kasid knew that Falak's team was desperate to find out who controlled this machine. Kasid scoffed at those fools. Falak must have realized that some of his team had betrayed him and he was taking his revenge on all of them. Falak had tied all loose ends before he had died. They would never find out who controlled the machine until he showed himself. Kasid realized that Falak must have had his own reasons for building such lethal machines and would never hand them over to anyone. Once again Kasid had lost all hopes.

But fate had intervened on Kasid's behalf one more time. Kasid could not believe his luck. A small time politician called Negi was looking for someone called Yanus. Negi had moved a lot of resources to locate the boy. At first, Kasid thought nothing of it as many such bits and pieces reached

Kasid through his spies. But then Kasid found out that this Yanus had killed men working for Babur and that Babur too was looking for him. Kasid's interest in Yanus grew. Anybody who was fool enough to take on Babur must be mad. Even Kasid would not mess with Babur. But still Kasid had doubts. It might not have anything to do with Falak. There was no information on Yanus' background either and Kasid eventually lost interest. A third piece of information finally reached Kasid and that convinced Kasid that it was Yanus that Falak had given the control of the machine to. One of the men whom Negi contacted to find Yanus was actually loyal to Kasid. The man reported to Kasid that Negi had mentioned that his target would be accompanied by a machine and that he must approach him carefully. The man had been instructed to inform Yanus that Negi could help him and that they must meet soon.

It did not matter why Falak had chosen Yanus. Like in other matters, Kasid knew Falak must have his reasons. Kasid laughed at how naïve this Negi could be: trusting people with such information.

It was only a matter of time before he had Yanus in his grip. Yanus had proved that he could fight. But Kasid had a lot of fire power at his command that would surely overcome the machine. He had to send enough men to weaken them first and then Kasid would take them down. It would take time and effort but Kasid knew that his reward would be worth it. Yes, Kasid thought…it was a matter of time.

Karim brought in the cup of tea and set it down on the table. Negi had put his legs on the table and was whistling cheerfully. He seemed to be in high spirits. Of all the people he had ever worked for, Negi was perhaps the one person he had enjoyed working for. Karim used to work for another high ranking government official. But Negi had spoken to the man and convinced him to let go of him so that he could hire him. Negi was well liked among his community and that too, Karim knew, was rare for a politician. What was even rare was the fact that the people in this area loved Negi. The man was tireless in his efforts to accelerate development. Karim knew that Negi was not too senior, but that didn't prevent some of the biggest names in the political arena calling at his residence from time to time. Kareem wondered what had the man grovelling at Negi's feet done. That he was a good man did not mean that he did not have claws. The man kept apologizing but Negi turned his attention to Kareem.

"Why don't you go have your lunch, Kareem?" said Negi

Kareem had been instructed never to leave his presence until told to. Kareem looked at the man one last time and left.

Negi patted the man on the shoulder and said, "Get up."

The man did as he was told but did not stop crying.

"Tell me, have you spoken to anyone else other than Kasid?"

"I didn't. I swear I didn't. I had to…" the man went on but Negi silenced him with a wave of his hand

Negi smiled inwardly. The poor soul didn't realize that he had always known that he was leaking information to Kasid. In fact, Negi had been feeding him the correct amount of information that Negi wanted Kasid to have. But Negi had taken a gamble and told him about the machines as he wanted Kasid to know about Yanus. The gamble had paid off. The fool had rushed to tell Kasid all that Negi had told him. But the man was of no use to him anymore. It was much too dangerous to have him set free. The secret of the machines had to remain a secret.

"You may go." Said Negi

The man looked at Negi in confusion. He stood where he was wondering if Negi was playing with him. That's what usually happened in this city. Benevolence was usually a garb over lethal intent.

"I said you can go." Repeated Negi

Not believing his luck, the man touched Negi's feet and thanked him profusely. Then he began to apologize again as he made for the door.

Negi looked at him and smiled again.

The man rushed out of the room.

Negi wondered what caused people to betray their friends. Negi lit a cigarette and blew the smoke in a ring over his head. Negi gave a little laugh. He wondered how such people got caught. Being dishonest and dumb was a dangerous combination.

His phone rang. He had been expecting the call. It was Jadhav.

"Mr Negi, I have your man. I just picked him up outside your house."

Negi exhaled the smoke out and spoke, "Make sure he is isolated. I don't want him speaking to anyone. And that includes you. Come up with some charge that will keep him there forever. Is that clear?"

"Yes Sir! What exactly did …?" said Jadhav but heard the line go dead before he could finish.

Jadhav threw a dirty look at the man now sitting in the back. The man was in a shock at the betrayal.

Sunny clicked his fingers excitedly. This was beyond his imagination. Sunny wondered what Babur might think of this.

"Are you sure, Raj? Are you absolutely sure?" asked Sunny again

"I am sure, Sunny. Those men worked for Kasid. Some of them have a high profile: Remnants of the old days who knew who to fight. Somehow Yanus got past them. The strange bit of news is that Kasid is prepared to lose more men before he can get to Yanus."

Sunny didn't have much information about Kasid other than the fact that he was based in Mumbai. Babur too had never mentioned him. But the fact that Kasid was looking for Yanus was interesting. How had Yanus earned the displeasure of a high ranking official? What was so special about this Yanus?

"One other thing, Sunny, I think you should know this. Word has gone out to look for the men that attacked Yanus. All of them have gone missing."

"What are you talking about?" asked Sunny

"Don't you see? It is the same thing that happened with our people too. Whoever attacked Yanus so far has disappeared off the face of the earth. All of them could not have…"

"I don't care about what happened to them. There are always more men." Said Sunny

"I know there are more men. The question is how many are we prepared to lose? Yanus has cost us too much already."

"What are you getting at?" asked Sunny

"Have you noticed that he is no longer attacking the camps?" asked Raj

"I did. What's your point?"

"Let it go, Sunny. I have a bad feeling about this. Kasid is moving heaven and earth to reach this boy. He is prepared to go to any length. I think we must wait and watch for developments."

Sunny glared at the floor and spoke through gritted teeth.

"There is no way I am letting go of this. I don't care about this Kasid. He can go to hell. I will find Yanus and kill him. Any who stand in my way will join him. Is that clear?"

Raj was about to speak when there was a knock on the door. A man poked his head through the door and spoke to Sunny, "Jadhav wants to speak to you."

"Bring him in here." Said Sunny without any hesitation

"Now what does he want?" asked Sunny

Raj put on a stony expression as Jadhav entered the room. Jadhav took a seat opposite Sunny and did not look at Raj. He was not in uniform. But he had his gun with him which he put on the table before speaking. Raj raised his eyebrows at this gesture.

"I have some news." Said Jadhav

Raj stared at Jadhav and waited for him to finish his theatricalities.

Jadhav went on, "Do any of you know of Negi?"

"What about him?" Sunny was losing patience

"He has asked me to find the boy that was troubling you. I have no idea what he wants to do with him."

"Yanus?" Sunny was stunned

"Yes, Negi had called me an hour after we arrested him that night. He instructed me to keep him there until he could come there and see him."

Raj leaned forward and stared in to Jadhav's oily face.

"Of course, I had your orders to bring him to you. So I…" Jadhav's voice failed him in the face of the two men staring at him like a pride of lions would stare at their dinner. Both looked more interested than he had thought they would.

"Why did you not tell us about Negi before now?" Raj's voice was barely above a whisper. It was a danger sign that Jadhav recognized.

"I didn't think it was important…"

Sunny leaned forward and slapped Jadhav in the face.

"A man like Negi does not look for people who are unimportant. You are an idiot, Jadhav. I don't understand why Babur bothers with a fool like you." Sunny was too angry to speak. He got up and began pacing the room.

"Why are you telling us now?" Raj was still eyeing Jadhav dangerously whose eyes were watering

"Negi called me and asked me to look for Yanus…"

"…and what did you tell him?" It was Raj who was getting to the heart of the matter.

Jadhav was trembling was head to toe but he had to tell the truth. "I told him about Yanus killing a few of Sunny's men…" Sunny stopped pacing when he heard this and nearly jumped on Jadhav. Sunny kicked Jadhav in the stomach and sent him reeling on the floor. Sunny kept kicking him and shouting at him, "You little piece of shit! How dare you? What do we pay you for? So you can blab to politicians about how I am getting beat? I'll kill you, you little…!"

Jadhav was in too much pain to even whimper. Sunny had driven the air from his lungs. Raj sat quietly looking at him writhing on the floor. He looked lost in thought.

"Get up and get out! Get out before I kill you." Roared Sunny

Sunny's voice brought half a dozen men running up to the door and a few of them barged in without knocking.

They saw Jadhav rolling in his blood on the floor and quickly made to leave. Sunny hailed the nearest one, "Throw this garbage out, right now."

Four men grabbed Jadhav and dragged him out, shutting the door behind them. Raj could hear Jadhav struggling on the other side of the door.

Sunny cooled down a little and spoke to Raj, "You two have a history, don't you?" gesturing toward the door

Raj kept his silence and said nothing. Sunny went on, "You have killed people for a lot less than what he did to you. Why is Jadhav still alive, Raj?"

Raj put his head back on the sofa and spoke without emotion. "Killing him won't satisfy me. It is too easy. I see his fear. He knows I can kill him at any time without any reason. That fear is what I want him to live with."

"I don't believe you. You will not let this go on forever. You know Babur won't mind…" Sunny made a face to suggest his understanding

"Oh! Of course he will die. But I want him to suffer before I kill him. Death is too final."

Sunny stared at the man seated in front of him. A man, they said, was feared perhaps more than him.

Sunny nodded his understanding.

Sunny changed the subject, "What do you make of Negi's interest."

"Apart from his sick hobbies?" asked Raj

Sunny made a face and gestured to Raj to share his opinion

"Before we do anything, I think we must find out why these people are after Yanus. Of course, we could follow the best way which would be to drop the matter and ignore Yanus. We don't need this problem."

Sunny waved his hand impatiently to suggest that such a notion was out of the question.

"That is not going to happen, Raj. I want Yanus and that is final."

Raj's expression was unreadable, "Very well, I am going to find out why Negi is after Yanus."

"What about Kasid?" Sunny wanted to know

"Kasid can wait. From what I have seen, it is Negi who will be difficult to figure out. This man enjoys a lot of support. Also I have heard that he is one of the most competent men in the country's political system." Said Raj

Raj picked up the gun that Jadhav had left behind in haste and walked toward the door.

"Take it as a souvenir." Said Sunny laughingly

Raj had a strange expression on his face as he left Sunny. His mind had travelled down a different road to search a different purpose for Jadhav's gun. But that would have to wait. First, he had to change his tactics with Yanus. Raj knew that Sunny would not budge from his position. He would keep sending people to attack Yanus until there were no more left. Whatever Sunny said, Raj was sure that Yanus had found a way to get past professional fighters and to defeat him, they would have to think of something different.

The time for covert operations had come and gone. Raj knew that there had been a time when only he and Sunny were after Yanus but the last few days had seen the arrival of Kasid and Negi in to play. Their motives too were unknown which was quite unusual. Politicians usually made no bones about their motives, even if they were illegal. It was time to approach both these men and find out why they were after Yanus. Raj was not intending to race them both to get at

Yanus. Nobody was that important. Raj just hoped Sunny understood that before it was too late.

Raj went through different arguments in his mind against meeting Negi. Raj decided that his decision was correct. He would have to meet Negi as soon as possible. Raj frowned to himself. A thought came to him that stopped him in his tracks. Negi had asked Jadhav to look for Yanus but had not given any specific instructions as to what to do with him. Kasid had sent men to attack Yanus and thus had made his intentions clear. But what did Negi want? Raj began walking again as another thought came to him. Negi had known that Yanus was in Jadhav's station. He had got to Yanus before Kasid. Somehow, a low ranking official was looking a lot more dangerous than a more powerful one. Raj quickened his step. He had to meet Negi as soon as possible.

Negi looked at the man and stared in to his eyes to detect lies. The man looked away and swallowed, understanding the gesture.

"Sir, the information is absolutely…" the man began but Negi cut him short with a wave of his hand

"I know it is the truth. You may leave." The man nodded his head and walked out

Negi put his legs on the table and yawned. It had been a difficult day. He wondered how he had survived for so long in this mad world.

Negi smiled to himself thinking about Yanus. He had gone further than he had imagined. Kasid, as usual, was underestimating his opponent. Negi shrugged to himself. Why did he give a damn? As long as Kasid led him to Yanus, it would be fine. Negi did not fear what firepower Kasid threw at Yanus. It didn't matter…

Negi was worried about one thing: Babur. Babur was a different matter altogether. Would Yanus be able to defend himself against Babur? Babur was sure to get to Yanus before Kasid did. Negi broke in to a cold sweat. If only that fool Jadhav had not gone to Babur that day, Negi would have had Yanus.

The phone on Negi's table rang with a sharp shrill bringing Negi out of his thoughts. Negi answered with a short, "Yes?"

It was the security asking for permission. Someone wanted to see him.

Negi groaned to himself. What was it this time? Negi hated seeing random people with their random problems. But this was his job and he had to fulfil his duties. No matter how random….

"Send him in." Negi put down the receiver and put on his "good natured uncle" face that he usually did when seeing people with complaints.

The man knocked and entered the room. Negi asked him to sit down and asked him for tea. The man refused and thanked Negi for his hospitality.

"What can I do for you?" asked Negi wondering if this man could top the list of 'most weird problem'

"What do you want with Yanus?" said the man in a deadly tone

Negi put his hand on the table and leaned forward, "Yanus?"

"Yanus, Yes. What do you want with him?" the man repeated

"And who are you?" asked Negi

"My name is Raj."

"Aah! You work for…Babur, don't you?" said Negi relaxing a little

"Yes, I do. Answer my question."

"I heard he killed some of your men." Said Negi casually

"That is not your concern, Negi. Why are you after Yanus?"

"I could say the same thing to you. Why are you so concerned about an orphan?" asked Negi

"Orphan?" Raj was genuinely surprised. He had missed that one

"Yes, didn't you know? Did you think none of the children you abused over the years would think to fight back? I am disappointed, Raj. I had heard better things about you."

Raj kept his silence. But he needed answers. *Think,* Raj told himself, *think.*

"I understand Babur is after Yanus. I am sure he has his reasons. But I doubt he goes down the street explaining his actions. Why do you expect any different from me?" finished Negi

"Well, you gave the reason yourself, Negi. Don't you understand? I am surprised at you. I had heard you were smarter than the others of your kind."

Negi broke in to a laugh. "You are good, Raj. You are really good. You mean Babur, don't you?"

"Of course I do. I still haven't told him that you are poking your nose in his business. May be he already knows. Do you think your rank will protect you against Babur? He will butcher you if you get in his way. Ask your friends."

"Like I said, you are good." Said Negi raising his hand in a mock salute and continued.

"But that would be applicable in ordinary situations. This is no ordinary problem we are facing, Raj. Surely, with your educational background and vast experience in analyzing financial data, you understand that much."

Raj dimly wondered how Negi knew so much about him. Raj pressed nonetheless, "What do you mean?"

"Do you know how those people you send to kill Yanus died?" asked Negi in a suddenly dangerous tone

"I presume you mean those people who disappeared. That happens all the time. What does that have…?"

"They were killed, Raj. They did not disappear. You know the truth of this. Are you going to pretend otherwise and insult my intelligence?"

Raj's estimate of the man rose a little. He surely had a powerful motive. But Raj still needed his answer and waited for Negi to go on.

"I am sorry, Raj. But I cannot tell you anymore."

"I am not leaving until…"

"No information on earth can help you to defeat Yanus. Do what you can, Raj. If you go down this road, eventually you will all die."

Raj was stunned. What did Negi think he was, a school boy?

"This is not the first time…"

"Yes, it is. This is the first time you are facing a threat of this kind. If it is any consolation, no one on Earth has ever faced anything like what you are now facing now. You have got in the way of the most powerful force that walks the Earth. In Babur's case, nature has just set him down a path where he will finally meet his end. Ordinary people were no match for him, so something a lot more potent has been sent by nature. And there is no way out."

"You know something, Negi. I will find out what is scaring you. Just sit tight and…."

"I will. Now leave."

"This is not over, Negi."

Negi looked past Raj and said with a heavy voice.

"I know your past Raj. I know where you come from. Had it been anyone else instead of you, I would have thrown him out. Please leave before I change my mind."

Somehow, Raj thought, this was not an idle threat. He knew a lost cause when he saw one. Raj got up and left.

Negi smiled to himself and put his feet back on the table. Lighting up a cigarette, Negi wondered what Raj was thinking now. If Raj had known about him, then he would definitely know about Kasid. Negi hoped Kasid used his brains when Raj spoke to him. Raj was right. He was smarter than most. Negi couldn't help but smile to himself.

Negi got up and picked up his phone. The crap was about to hit the fan.

Raj stopped at a red light and put his head on the steering wheel. It was one thing to go after an individual. Hits had been ordered in the past and there had been conflicting interests between politicians, businessmen, and men like Babur. But there had always been a middle ground. There had always been a way to resolve conflicts in the interest of all. That was the key to survival. Being strong headed was one thing and being pig headed was another. Stubborn people who did not listen were usually the scapegoats that were sacrificed at the first hint of trouble. But this was different. Not only was Negi not revealing what his intentions were, he had actually hinted that Babur would not be able to defeat Yanus. Raj lifted his head and took a deep breath. There was no way anyone could know that and considering Babur's resources, that was highly unlikely. But the question that was burning in Raj's mind was why Yanus was being hunted? Raj drove off toward the office of Kasid hoping that Kasid would be more forthcoming.

Raj smiled at the big man standing guard at the reception. The large room did not look like a reception at all. It was unwelcoming and had a sinister feel to it. The men sitting around the table had stopped talking and were looking at Raj with a rapt expression. The few sitting on the sofa had got up immediately and surrounded Raj as soon as he walked in. Raj looked around at the big man standing outside who had let him in. There was no expression on his face as he too stared at Raj.

"What do you want?" asked one of the men in surrounding him

"I told your friend outside. I want to see Mr. Kasid." Raj turned around to face them

One of the men stepped forward and stood toe to toe with Raj.

"And why would Mr. Kasid want to see you?"

"That is between him and me. Now get out of my way."

No sooner had Raj finished his sentence, than the men at the table got up and walked toward. Raj was in danger of being suffocated by all the men surrounding him.

The man nearest Raj held Raj's chin and shook it, "Go home. If I ever see you here again…well, we don't want you peeing in your pants now, do we?" the man laughed as he patted Raj's cheek. The men laughed at the joke.

Raj began to laugh as well. He had once seen this happening in a movie. But he couldn't remember when or which movie it was. The outcome was never conducive for those who laughed first.

The men stopped laughing as the man suddenly grabbed Raj's neck and spoke angrily, "Think you are smart? You want to see….?" The man began but could never finish his threat.

Raj raised his arm and hit the man's elbow as it came up. The man screamed in pain as his arm broke at the crook of the elbow, sending him to the ground. The men, stunned, advanced toward Raj.

Raj's long leg connected with one of the men in the chest sending him crashing in to the two behind him. Raj whirled about and brought down his fists on any one who came close. Raj never bothered going to them. They would take care of that. One of them caught hold of Raj from behind and tried to throttle him. Raj poked his fingers in his eyes. The man released Raj and fell back screaming. Raj waited for the next wave of gentlemen.

But before they could reach him, one of the men on Raj's right was lifted off his feet and flew past Raj. Raj stayed rooted to the spot as he saw the black robes billowing about as if in a wind. The men stopped in their tracks and turned to their chief.

Kasid's eyes found Raj and for the first time since he had met Babur, Raj felt a profound sense of power surging through an individual. Kasid's eyes were on Raj as he lifted his own man and turned him around to face him.

"What are you doing?" the voice was of steel grating on stone.

The man was smart enough to realize that any answer would attract punishment. It was better to mumble. Kasid let go of the man and gestured to Raj,

"Come in, Mr. Raj." Raj did not show his surprise that Kasid knew about him too, just like Negi.

Raj followed Kasid in to the room from where Kasid had apparently appeared from. If the room outside was unwelcoming, the room inside was warm and had a welcoming feel to it.

"Please sit down. Let's get this over with quickly." Said Kasid

Raj took a seat opposite to Kasid and spoke without wasting any time.

"I have come here on behalf of Babur. I am sure you know…" Raj waited for Kasid to answer

"Of course, I do. I have immense respect for men of courage and almost always know about such men in my city. That is why you are sitting here."

"Why are you after Yanus?" asked Raj wanting to finish this quickly

"Do you not know? Is that why you are here? To ask why I am after Yanus?"

Raj betrayed a hint of confusion, but realized that there was no time to play games.

"There are many areas where my mind is occupied. Yanus is of special importance to Babur. I want to know why you are after his mark. Is it…?"

"There are many powerful forces at the moment who are trying to find and destroy Yanus. I am one of those who want to see if he can be controlled…before I too decide to kill him. Obviously, this is not as easy as it sounds. He is heavily protected, as I am sure, you too have found to your cost."

Raj was not sure what Kasid was getting at.

"How is he protected? All he has is that old man."

"That I am afraid, you will have to find out yourself. Even if I tell you, it will not deter Babur."

"Is that why you are after him? Yanus has some weapon that you want?"

Kasid leaned forward and spoke in a whisper, "Yanus is the weapon, Mr. Raj."

Raj did not have the information that he wanted, but he had what he needed. He drove as fast as he could. It was late in the evening. He would be with Babur. Raj was convinced that this war with Yanus was foolhardy. There were too many unknown factors which could jeopardize their operations in other areas. There was no point in endangering so much for so little. Raj hoped to convince Babur and Sunny of this fact. Raj feared that Sunny might still not agree to back down and Babur would go along with Sunny's decision. Fearing the worst, Raj got out of the car and took the stairs to Babur's quarters. It was the same old damp room that he stayed in during the evening. Raj was sure that this old room had some connection with his past. Babur had many properties in and around the city but he rarely visited any of them. This was where they all came to see him. The lion would be found in his den and on his terms.

Raj entered the room to find Sunny settled down on the ground opposite Babur who had lit up his pipe. He did that rarely and Raj was surprised to see Babur smoking. Raj wondered what the occasion was.

"What did Negi say?" asked Sunny

"He did not reveal why he is after Yanus. But he won't back off, and neither will Kasid."

"They are aware that I want this boy." Said Babur

"Yes they are. But it is what Kasid said that is interesting."

"Kasid! I haven't heard anything about him for years." Said Babur

"He said that Yanus has some protection or a weapon. That is what everyone is after."

Babur made a face and that is exactly what Raj knew he would do. Even Sunny laughed a little.

"What does he have, a pocket atom bomb?" laughed Sunny

"They both told me one thing: we will not be able to defeat Yanus." Said Raj

"I have been told that before…"

"You don't understand, Sunny. Kasid attacked Yanus with a lot of firepower that even we might not be able to manage. Yet, he killed them all. And yes, they were all killed. Negi told me." Said Raj seeing the look on Sunny's face

Sunny's expression tightened further and he looked away.

"That he may be heavily armed is irrelevant, Raj. What must be done, has to be done."

"Babur, please try and understand…."

Sunny rose up in one swift motion and addressed Raj, "No! You understand. Yanus killed my men. He will not get away with it. You asked me to wait for this. I did. That is the only courtesy I can extend you, my friend. Now I will find him and kill him. That is final."

Raj looked imploringly at Babur. But there was nothing there. Babur looked at his hands and finally spoke to Sunny.

"Take all the men you can and bring me this boy. I don't care if he is dead."

Raj raised his arm in a half hearted attempt to stop Sunny from leaving the room but Sunny rushed out leaving Raj alone with Babur.

Raj glared at Babur and said, "He does not understand. But I know that you do. You know that you are sending him to his death. If Sunny attacks Yanus…."

"There really has been no turning back since a long time, Raj. You obviously know this, don't you?"

Raj did not understand and continued to glare at Babur. Babur smiled and went on, "I have known for a while that Yanus had the means to defeat Sunny. But such are the ways of men like Sunny, Raj. I could not stop him. The least I could do for the man who has been loyal to me for so many years is that I would not get in his way. Who knows? Maybe Sunny might survive... and even win."

Raj gave a weak laugh, "That is the biggest pile of crap I have ever heard. What is this fight for? To massage bruised egos? What will we lose if Yanus lives? Is this worth a life?"

"That does not suit you, Raj. You have killed people. Did you ever rationalize the purpose?"

"Yes, I did. And I am not concerned about the purpose. My question is whether Sunny has to die for this."

Babur got up and stood in front of Raj and answered, "That my friend, is the answer that Yanus will give us soon. Then it will be our turn."

Raj was astounded at the carelessness. He could not believe how easily Babur had let Sunny go. Raj was sure that Yanus would kill him. Sunny was an intelligent man but this was not a matter of intelligence. Babur too knew this. And he had let him go. Raj looked up to see in to the eyes of Babur. There was nothing there as usual. Raj turned around and left.

Babur watched from the window as Raj got in to his car and drove away. Babur once again settled down on the rough floor and lay down. He remembered the old days when he had held his first meetings here. Those were different times, different men, and a different calibre. Times had changed. Everything had changed. Babur remembered how he had started his married life here all those years ago... and how everything had burned. It had burned right here, in this room. Babur closed his eyes to block out the images and waited for the news.

Chapter 6

The Rise of Cyclone Rx

Sunny's car screamed through the traffic. There was a reckless rage coursing through him that demanded action. For far too long the boy had played with him. But this time he would get Yanus. For good measure, he would take care of Singh too. He was the one who had guided Yanus all this time. It was only a matter of time before one of his sources found out where they were hiding. Sunny gripped the wheel harder as his anger boiled over at Raj. How could he expect them to do nothing? Raj knew the code. He knew how the business functioned. It was a "live and let live" world but there were limits. There was a line that you couldn't cross and Yanus had crossed it. There was only one possible course that events would now take. Yanus would pay with his life and become an example.

Sunny's phone buzzed. Sunny hit the green button and answered, "Yes?"

Sunny listened to the man on the other end and his face lit up. Sunny slowed the car to a crawl and mounted the pavement on the far side, bringing the car to a stop.

"Are you sure?" asked Sunny

Sunny listened for a few seconds and disconnected the line.

Sunny swerved the car around and dashed back the way he had come. The fools were cornered. They were not as smart as he had thought.

"I hope you know what you are doing!" said Singh

Yanus was perched on a big rock and eyed Singh with a smile.

"He is coming here for me. You should not get in the way."

Singh had a suspicious look on his face, "You remember what I told you. There is no need to…"

"How can I forget it? You must have said it a hundred times. I am not daft." Said Yanus

"I am not saying it because I think you are daft. You know why I am saying it."

Yanus nodded and looked at the setting sun. It was a beautiful sight. He wished Singh had brought them to the woods more often. It was a whole lot better than hiding out in the warehouses and slums where you had to be careful. It was much safer here and much more peaceful.

"You sure we were seen?" Asked Yanus

"Yes, they will be here soon. Are you prepared?" asked Singh

"We will know."

Singh did not like Yanus's tone. But there was nothing he could think of say that could change Yanus's mind.

Darkness fell over the woods and the immediate area was washed with the blue glow of the machine. It drifted idly beside Yanus waiting for a command. Yanus closed his eyes and wondered if Babur would send someone tonight. Would it be Sunny? All this had begun with him. He had seen what Sunny was doing to those children the night he had escaped with Singh. Yanus clenched his fist and felt the rage ignite. He hoped it was Sunny.

"Yanus, they're here." Singh leapt to his feet and squinted in the darkness.

"I can hear them. They know we are here. You must leave now, Singh."

"Yanus, please think about it again. There is still time."

Yanus was not even listening. He stood still facing in the direction of the voices and faint glows emanating from tiny flash lights.

Singh pursed his lips. There was no time left.

Sunny was the first one to lay eyes on the solitary figure standing in the clearing. Sunny signalled some of his men to circle around and surround Yanus. Yanus kept his eyes on the large group now advancing through the trees and paid no attention to the men now appearing behind him.

Sunny stood at the edge of the clearing, backed by his little army.

"How are you going to get out of this, Yanus?" asked Sunny

Yanus did not answer and waited.

Sunny started forward and came to a stop in front of Yanus. Sunny was slightly taller than Yanus and looked down at him.

"You are going to die. But before that, my people have something to say to you. They have been waiting for a long time. I hope you don't mind the delay." Sunny smiled and turned back

Yanus watched as Sunny went to his men and sat down on the ground as if settling down to enjoy a picnic. Yanus stood ready as the men advanced. So this was how it was going to be. Yanus waited till they were ten feet away. Then he sprang in to action.

Yanus rushed at the nearest man and grabbed his arm turning him around, ramming him in to the next man. Both took the hit badly and went down. One man used the opportunity to attack Yanus from behind and grabbed hold of his neck. Yanus kicked the first two men who advanced from the front in their faces sending them to the floor. Yanus shifted his balance and crashed his elbow in to the man in the back. Staggering back a little, the man exposed his left flank. Yanus kicked him hard in the ribs, dispatching him too. Sunny watched in amazement as one after the other his men dropped. Yanus side stepped one of the men charging at him and yanked him around with his arm. The man cried out holding his shoulder and staggered to the floor in agony. Finally it came to a point when the men began backing away. Yanus waited in the centre for Sunny.

Sunny watched his men angrily. Finally he got up and strode toward Yanus. This time, Yanus charged Sunny. Sunny however, was a lot smarter than the men he commanded. At the last moment, Sunny side stepped and drove his arm straight in to Yanus's chest. Yanus was expecting Sunny to come up front and didn't anticipate this move. Yanus faltered and sank to the ground. His chest began to burn with pain and it was getting difficult to breathe.

"Did you think I was going to be easy?" asked Sunny

Yanus tried to get up but Sunny caught his neck and pulled him up to his feet and lifted him clear off the ground. Yanus began to choke and struggled to get free but Sunny was strong and Yanus had spent a lot of energy fighting his men. Then Sunny dropped Yanus on to the ground and said, "It will not be this easy for you, Yanus." Sunny slapped Yanus as hard as he could on his face. Yanus felt his face burning and his eyes began to water. Yanus was struggling to find his feet. He still couldn't get a full breath. Sunny slapped him again and the blow sent Yanus sprawling on the ground. Yanus tried to get up but Sunny put his foot on his back, pinning him to the ground. Sunny pulled Yanus's head up and unleashed a powerful blow behind Yanus's ear. Yanus could feel his strength waning. Sunny was too strong and that one strike on his chest had weakened Yanus a lot. Yanus tried to crawl out from under the foot but Sunny slammed the foot on Yanus's head causing it to bang on the ground. The pain nearly made Yanus pass out. Yanus took in rapid breaths to keep conscious. He could not afford to faint. He could not fail. Yanus dragged himself forward out of the reach of Sunny's foot. Sunny moved forward to kick Yanus but Yanus rolled to the side and avoided the kick. Sunny laughed and followed Yanus as Yanus tried to get to his feet. Sunny caught Yanus's collar and turned him around to face him. Yanus shielded his punch behind his body and caught Sunny by surprise on his head. Sunny felt his knees buckle. He felt another punch on the other end of his head that brought him down on all fours. Sunny looked up to see Yanus swinging his leg and felt his jaw break with the impact of the kick. Sunny was suddenly in a lot of trouble. He tasted blood in his mouth and found it difficult to block the blows that Yanus was now unleashing at him. Sunny tried to back away but Yanus landed blow after blow on his face and chest. Once Yanus got the upper hand, Yanus did not relent and punished Sunny relentlessly. Sunny realized he was losing. He shouted as loudly as he could through Yanus's punches, "Shoot him. Just shoot him."

Sunny looked at Yanus and was surprised to see him smiling.

"Your time is up, Yanus." Sunny gasped as he spat blood from his mouth

The men all around Yanus were advancing and were preparing to shoot him from point blank range. It was time. Yanus looked back in the woods and whispered, "Kill them."

Sunny wondered who he was talking to when suddenly a blue light lit up the trees around them. At first Sunny thought it was a siren but then the machine came in to view. Sunny scrambled backwards to get away from it. Sunny realized that this was going to be trouble and he had to get away from it. But he was wounded and it became a huge struggle just to move. Sunny looked up to see the tall body drifting in silently in to the clearing. The men recognized the danger and let loose their weapons at it. Two seconds later, an intense discharge of light erupted from the machine. More than half the men disintegrated in to nothing. Sunny was too terrified to even scream as another discharge blasted the remaining men. Sunny knew he had seconds to live. He was going to go the same way as his men had gone. The same way Rohan had gone. Nobody would even find his body. Sunny waited for the same blue light to hit him. But it didn't come. Sunny looked up to see the machine hovering silently a feet away where it had appeared.

"You don't deserve to die like that, Sunny. You deserve pain."

Sunny tried to put some weight on his legs but he couldn't. He got up on his one good leg and limped toward Yanus.

Yanus smiled at the temerity of the man. But he had expected no less. Yanus waited till Sunny was almost on top of him. Just as Sunny reached him, Yanus swept his leg under Sunny tripping him up. Sunny went crashing down on his face. Yanus kicked Sunny twice in the head as hard as he could. Yanus bent down and reached in to Sunny's pocket pulling out his knife.

"How many times have you used this knife?" asked Yanus

Sunny was no longer coherent. He knew he was going to die. He was losing control of himself. Yanus realized he had little time. He wanted Sunny to feel this. Yanus twirled the knife in his fingers and began.

Singh ran as fast as he could. He had heard the twin blasts of the machine discharging its weapon. It must have been all over. But uneasiness had been creeping up over him since the time Yanus had proposed this plan. Yanus was not just determined to punish Sunny and Babur, he had become obsessed. There was a hint of madness in his eyes that Singh was becoming uncomfortable with. Then Singh heard the screams. It did not sound like Yanus at all and Singh sped up. He knew what this was all about. It was about revenge. It had become personal. Singh ran faster and reached the clearing in less than two minutes. But those two minutes were all that Yanus had needed. Yanus stood over the body of Sunny with a bloodied knife in his hands. Slowly, Singh approached Yanus and looked down at Sunny. Sunny was dead. Yanus had stabbed him with his own knife. And Yanus had cut his eyes out.

"What have you done?" Croaked Singh

"I have done what he wanted to do to me."

Singh caught Yanus's collar and pulled him around. "So you have become like him, Yanus. Is that it? You want to be a murderer?"

"Stop it, Singh." Said Yanus as he pulled himself free and continued, "He deserved it."

"Yes, he did. But why did you kill him? We agreed to...."

"What did you expect me to do? Did you think this was a slapping contest? He came here to kill me. Only I killed him first. And what is your problem?"

"He had been injured. He…."

"And that would have made no difference to anything. We are done here. Let's move."

"I am not coming with you, Yanus."

Yanus stopped in his tracks and turned around.

"What do you mean?" asked Yanus

"You have become a monster, Yanus. Every time you have fought has only increased your cruelty. I don't even recognize you anymore. I promised to help you fight Babur. Killing Sunny was not going to help. Not only did you kill him, you even…."

"Yes, I did." Said Yanus defiantly

Singh nodded. There really was no other way to do this. It had to be this way.

"Good bye Yanus. I hope that you find some peace in you."

"I am sorry that you feel this way, Singh. But this is how it will be. There is no peace. There are only horrors. I knew you wouldn't understand. Perhaps this is for the best."

Singh nodded again. One last time, Singh looked in to the eyes of Yanus. There was no remorse. Is this what Jabar Falak wanted? He would never know. Singh realized that he didn't care and began walking.

Yanus watched as Singh disappeared in to the night. Yanus whispered, "Good Bye, Singh."

It was still night when Babur was shaken awake by one of his guards. Babur was having nightmares and woke with a start. But the expression on his guards face sent a chill down Babur's spine.

"What is it? What happened?" roared Babur

The man simply looked away and hesitantly walked toward the door

Babur knew something was wrong the moment he stepped out of the room. There were about a hundred men gathered on the ground below and the stairs leading up. None of them looked his way and none of them made a sound. An ambulance stood in the grounds with one of its back doors open. Raj stood next to the closed door and there was a murderous look on his face. Babur clenched his fists and walked down toward the ambulance. People made way as Babur walked slowly toward the ambulance. He knew what was inside. But he could only delay the inevitable, not avoid it. Babur came face to face with Raj. There was a fire in his eyes that Babur had seen in him only once before. That was the day Babur had met him for the first time.

"Sunny has paid the price of your arrogance with his life." Said Raj

Babur reached for the door of the ambulance and opened it. Babur had seen much death. But the death of a loved one was different. Babur realized that he had never told Sunnil Thore that he was more than a son to him. He would never be able to say it now. Sunnil was gone. The men had lost their leader.

Babur watched as Raj walked through the crowd and disappeared. Raj's loss too was great. Sunny had been like a brother to him. It was Sunny who helped him all those years ago when Raj's family had been killed. It was Sunny who realized that Raj could be an asset to them and had silenced all who opposed Raj becoming a part of Babur's family. Babur realized that he could never have done the same for anyone. No one would have, not in his time. But this generation was better. This generation was much more comfortable in sharing their glory and their power. Just like Sunny had. Now he was gone. Yanus had killed him. Babur put his hand on Sunny's forehead and pushed the hair out of the empty eye socket.

Babur tightened his fist and made a plea for forgiveness. Babur turned to the man who had awoken him just a few minutes ago.

"Take him away."

The man nodded and gave urgent instructions to his fellows. The men leapt in to action. Within seconds, the ambulance had been driven away. Babur stood where he was feeling the eyes of a hundred people on him. They waited for instructions. But none came as Babur stood silent among his men staring in the direction where the ambulance had gone. One after another, the men left. The silence had been an instruction too. It was an instruction to leave Babur alone. The silence was an indication of the storm to follow. Babur would himself deal with this. It was time for the king of the jungle to enter the battle.

Mani turned the pages around one by one. Samar looked at him expectantly. Clearly, it had something to do with the Cyclone. But Mani could make no sense of it at all. But he was careful not to let Samar know that. Mani looked up to see Samar hopefully watching him for a sign of some revelation. Mani had to disappoint.

"Well, what are these?" asked Samar

"I will have to get some people here to look at this." Said Mani

"And you?" persisted Samar

"I didn't deal with this."

"Then what did you deal with?"

"I'll tell you some other time. But this won't help us to control that Cyclone." Samar looked dejected. He had thought it could be of some help. After all, these were the only documents related to Cyclone that were kept in his father's office. It had to be of some significance. Samar got a faint feeling that Mani was not being entirely truthful about something.

"What do you want to do now?" asked Samar

"I don't know. I just want to get rid of that infernal machine so we can get our work back on track."

"What track?"

"First things first, shall we? Was there anything else in the safe that could be useful?"

"There were old records of Dad's business deals, nothing technical like what I just gave you. Why don't you get that checked? May be something in it might help?" Samar was still hoping against hope.

"I told you. It doesn't look like it is important at…."

Mani was interrupted by the buzzing of Samar's cell. Mani put up his hands and gestured toward it. Samar quickly flipped it open and answered it.

Mani watched Samar's expression darken as he listened to a female voice on the other end.

"Okay. Give him the…Hello Sir. I believe…." Samar had been cut short by the person to whom the woman had given the receiver. Mani stood up and leaned closer to Samar. He still couldn't hear the voice properly. Samar listened for a few seconds.

"Please stay there. I will get there as soon as I can." Samar flipped his cell and cut the call.

"There is someone we have to meet at my office. Come on."

"You want me to come with you? Are you sure?"

"Don't worry. The machine is not going to show up now." Said Samar drily

Mani was surprised. "What do you mean? How do you know?"

Samar looked at Mani and said, "Your machine is busy elsewhere."

Samar had a look on his face that Mani did not understand.

Mani and Samar walked in to the office and strode past the reception area. Samar's eyes fell on the man standing next to the reception counter.

"Mr. Samar." Singh said and nodded

"Follow me, please." Said Samar and walked inside his cabin followed by Mani.

Singh took a deep breath and entered the cabin after Mani. Samar was already seated and Mani had placed himself at the sofa and looked more relaxed.

Samar motioned Singh to take a seat while he spoke a few words on the phone to the woman outside. Samar did not want to be disturbed. This was a good sign, thought Singh. Singh eyed the man on the sofa and wondered who he was. It didn't matter. He just wanted this over with.

"Can you explain what you said on the phone?" asked Samar

Singh looked again at the man on the sofa. He didn't seem interested and was studying the carpet.

"Like I told you, I knew your father." Singh said simply

"And?"

"You father asked me to look after a boy…a few years younger than you. He was raised in an orphanage…your orphanage. We escaped from there when it was attacked by Babur's men. Do you know who that is?" Singh wanted Samar to understand this much before he went on.

"What is the boy's name?" asked Samar ignoring the question

"I told you, his name is Yanus."

"Yes, you did. You said that Yanus has something that might belong to me."

"Have you lost something, Mr. Samar?"

"What do you mean?"

"I just want to ensure that we both are talking about the same thing. Jabar asked me to keep Yanus safe. I did what I could. But things are beyond my control and I just want to know if Yanus is where Jabar intended him to be."

"How would I know?" asked Samar

"You are his son. You are sitting where he once sat. You should know."

Samar felt irritated at this man. Why did people always think that he was his father?

"I am sorry. I don't know what you are talking about. I too am looking for something. It sounded like you knew where it was. Thank you for your time." Said Samar and began to get up

"Did you make that machine?" asked Singh freezing Samar on the spot

Samar sat down and swallowed.

"Do you mean to say that Yanus is controlling Cyclone Rx?" asked Samar incredulously

"Is that what you call it? Do you have any idea how many people it has killed?"

Samar was about to give a caustic retort when Mani cut in.

"We named it Cyclone Rx and it has killed a lot more people than you think, Mr. Singh."

Singh turned to look at the man in the crisp black suit.

"And who are you?" asked Singh

"The machine belongs to me...or Mr Samar here." Said Mani when Samar raised his eye brows

"Tell that to the machine. It follows Yanus like his pet dog." Said Singh

Singh turned to Samar and continued.

"Children that were abducted from your orphanages were rescued by Yanus. He was the one who kept sending those children back. You got the letter?"

"I did. I thought it was just someone picking children up from the streets. I doubled the security around those places and armed a few of them to ensure it didn't happen again. I didn't think about that again."

"We came to your office to meet you. But you were not here and the cow outside wouldn't even give me your contact details. This was before the machine came to him. Then... everything changed."

"How many people know that Yanus is controlling Cyclone Rx?" asked Mani

"All those who know are dead. Yanus slaughtered them all." Said Singh simply

Mani nodded and said, "It killed a lot more people before it finally went to Yanus. I wish it had done sooner than it did."

Singh gave a mirthless laugh, "Yanus is not using it to plant trees. He is killing people as we speak. Do you understand? The machine is killing everyone it comes in contact with."

"Who is he killing? Who is he after?" asked Samar

"He wants to kill Babur. He is the one who attacked the orphanage. Yanus saw one of his men injuring children...to beg, I think. That is what they do. Yanus killed that man last night…"

Samar could see that Singh was getting uncomfortable. This had affected him more than he was letting on. Samar could not believe that all this had been happening right under his nose. And he had never known.

Samar turned to Mani, "Does this mean anything to you?" indicating Singh

"Yes, it does. But I need some more information from someone else. I need answers too."

Samar smiled wryly. Apparently, all this foxed Mani more than him. Samar was not supposed to know this. But Mani had lived with all of it and yet….

"Why did my father ask you to look after Yanus? Did he tell you?" Samar asked Singh

"He never did. All I know is that he was looking for Yanus for a long time before he found him. He had been brought to the orphanage when he was still very young."

"And how did you fit in?" asked Samar

"I…was stationed in Gujarat at the time. I was ordered to take the responsibility of protecting the child till Jabar was ready."

"You were ordered? Who ordered you? Were you in the army?" asked Mani

"Yes, I was. The orders were to assist Jabar in protecting Yanus. But no names were taken. I do not know who Jabar approached. But it had to be someone high up enough to disrupt my career." Finished Singh

So that was it, thought Samar. Singh was bitter. Somehow his father had caused Singh to lose his career in the army and forced him to do guard duty for a baby. Jabar had turned a soldier in to a babysitter.

"But why you?" asked Samar

"I have no idea. May be Jabar thought I was the right person for the job. I never knew your father to make mistakes. It had to be important."

Samar made a face, "Of course it was important. These gentle men rarely deal with the ordinary. Don't you, Mr. Mani?" asked Samar sardonically

Mani got up and sat down next to Singh.

"Tell me more about Yanus. What is he like?" asked Mani

"Yes, tell us what is so special about this Yanus." Added Samar

Singh looked from one face to another. Both the men seemed to have their own agendas to follow. Singh realized he was unsure about both of them.

"Yanus was one of the boys at the orphanage. There was nothing special about him. He liked to stay alone. Only once did I see him get close to someone…a girl brought to the orphanage a few years ago. But she disappeared. That happens sometimes though she didn't look the kind to run away. Anyway, Sohrab didn't report the matter and nobody came looking for her either. Before and after that, I never saw Yanus being friendly with anyone. He kept to himself. I had to warn Sohrab not to touch Yanus."

"Sohrab hit the children, didn't he?" asked Samar quietly

"Yes, he did. I am sure he did."

"Why didn't you report him to my father?"

"I never saw your father after that day. There was nothing I could do."

"You could have warned Sohrab. I am sure you could have done that. An army guy like you…."

"Army guys are disciplined and we know how to follow orders. My business was guarding the place. I had no authority over what happened inside its walls. There were times when I was not on duty." Singh shook his head and continued, "There was nothing I could do to stop him. Nobody could."

Samar nodded and wondered if Yanus was after Babur because of this. Anyone left too long in a place like that would go mad. He was sure that Singh probably did not know everything that went on in there. Yanus must have seen it. He must have known. Killing Babur was his way of getting back at them all. Perhaps Yanus saw him as the enemy as well. After all, it was his orphanage. Why did father not look in to this more often? How could he allow such cruelty to go on under his roof? Was he that busy? He probably was, thought Samar with a sad shake of his head.

Samar looked at Mani who seemed lost in his own thoughts. He had been like that for a while. Samar was sure that Mani had just been surprised by Singh. He obviously did not know about Yanus. Samar smirked to himself. His father had not even told him.

He had trusted a stranger and an orphan but had not seen it fit to trust him with his greatest secret. Samar felt a pang of bitterness. He also felt jealousy. He was jealous that Yanus had been chosen by his father to command a machine. A machine built especially by his father. What was the whole purpose of the machines? Why were they built? And why should an unstable orphan be trusted with such terrible power? Yanus was at this moment following his own agenda. He was using his father's machine to take revenge on the people who hurt him. Is that what his father would have wanted?

Samar got up and walked to his favourite window overlooking the sea. The sun was shining brightly and it was nearly time for lunch.

Samar decided that the original idea of the machine, whatever it was, was being corrupted by Yanus. His father had not built it to fulfil a vendetta. Samar had to meet Yanus and find out more.

Samar turned to Singh, "Do you know where Yanus is?"

"He could be anywhere in the city. Why do you ask?"

"Could you arrange for us to meet?" asked Samar

Singh put his hands up and made a face.

"I did what I could. I don't want any more of this. I am leaving tonight for home. I am sorry."

"Yanus will need your help before this is over. You helped my father all these years. Now I am asking you for your help. You are the only one who can reach Yanus."

"Please Mr. Falak…"

"Jabar would never have asked you to do what you did if he did not trust you." It was Mani

Singh looked a little tired and answered wearily, "Maybe he was wrong. I am done."

Singh got up and turned toward the door.

"Just get me a meeting with Yanus. I will ask no more." Said Samar loudly

Singh stopped with his hand on the door.

"Just help me this one time. I will not ask you for anything else." Added Samar

Singh wondered if he was losing his mind. He nodded and left.

"What did you make of that?" Samar asked Mani

"Why do you want to meet Yanus?" asked Mani

"Isn't that what you want? I am helping you." Answered Samar

"Perhaps you are. But I need certain answers. I need to get going too." Mani got up

"Going to get some fresh air?" Samar wondered what was going through Mani's mind

"Let me know when you are going to meet Yanus. I will call you as soon as I have…some information."

Samar nodded. Mani seemed to be in a rush to leave.

It had been a while since Mani had been able to drive freely without the fear of being blown up. But the price, Mani decided, was too high. He knew Jabar had been lying to him. He had given the control of the machine to someone else. Only one person would know about this. This time Mani would not leave him until he had all that he wanted.

Mani strode through the double doors and ignored all the greetings. He had no time for this now. Mani walked up to a blank wall and pressed a button on it.

"Are you in?" asked Mani

"Yes." Came the reply

Mani stood back as the entire wall lifted off the ground and slid up in to the ceiling to reveal an opening. Mani got in and waited. The elevator came to life and began to rise. It came to a stop a few seconds later and the doors opened to reveal a spacious cabin. There was no other way to go. Mani stepped out and approached the man seated on the sofa.

"Learn something new today, son?" asked Suri Chetwal

"Did you know about Yanus?"

"Yanus, is it? Yes I did." Said Chetwal

"You knew and you said nothing. All those people died and you sat here while…."

"Sit down my boy. It looks like you have been caught up in your own game." Said Chetwal

"Don't play with me Chetwal…" Mani was absolutely livid

"You are the one who started this. That machine has been hunting us without Yanus's help. He has nothing to do with it."

"But you could have stopped it."

"Are you mad, Mani? Is that what was going on in your head when you forced everyone to betray Jabar? They believed your nonsense and look where it got us. I had no idea whether Cyclone R would still follow Yanus after your little coup. Falak shut us all out when you forced everyone here to isolate him. This madness had nothing to do with Falak's original plan."

"That's who it is with, Chetwal. Yanus is using it to go after gangsters who blinded his friends and forced them to beg. Falak chose an orphan boy living in an orphanage to control the deadliest creature on earth. And you let that happen…"

"The boy is attacking gangsters? Hmm. That is a worthy cause. I wish him luck. But I assure you that I had no idea that the boy's name was Yanus." Chetwal was almost smiling.

Mani realized that Chetwal was enjoying this. He had never been comfortable when they had accused Jabar of betraying the country. Chetwal had seen through the lie, but he was unable to do anything about it. Now he was taking his revenge on Mani for engineering Jabar Falak's downfall.

"What else do you know that I don't?" asked Mani

"That's all." Lied Chetwal

"I don't believe you. I will get to the bottom of this. I will find this…."

"Actually, you are not going to be doing anything." Said Chetwal in the most condescending tone he could manage

"What do you mean? You can't give me orders, Chetwal. My mission is to...." said Mani but Chetwal cut him short

"My dear boy, I couldn't care less about your mission. You will soon see. Now get out. I have important things to attend to." Chetwal got up and gave Mani a very cool look

Mani was sure Chetwal had found something out that he was hiding. No matter, thought Mani. He was good at finding out secrets. Chetwal will be sorry about this.

"I will be seeing you soon, Mr Suri Chetwal." Said Mani

"No, you won't. Or at least I won't." Said Chetwal with a smile and gestured toward the waiting elevator

Mani nodded curtly to Chetwal and walked in to the elevator. The two men shared a decade's worth of loathing. In those few seconds as the elevator rose up and out of sight, they glared at each other. It would be the last time.

Mani got out and made his way to his office. Mani froze in his tracks. There was already someone there.

The man turned around to face Mani as soon as Mani opened the door.

"Good evening, Mani." Said the man

"Who are you? What do you want? How did you get in here?" Mani did not like the smug look on the man's face

"A few years with civilians and you have lost all sense of discipline. Not to mention your powers of observation. You didn't think that we would tolerate such failure and insubordination, did you Mani?" the man took an envelope from his pocket and handed it to Mani.

Mani took the envelope and with shaking fingers, opened it to the read the letter.

The colour of Mani's face paled as he read the document. His legs gave way as he struggled for balance and collapsed in the chair.

"How would you like to get this done? Will you come willingly? Or do I have to drag you out?" asked the man

"You can't do this to me. Please, my career...." Mani was nearly in tears

"You should have thought of that before. Your mission was to observe and report on events, not to influence them." The man waited for a few seconds and walked out of the room

Four men walked in simultaneously and surrounded Mani. One of them leaned forward and said,

"Sir...?"

Mani raised his hands as if to surrender and got up from the chair to walk out. The men followed him out of the facility and shepherded him in to the jeep. Mani buried his face in his hands as he cursed the irony of it. He was being destroyed in exactly the same way he had destroyed Jabar Falak.

Chetwal took out the papers he had been studying before Mani had come in. He wished he had been able to see Mani's face when was taken away. Chetwal knew that he had been too late. He should have stopped Mani a long time ago. The price of his inaction had been too great. Chetwal focused his head back on the papers. He had taken these from Mani's locker the day Samar had given it to him. Mani obviously could not understand what the papers contained. He was not a man of science. But Chetwal too had been unable to figure out what the calculations and scribbling were all about. But then Chetwal had looked deeper. The equations and notes were beginning to reveal something else entirely. Chetwal screwed up his concentration and worked faster.

Yanus opened the parcel and ate greedily. It had been his first meal since a while. It had become quite difficult to survive without Singh. For nearly two days he had struggled for his next source of sustenance. Everyone had been driven out of his mind. All he could think of was of food. Even life at the orphanage provided some food. This was different. Yanus coughed a little and tried to gulp down the dried bread that he had got from the shop. It was all he had. He had no money and he had no shelter. All he had was the machine. He had not liked to steal. But it was the only option he had. Either steal or starve. Besides one day, he hoped, he would pay the shopkeeper. Yanus decided he was not a thief and hated himself for depending on stolen food. Yanus wondered if that is how people end up becoming animals. It had been only two days and he was prepared to go to any length to get a morsel of food.

Yanus got up and started walking toward the small path that would lead him back outside the city. He had left the machine there. It would be a bad idea to keep it with him all the time, especially during the day. Yanus realized that with the departure of Singh, he had to shift his priorities a little. He had to find a way to feed himself and find a permanent shelter. The shelter was not much of a problem. His present abode was outside the city and away from prying eyes. Yanus had not seen anyone come close to it at all since the time he had got there. It was rough, but it was safe. It was perfect to hide the machine as well. Food was a different problem. Yanus needed money to buy food. He didn't have a single rupee on him. He had never even held any money in his hand before. Yanus jumped down from the little wall he was walking on and crept inside the building's boundary wall. It was the last building before the little path turned in to a huge road that connected this city to the next one. Yanus had no idea which one. Quietly, Yanus opened the tap connected to the hydrant and drank. He drank as much as he could. It had to sustain him till tomorrow morning. There was no water anywhere near where he was now hiding. Yanus shut the tap and jumped back on to the wall.

Fifteen minutes later, Yanus was walking parallel to the path and the huge paved road. He was the only one walking there, though he could hear the zipping of cars. The path turned away from the road until Yanus felt he was walking on a desolate wasteland littered with huge rocks. There was nothing here. Yanus stopped walking and sat down looking at the expanse of the rock formations. There was a glow about them in the moonlight. Yanus wondered what it would be like to get lost within those rocks. The dark of the rocks looked inviting and Yanus felt tempted to explore. But it was still a long way to go. Somehow, the return journey was a lot longer. Yanus promised himself that he would think of a concrete way tonight of getting some food. This was ridiculous. He felt himself getting weak.

Suddenly he heard a rumbling. It was the sound of an engine. Yanus frowned. That was impossible. There was no road here that led anywhere. Yanus saw the headlights of a car in the distance. The glare was facing him and Yanus picked up his speed in the opposite direction. Yanus kept looking back to see if the car had changed direction. It had not. It was moving quickly. Then Yanus saw another pair of headlights behind the first one. Yanus wondered if it were just some kids looking for some privacy. Yanus shook his head. Kids wouldn't dare to come here. Something was wrong. Yanus sprinted in a new direction and kept his eyes on the leading car. To his dismay, the car swerved to face him again.

Yanus looked around for a place to hide. There would be too many people and he was alone. If it came to a fight, and Yanus knew it would, it had to be on his terms. Yanus turned toward the glow and made a decision.

Yanus squatted down and rested his head on his knees. It would begin soon. He had waited till the last moment and ensured that they had seen him disappearing between the natural stone walls. Yanus was surprised that there were no people living here. The space inside was gigantic. There were tunnels and passages that led further in and Yanus hoped he wouldn't have to go in there tonight. Some other time, it would be a perfect place to hide.

The diffused light inside the cave was pierced by the harsh glare of flash lights. Yanus could hear voices and footsteps echoing on the hollow walls. Yanus crawled behind a wall and spied the men coming closer. As Yanus had feared, they were carrying guns. Yanus sat down with his back to the wall and cursed his stupidity. Every time he took a chance, it brought him trouble. He wished he had the machine just now. He could have fried them on the spot. Once again, Babur had sent his men. None of them looked like the man Singh had described. Yanus wondered what it would take for the man to come down and hunt him. Did he really think these dogs were up to it?

"Stop hiding, Yanus. We want to talk to you." The voice echoed around hurting Yanus's ears

Yanus stayed where he was and thought that it was too late for discussions. What did they want, anyway? Yanus peered through the gap and saw that the men had split. This was good. Yanus followed one of the men and waited till he was level with a gap in the wall behind which Yanus was waiting. The man approached the gap with his back to it, gun at the ready. Yanus crept up behind it and grabbed his throat. The man fell backward on Yanus with his arms flailing. Yanus slapped his hand away from the gun and kept the pressure on the neck. Yanus pulled him to the ground and waited for the limbs to stop jerking. Yanus patted the man on the cheek and stood up. The dead eyes seemed to be accusing Yanus of theft. Yanus had picked up the dead man's gun and tried to figure out.

"Thanks!" whispered Yanus and walked out from the shadows

One of the men had waited at the clearing and was pointing his flash light in the opposite direction of Yanus's approach. His focus was on the illumination provided by his flash light and didn't hear Yanus walking toward him. The man flinched when Yanus came up right behind him and in his haste dropped the light and fumbled with the gun. It was all the time that Yanus needed. Yanus dropped him with a punch to the head. Yanus looked up and heard the men calling out to each other. Their courage was failing in them in the dark. Men who boasted of strength and flaunted their power over the weak were discovering their own impotency. Out here, there was no one to scare with rhetoric. Yanus disappeared back in to the shadows.

Yanus followed the voices and took them out one after the other. Not only were they scared, they were also inept in combat. Not one posed Yanus a challenge. Most of them struggled to stay alive till the end. Not one thought to fight back. These were men who were used to their opponents lying down for them. Not one of them had been in a fight for their life. Their only advantage was that they were too many. Yanus knew that he could not leave any of them here and run away. It was open land on all ends. If they figured out that he had escaped the caves, they would catch up with him in no time. There would be no refuge. He had to get them all. Yanus could still hear voices. But now the voices were excited and a lot louder.

"Come out if you have the guts. What is the matter? Afraid to come out?" the voice had come from the direction of the clearing. Yanus hurried back to his vantage point and looked out. Around seven men were gathered there. They had obviously discovered that their friends had been killed. Yanus looked at his hands. He expected to see blood on them. But they were clean. For the first time ever Yanus picked up the rifle and took aim.

"Come on out, you coward. How long will you…." The man could never finish his sentence. A single rifle shot had hit him in his throat. The men saw him fall and instantly took cover. Some fired wildly in all directions as they ran. Yanus saw the man fall and put down the gun, amazed that he could aim that well. He noticed that his hands were shaking a little. One of the men looking for a good place to hide, in his haste had stumbled exactly where Yanus was standing and instantly took action. The man raised his gun and attempted to fire it. But Yanus slid down beneath him and the man's momentum caused him to trip over. The man fell on Yanus and died instantly as Yanus broke his neck as soon as he had landed. Yanus shook him away and got up. Yanus looked at the man. He looked young. Yanus shook his head and reached down to put the light out. When Yanus looked up, he felt a shoe connect with his face. The kick had rocked him sideways in to the hard wall and Yanus felt his head bang on it. Yanus tried to jump out from the gap in the wall on to the other side. But the man caught Yanus in mid air and slammed him back on the ground. Once again, Yanus felt his head ring like a bell. The man took the opportunity to call out to his friends. Yanus saw him looking the other way to call out and took his chance. Yanus kicked between the man's legs. It was an awkward angle and the kick was not well aimed. But it did the job. The man collapsed slowly holding his groin. Yanus quickly got up and rammed his knee to the man's ear. Even in pain, the man had the presence of mind to reach for his gun. But Yanus got to his knife first. The man had not even lifted the gun when Yanus plunged the knife in his chest. The man had already been injured and the knife wound took the fight out of him. He lay down without moving. Yanus stood up over him to deliver the final blow. Yanus wiped the blood from his hands and decided against it. He would die slowly.

Yanus jumped out of the gap and landed on the other side once again moving toward the clearing. Three men ran out from behind him toward the spot Yanus had just left. Yanus shot two of them down before the third ducked for cover. Yanus did not hide now. He could finish this.

"Okay, I am here now! Someone wanted to talk?" said Yanus

The man who had hid in the shadows came out but didn't approach Yanus. Yanus felt another pair of eyes on him. He turned around to come face to face with a bald man with a piercing glare.

"I hope Kasid kills you for this." Said the bald man softly

"Who is Kasid?" Yanus was genuinely confused

"We would have preferred to take you alive, but you had to do this." Said the man waving his arm about

"Of course, you would have. But who is Kasid?"

"You will find out soon."

Yanus felt his nose break as the man without warning butted his head on it. Yanus stumbled back and lost his footing. The gun fell from his hand and his eyes began to burn. Yanus felt a hard object hit his mouth that sent him flying backward on the ground. This, Yanus thought, was ridiculous. The man raised his gun to finish Yanus off but Yanus sprinted toward the man and hugged him tightly. The strength of the grip pinned the man's arms to his sides and prevented him from firing his weapon. Both men were equally strong and tried to get leverage. Yanus brought his head down and tried to break the man's nose or at least injure him. Yanus connected twice and felt the man's nose break under his head. Yanus prepared to slam him on to the ground when he felt his hair being pulled. The last man had finally decided to intervene and didn't let go of Yanus until he had dragged him to the ground. Yanus punched him as hard as he could and as many times as he could. But it was too late. The man swung himself out of Yanus's reach. The two men watched Yanus getting to his feet and cocked their guns.

Yanus began to laugh. This was too much.

"Good to see people laughing before they die. I will tell Kasid of your bravery. Good Bye Yanus."

"Yes! Good bye, whoever you are." Said Yanus and gave the signal

Yanus shielded his eyes to block out the intense glare of the blast. The heat vaporized the men. Not even their guns remained. Yanus waited for the smoke to clear. It cleared to reveal a blue sheen all over the massive cave. The machine drifted toward Yanus and stopped where the men had stood. Yanus shook his head. This really was too much. The machine had found him. It had known that he was in danger. Not only had it found him, it had protected him. Yanus patted the machine. Not a day went by, when it did not surprise him. This was something that Yanus never imagined that it could do.

"Thanks." Whispered Yanus as he walked toward the man he had shot and inspected his pockets.

Yanus found what he wanted. It was time to get out of here.

Yanus settled down and gazed in the direction from where he had come. Nobody would find those people in those caves. Where had they come from? Who was Kasid? What did he want? Was he a friend of Babur? The man had said that he would have preferred to have him alive. Yanus felt an intense frustration at all this. Why do these people never do their own work and send others to die for them. How many would he have to kill before they realized this? Yanus punched his thigh as he felt his anger rise at everybody. This time he would know how to reach his adversary. Yanus eyed the cell phone he had picked up from one of the men. He couldn't call anyone. He could not understand the numbers. But he was sure, the call would come. It would come tonight.

Kasid rarely travelled outside the office. He felt his control over events diminishing whenever he had to travel. Control was people coming to him. But this, Kasid realized was different. Yanus had finally been caught. He was in his power. He wondered how his people had overpowered the Cyclone with him. May be Yanus had agreed to talk. That was what Kasid had instructed anyway. Yanus must have been tired living on the streets. Kasid thought that perhaps Yanus needed him more than he needed Yanus. It didn't matter. Kasid tried to go over in his mind the arguments that he would put forward to convince Yanus to join him. Kasid knew he had a difficult task ahead of him. He had to be careful not to sound too desperate. Yanus might not want to share his power. But what was power without control? Kasid could be that control. Yanus could not survive forever in this manner. Surely, he knew that. Kasid could provide Yanus a direction to follow. That is what had been in his mind ever since he found out that Jabar Falak had given the control of the machine to someone else. Surely, whoever it was couldn't be as unreasonable as Falak. The effort of all these years had finally paid off. Kasid didn't mind journeying to a desolate wasteland to meet the man who controlled the deadliest fighting machine in the world. A hotel would just not be right, thought Kasid amusingly. Kasid swerved out of the main road and drove toward the small forested area that was between the two cities. Kasid marvelled at Yanus. He had chosen the perfect spot to hide. It was away from prying eyes and interfering authorities. Kasid slowed down to negotiate the huge stones littering the ground. Finally the ground cleared and Kasid was able to travel faster. Soon he was able to see the trees at the edge of the forest. Kasid entered the area and brought the car to a stop. There was enough moonlight to provide visibility, so Kasid turned off the headlights. Kasid honked a few times to announce his arrival but there was no one around. Kasid couldn't see his people anywhere. Kasid remembered the short conversation he had with his man. It had been cryptic. Kasid had called to find out what had happened. The man on the other end had said that Yanus was ready to talk and that the meeting had to take place here and immediately. Kasid had not asked any more questions and had set out right away. Kasid began to sense a trap. Where were his people? Where were the cars they had travelled in?

"You must be Kasid." Said a voice that made Kasid spin around

His black robes billowing behind him, Yanus thought that Kasid looked imposing. But Kasid's eyes were not on Yanus. They were staring at the machine behind him.

"So this is Cyclone." Whispered Kasid

"How do you know what it is called?" asked Yanus

"A lot of people know what it is called. Few have laid eyes on it. And only you can control it. That is the Cyclone." Said Kasid

"What do you want?" asked Yanus getting to the point

"Where are my people?" asked Kasid knowing that he had been duped.

"They are dead."

"I thought so. That was you I spoke to on the phone?"

"Yes, you should have known the people you sent to their deaths a little better."

"I can help you, Yanus. There are too many people wanting that machine. I can protect you. I can guide you."

Yanus nodded and walked closer to him.

"I have seen the help you have given me."

Kasid noticed now, that Yanus was injured. His men had botched it up. He should have done this himself.

What was the price of this mistake?

"Yanus, do you think you can survive in here forever. They will hunt you down."

Yanus didn't feel like asking who they were. It was immaterial to him.

"Is there anything else you have to say?" asked Yanus

Kasid knew what was about to happen. Without warning, he lunged at Yanus's throat. But Yanus was prepared. A stiff arm in the chest pushed Kasid back. Kasid stumbled back prepping himself up to allow Yanus to deliver a massive blow to his face. Kasid stumbled further and collapsed on the forest floor.

"You have been some help to me, Kasid. I extend my gratitude to you." Yanus tried to kick Kasid in the neck to finish him off but this time Kasid was prepared. Kasid swerved out of the way and head butted Yanus in the stomach. The pain doubled him up. Kasid rose up eyeing the Cyclone. Yanus was almost on his feet. Kasid brought down his arm on Yanus's back. Yanus cried out in pain and collapsed again on all four limbs. Kasid rained down punches on Yanus pummelling him to the ground. Kasid grabbed his shirt and pulled him up. Kasid looked in to the eyes of Yanus. Kasid lifted Yanus clear off the ground and slammed him back on it. Yanus took a lot of kicks in the stomach and head until he was woozy. Finally Kasid stopped and pulled him back up again by the scruff of his neck. Kasid looked at the young boy. He looked like a tramp. This is who Jabar Falak had chosen? And this tramp had dared to stand up to Kasid. Where, so many had failed, this tramp had hoped to succeed. Kasid was amused.

"Does your Cyclone understand that you are moments away from death? It does not seem to want to protect you. May be it has realized that you are a loser. And that you do not deserve such power. What do you think?"

Yanus smiled as wide as he could. He was struggling to find balance. It was time to end this.

"It senses that I do not need it, you arrogant fool."

Yanus punched Kasid squarely in the neck. It was a powerful blow that ruptured his wind pipe. Kasid's eyes widened with surprise as his legs folded under him. Kasid clawed the ground in desperation to get air. But it was too late. Yanus sat down beside him watching the life drain out of him. A few moments later, Kasid became still.

Yanus got up and walked up to the machine. It had almost settled on the floor while Yanus had fought with Kasid. Something came to Yanus's mind. It was a realization that had come with the death of Kasid. He should have felt anger and frustration at all the abandonment. His parents, the orphanage, and even Singh had been nothing but disappointments. But Yanus felt nothing. It was cold and dark where his thoughts were born. His fear had left him the day when Tara had gone. Tonight, Yanus felt something else die inside him.

Yanus stepped forward to the machine. He wondered how these words had come to him.

"Cyclone…Rise."

The blue light recognized its master and came to life.

Chapter 7

The End of The Lion

Jadhav waited for the constable to open the umbrella. Cursing his bad luck, Jadhav stepped out of the car and in to the rain toward the station. The hordes of reporters prevented him from making much progress.

Don't these people have homes to go to? Thought Jadhav

All of them seemed to be speaking at once. And most of them had the same questions to ask. Who was behind the murders that were taking place in different parts of the city since the last few days? Was it one person? Was it a gang? What did they want? Was it a serial killer? Are the murders connected? What was the police doing about it? What chances did the common man have if even ministers with security were being killed?

There he was again, thought Jadhav, the common man. The common man greatly resented being born common, and yet felt comfortable to hide behind his commonness to watch, complain, and then do nothing. Jadhav was wondering when the common man would make his appearance to make his opinions heard. Jadhav thought, actually, the common man had a great job.

Jadhav slowly made his way to the station. He had to make a statement. Once again, he rued why everything had to happen to him. Well, at least Kasid was gone. One of his tormentors was dead. Jadhav climbed the few steps leading to the entrance and turned around with some drama. Like a king addressing his subjects, Jadhav raised his hands and requested some quiet. The reporters fell silent and waited for Jadhav to answer.

"I appreciate your concern in reporting the facts. The truth is that I do not have facts at the moment…that I can share with you as they are part of the investigation." Jadhav added quickly seeing the look of delight on everybody's faces. The faces fell as he completed the statement.

"Have you made any arrests?" asked one

"Like I said, I cannot disclose anything. We are close to reaching a conclusion and hopefully you will all get to report some good news."

"Have you noticed that all these murders have taken place in your jurisdiction? Is that a coincidence?"

Jadhav wished for once that he could tell the truth.

"I doubt you are aware of what is happening Mr…?"

"My name is Charan."

"Yes…Charan. You do not know much of what is happening. I would appreciate it if you could refrain from printing anything that would cause panic. Now please.…"

Jadhav made to turn around and was bombarded with a variety of questions. Jadhav marvelled at the creativity some put in their way of asking questions.

Wet and irritated was how he felt. He had Yanus under his control that day. But Sunny's stupidity had caused him to escape. And his own incompetency…thought Jadhav sadly. But Sunny had hounded Yanus till Yanus had learned how to fight back. And his stomach for a fight had stunned Sunny. In the end, Yanus had proved too much for Sunny, as he had proved too much for Kasid. In the end, the two of them had created a monster. Jadhav mused that since

Sunny had died, no one seemed to have bothered him to find Yanus. Jadhav knew that Yanus had to be stopped. It was only a matter of time before his seniors started asking questions and demanded action. This was not a case where he could twist the facts to save face. It was only a matter of time before Yanus became the next Babur. The police force would never allow that. Men like Babur were no longer required in the society. They were remnants of a past era. The rise of Yanus in Babur's shoes would mean another few decades of head ache for the police and the authorities. A subdued population that feared and respected the authorities was what the bosses wanted.

Yanus would never submit or surrender. He had to be killed before he got any stronger. Jadhav made up his mind and went back to his car. Jadhav nodded to the driver and sat back. The driver knew where he was supposed to go.

Jadhav knocked and waited for an answer. The door opened suddenly to reveal the blood shot eyes of Raj.
"Hello Raj." Said Jadhav as pleasantly as he could
"What do you want?" asked Raj as rudely as he could
Jadhav mustered his courage and managed a squeak
"I want to speak to Babur."
Raj nodded a little and opened the door to let him in.
Babur was sitting on the floor as usual. Jadhav sat down next to him.
"I am sorry about Sunny…"
"I doubt that. What do you want?"
Jadhav decided that the best tack would be to be frank.
"I need to talk about Yanus."
"Do you know where he is?" asked Babur
Jadhav shook his head. "No one knows where he is."
Babur looked a little disappointed

"Then why have you come here?" asked Raj

Jadhav turned to Babur. "With Kasid gone, Negi has a clear field. He could reach Yanus anytime. There is no guarantee that Negi too will fail like Kasid. Negi is a lot smarter than Kasid and he will offer Yanus a lot more. With Negi's support, Yanus will be impossible to beat. All he requires now is some political muscle."

"So what's your problem? Politicians are no big deal." Said Raj

"I do not mean any disrespect but I don't think any politician you have gone up against had someone like Yanus at their disposal. This man is not a fool. He knows how to fight...."

"You would know that." Said Raj mockingly

"So would you." Said Jadhav with equal venom and surprising Raj

Jadhav went on with his eyes on Raj but addressing Babur

"There are scores of people out there who would want to settle scores with you. Yanus will become more potent with Negi's backing. And Negi would become...."

"And since when do you care about the changing power equations?" asked Raj again

"There will be...consequences." Said Jadhav

"Such as...?"

It was Babur who answered. "Nobody would want Yanus becoming powerful enough to cause them problems, including the police."

Jadhav was glad that Babur understood.

"If Yanus is killed, I could tie him up to the recent murders that have taken place. We know he is partly responsible anyway. It would shut everyone up. You are happy and so...."

"And so are you." Raj finished for Jadhav

"And so are my seniors." Jadhav corrected Raj

Jadhav took the opportunity of the continued silence to finish.

"That is what I wanted to say. You have been good to me all these years. I just thought that...."

"I have understood what you had to say. Is there anything else?" asked Babur

"If there is anything I could do...."

"There is nothing I have to say to you. I had already decided to kill Yanus. Your point is of no worth to me or to my business." Babur pointed to the door

Jadhav got up and stood in front of Raj.

"I will take my leave."

Raj glared in to Jadhav's eyes for a long time before he stood aside and let him go.

"You will listen to a worm like Jadhav but not me." said Raj to Babur

"That worm does not know that he spoke the truth. He is only protecting himself. Yanus is not only my enemy but also dangerous for balance."

"You mean him and Negi becoming...."

"I cannot say what his alliance with Negi will result in, even if it does. But it cannot be conducive to us. What political games Negi plays and who he uses Yanus against is also not my concern. But Jadhav was right that it will make Negi powerful; perhaps powerful enough to challenge my authority."

"Do you really believe that?" asked Raj

"I have to assume that it will. Sunny's death has not gone unnoticed. My good friends in this world are already speaking about the tramp that killed him. In the rare case of Negi supporting Yanus, my friends will rally around Negi and show me their true colours. Negi's ambitions of power will also take flight."

"Babur, can one man make such a difference? Can so much be influenced by one man?"

"Yes it can. I have seen it before. It is rare these days. The halls of power in this city are filled with cowards and opportunists who know only how to prey on the weak. Unfortunately for us, the one rare man of force that comes around in a great while is arrayed against us. Yanus will cause a shift in the power structure of the city. This happens every time someone like him is forced in to our world. Thankfully I have the other such person with me."

"Who are you talking about?" asked Raj suspiciously

"I am talking about you, of course." Said Babur

Raj smiled for the first time since Sunny had died. "I am no man of force. That was Sunny."

"You are one if I say so. But now I must ask you for something that you will not like."

Raj knew that this was going to happen. He had been prepared for it since Sunny died.

"I want you to leave Yanus to me." Said Babur

"And what do you want me to do?" asked Raj

Babur took a deep breath and answered, "I want you to leave. Your time here is done, Raj."

"After all that I have done for you, you want me to leave now. I thought you wanted someone like me."

"I do. But I have to do what is right. You must leave before it is too late."

"Too late for what...?"

"I don't want you to waste your life here. You can start a family. Get a new life."

"Get a new life?"

"Yes, a new life. I will get Yanus. But I cannot live forever. After me, you will take my place. And that is something I do not want."

"You are taking Jadhav's words too seriously."

Babur shook his head and said, "Jadhav is only talking about what little he understands. But I know better. The truth is that my legend must die with me. There must not be another Babur. That includes you or...Yanus."

Raj put his head back and closed his eyes.

"You will not reconsider?" asked Raj through closed eyes

Babur said nothing and kept staring at Raj. Raj tried to clarify his question. "Is Yanus...?"

"I must do what I must. And so should you." Babur understood and answered as simply as he could

"You must do this for me. Consider this as my final command." Said Babur

Raj got up and Babur followed him up.

Both men shook hands. No more words were necessary. Raj knew that Babur had made up his mind.

Raj left before he lost control of his emotions.

Alone in his car, Raj did what he had last done when his wife had died. He began to cry. His tears flowed for his dead family and his dead friend. Raj punched the steering as hard as he could in anger. Raj thought about what Babur had said. It was all about balance. To keep the balance, sacrifices had to be made. Raj decided that he too would work toward maintaining the balance.

Babur woke up near morning and sat alone in his room. It had not been easy asking Raj to leave. But he had never balked at taking difficult decisions. It was something that was missing in today's generation. The will to survive and the courage to rush head on toward an enemy were rare commodities. Without these qualities, there could be no Babur. Babur walked to the window and looked out at the dark sky. The entire area was covered in darkness. It would be light in a few hours and the daily grind of the day would begin. Babur looked at his watch. His people had not returned. It was too late for them to get back with any useful information. Babur was a little disappointed. He was sure that Yanus would be looking for him. But Babur had been disappointed before. His men would search him out. Yanus could hide as much as he wanted. But this city belonged to Babur and there were no places deep enough to hide from him. Babur gripped the metal bars and tightened his fists. So the boy would survive another day. Babur turned around to go to bed. The night had been wasted.

Babur froze in his tracks.

He turned around again to look at the street below. Somebody was pushing a cart along the middle of the street and approaching his building. Babur looked below to see his men watching the cart too. They looked a little surprised. Something was wrong. Babur sensed trouble and quickly dashed out of the room toward the stairs. Barely had he reached the top flight when Babur sensed the air from the room being sucked out. There was a blue flash and the silence of the night was torn apart with a huge explosion. One end of the short rectangular building buckled and began to collapse. Babur jumped to the bottom of the stairs and collided with the opposite wall. Babur ran away from the falling debris and reached the open space.

The fire had engulfed the neighbouring buildings and people were rushing about trying to put the flames out. His men too had rushed to put out the flames. There were some men lying about injured or perhaps dead because of the explosion. Babur turned toward the remains of the cart. There was nothing inside it.

"Babur!"

Babur spun around at the voice. The source of Babur's pain stood amidst the smoke like a dark shadow. Yanus stepped forward toward Babur and came toe to toe. Babur looked in to the eyes of the man to measure him. This was the one who had killed Rohan. This was the one who had killed Sunny. Babur was glad that he was not disappointed after all.

Babur suddenly gripped Yanus's chin and pulled him closer. Yanus could not have imagined a more ferocious man or a more tenacious grip. But the man was clearly past his physical prime and had not taken Yanus seriously either. Yanus brought up his knee and smashed it in Babur's groin.

Babur smiled. "You have a lot to learn, son." Yanus looked surprised at the lack of pain in Babur's eyes. He had not even flinched. The grip tightened and Yanus felt his feet leave the ground. Babur had lifted Yanus clear off the ground and hung him in mid air. Yanus struggled to get free but Babur was an incredibly strong man. Yanus punched and kicked Babur from his higher position. Yanus's blood turned cold to see Babur smiling through the blows. Suddenly Babur shifted his weight and slammed Yanus on the ground. Yanus had been slammed like this before but this time he thought that the slam was intended to bury him. Such was the force of the slam that Yanus bounced once on the rough floor. Babur waited patiently for Yanus to get up.

"It's a different game, isn't it?" asked Babur

"No, it is just a different level." Said Yanus

Babur smiled and moved forward. Babur made to grab Yanus's throat but this time Yanus side stepped Babur and rammed his fist to the side of Babur's neck. This blow slowed Babur a little. Babur took a second to recover and Yanus took his chance. Yanus dropped himself and swept his leg around to trip Babur. The big man lost his footing a little but did not go down. Instead he lifted his foot to kick Yanus in to the next world. That is what Yanus had wanted. Yanus had positioned himself well and grabbed Babur's leg with both his arms and pulled. Babur could not balance himself to counter attack and lost his footing. Babur fell to the ground with his feet spread apart and was unable to get up immediately. His large size and age made it difficult for him to move quickly. Yanus had lost no time in getting on top of him.

Yanus began to pummel every inch of Babur's face and neck. Babur was a strong man but Yanus's blows had a lot of power. Babur tried everything he knew to shake Yanus off. He punched him in the stomach which was the only place he could reach. But Yanus ignored the pain. Babur knew he had to get on his feet. But Yanus would not yield an inch of his grip and continued to hammer at him. Yanus grabbed Babur's head and banged it on the ground a few times. Babur knew he would lose his consciousness soon. Babur summoned every fibre of his strength and lifted Yanus a few inches with his back. It gave Babur sufficient space to spin around and slip out. The move took Yanus by surprise and he jumped on Babur's back to pull him back to the ground. Babur was still disorientated and took a while to recover his senses. His head and face were bleeding and he was struggling to stay on his feet. Yanus kicked the back of Babur's leg to buckle them but Yanus realised that this man was made of much sterner stuff. Yanus lunged forward to launch another kick but Babur without looking, punched backward in Yanus's face. The blow tore through Yanus's cheek and pushed him away. Babur turned around to see

Yanus stumbling but recovering quickly. Both men stood a few feet away from each other. There was an intense glaze in their eyes that would have melted anything in their path.

Bleeding and broken, both men launched themselves at each other with equal ferocity. Both men fought to kill. None had the slightest inclination toward mercy. There would be no second chances. Yanus had broken the sheen of invincibility around Babur. That this was the toughest man he had ever encountered, Yanus had no doubt. Yanus had driven punches and kicks with enough force to kill any other man. But Babur had smiled and kept coming. Yanus knew that this man would have been something else when he was younger. It was his age that slowed him, not lack of strength, guts, or skill. The difference in age began to tell. Babur began to tire. He began to slow down. Yanus kept pushing him to prep him up to punch him harder. Babur let in more punches through his defences. Yanus kicked him in the guts to slow him down further. Yanus realised a few seconds later that Babur was not punching back. He was too busy defending himself. Yanus blinked through the blood in his eyes. Babur was barely able to stand. Yanus stepped forward and gave Babur a small push. The big man slowly collapsed. Yanus could not bring himself to kick him to the ground. Instead Yanus hammered his elbow on Babur's back. The blow caused Babur to fall completely to the ground.

"For all that you and those like you have done, Babur, you deserve a special end."

Babur looked up at Yanus through one eye, and that too was half shut. Yanus was not alone. Babur tried to make out what he was seeing. Behind the dark figure of Yanus had risen a taller shadow. Babur had not seen it earlier. Then Babur remembered the explosion. This must have caused it. He remembered the blue light that he had seen. It was now coming from the top of the figure now coming close. So this was how he had got Sunny. Babur prepared himself to die. He had lost.

"Yanus!" Babur recognised the voice

Raj stood twenty feet away from them.

"You were about to miss the party, Raj. I am glad you could come." Said Yanus

"Sorry Yanus. I brought my own party." Said Raj

Yanus looked past Raj. A man stood with something on his shoulder. Yanus took an instant to recognise the weapon. He had seen it before. Yanus turned around and screamed, "Get back!"

The machine began to drift away from Yanus. But it was too late. The man fired the weapon and the projectile hit the Cyclone with a deafening blast. Yanus was thrown backward because of the explosion and instantly lost consciousness.

Yanus opened his eyes. The heat from the flames was still pushing people away at the far end of the building. Yanus was alone where he had collapsed. Raj was gone. And he had taken Babur with him. Yanus screamed in frustration. Not only had Babur escaped, but Raj had destroyed the Cyclone.

Yanus frowned. Why had they not finished him then? Raj could have done it easily.

The blue light answered his question. Yanus's stared in amazement. He had seen it being hit with that missile. But there was not even a scratch on it. The Cyclone drifted idly in the same position where it had been hit. It had not retreated any further despite Yanus's command to back away as it had sensed Yanus in danger. Yanus looked at the people running about in the distance. The fire had engulfed the entire building. It was time to disappear before they were spotted.

Jadhav waited for the man to approach him. There was no need to rush toward bad news. The scene told him what had happened. The entire row of the short building had been burned to the ground. No one had called the fire brigade until it was too late. The fire fighters had arrived to find the fires still raging and out of control. Jadhav had arrived around the same time. Looking around, Jadhav noticed an unusually large crowd gathered. Obviously, they all wanted to witness the burning of the kingdom of Babur. This was the place from where the old lion had ruled the city through his network of influence and connections. But no more… as was the case with such people, they always came with an expiry date. Jadhav cursed himself. It had been merely hours before that he had approached Babur. Now there was no sign of him. The bodies had been pulled out. The fires had finally been put out and the extent of the damage was becoming clear. But Babur was not among the dead.

"How did it happen?" asked Jadhav

"I have no idea. I have never seen anything like it. We couldn't even put the fire out. It just died after a while." The chief of the fire brigade looked harassed.

"Any idea where…?" began Jadhav tentatively

"He is not here. His room was open but there was no one inside. It has been completely destroyed."

"Yes, I can see that. I can't say I am sorry though." Said Jadhav

The chief stared at Jadhav. He shook his head and walked away to a group of men waving at him at the far end of the building, leaving Jadhav alone.

Jadhav understood the reaction of the chief. He had seen that look on people's faces too often. Many people revered monsters like Babur. They looked upon them as saviours. Any person who stood up to the authorities and usurped the natural order of things was a hero. It didn't matter if that hero murdered them at will. Jadhav bit his lip in frustration. It was obvious that it was Yanus who had done this. This little war was now spilling out in the open. Either Babur was dead or he was incapable of stopping Yanus. This would be the beginning of a new era of crime with Yanus at the top. Jadhav had hoped that it would not come to this. With Babur gone, there was no one to stop Yanus. Jadhav weighed his options. He had to answer his superiors for the loss of law and order in his area. He had to do something...anything. There was only one option left.

The chief squatted down and ran his finger through the dark powder. His assistant was standing right behind him. The chief looked back and looked at him with raised eyebrows.

"Is that what I think it is?" asked the young assistant

The chief shook his head and got up. The young man followed the experienced chief to listen and learn.

"I have seen the aftermath of a fire caused by heavy ordinance. Whatever caused this little patch to burn could not have caused the entire building to burn the way it did. The fire in the building was different, though it started at around the same place."

The assistant considered the chief's words. "So this little fire on the ground was caused by...say a bomb or something..." indicating the black patch on the ground, "...but what about the building? How did the building catch fire?"

"I wish I knew. I am sure the investigation will throw up some answers." Said the chief

The chief patted the young man on the back and pushed toward the men waiting at the fire truck waiting for instructions. The chief looked at the blackened mass that was once alive with people. The chief didn't want to lie to his assistant but he had been around fires for a very long time. He had seen all kinds of fires of all magnitudes. The chief was sure of one thing; there was no way any investigation would be able to figure out what had caused this fire. He could bet his 35 years of fire fighting experience on it.

Negi looked terrible. His face was heavily lined and there were black marks under his eyes. Jadhav thought that Negi looked a little ill.

"Are you all right, Sir? Asked Jadhav

Negi's head snapped up and he glared at Jadhav.

"Of course I am all right. It's been a week full of fun." Snapped Negi

Negi glared at Jadhav till he looked away in embarrassment. Negi had a bad week. Most difficult had been the death of Kasid. Negi thought that somehow, he too was to blame for his death. Negi and Kasid were after the same thing. But each had different reasons. Kasid had wanted power. That desire had blinded Kasid. Negi wondered if his purpose too had been corrupted. Negi hoped that it had not. He had felt sorry for Kasid. Ruthless and ambitious though he was, he didn't deserve this fate. Negi again wondered if he too was heading for the same destination as Kasid had. Negi shook his head. He had a reason for doing what he was doing. Personal ambition had nothing to do with it. But for now, given Yanus's temperament, Negi had to play a different tune. Kasid and Babur had proved that force was not going to work with Yanus. A different approach was needed. Negi looked at Jadhav looking at him intently. The worm, it seemed, had grown a brain. Jadhav had yet again proven how unreliable he was and how quickly he changed his loyalties. Even in a world of shifting priorities, Jadhav had crossed a line. Though he didn't know it, he would pay for it...soon.

"What have you thought about Yanus?" asked Jadhav

"What did Babur have to say?" asked Negi instead

Jadhav once again looked a little flustered.

"I don't know where he is."

"Didn't you go looking for him?' teased Negi

Jadhav kept his mouth shut.

"Yanus is not your problem anymore, Jadhav."

"But Sir...."

"You came here to tell me how big a problem Yanus is going to become for me in the future. My guess is that you told the same thing to Babur. I have listened to your problems. I have taken note of it. Is there anything else?" Negi's tone was dismissive

Jadhav was used to a less than warm welcome everywhere he went. But Negi didn't seem to be interested in him at all. No matter, he had done what he could. There was nothing more that he could do. Jadhav got up and walked out of the office.

Negi picked up the phone and called the number hoping against hope that it would be answered. Ever since Jadhav had mentioned about Babur disappearing, he had feared the worst.

"Hello!" The response from the other end was as alert and crisp as Negi had heard it the last time.

Negi breathed a sigh of relief and began to speak.

Raj got out of his car and walked toward Negi's. It was one of those nights. The rain had begun to really pelt the city. It was one of those showers that rid the city of its filth.

Not all of it, but enough to prepare the city for the next year. Raj did not knock on the window and quickly got in.

"Amazing weather, huh?" asked Negi

Raj grunted. "What do you want?"

"I need your help." Said Negi appreciating Raj's business-like approach

Raj glared at Negi. But it was not Negi's fault that Sunny and Babur had not listened to him. Negi had given his warning too.

"What possible help can I give you?" asked Raj

Negi lit a cigarette and offered one to Raj. Raj raised his hand to decline. Negi blew some smoke and considered how to begin. "You saw the Cyclone, didn't you?"

Raj was a little confused. "I have witnessed many of them. Which one are you talking about?"

"The one that killed Sunny and...Babur."

Realisation dawned upon Raj. "It didn't kill Babur. He is alive...but hurt."

Raj looked out of the window, "It did kill Sunny though."

"I tried to warn you about Yanus. I tried to tell you that he was heavily armed."

"In the world we belong to, Mr Negi, heavily armed means guns, not flying machines. Why did you not tell me about that...thing? Asked Raj

"The Cyclone? It would not have made any difference. Just as you and I know to approach such power with caution, men like Sunny and Babur would throw caution to the winds just to prove a point. I seriously hope that I am correct in my estimation...at least about you." Negi spoke while exhaling more smoke

"What do you want now?" asked Raj

"Do you know about Kasid?" asked Negi

Raj nodded.

"Do you know why he attacked Yanus?"

Raj once again, only shook his head.

'For years, a certain team had been developing that machine you saw. Kasid and I had known about it for many years. And I am sure there are others too who know about it. Most of everyone I know wanted to know how to control that machine: The machine that they called The Cyclone. As you saw for yourself, it is incredibly powerful. But it has a flaw."

Raj understood at once. That was why it had not attacked them when Yanus was knocked out. It needed someone to command it.

"That is not a flaw. It is a safeguard." Said Raj

"Considering the given situation, perhaps you are correct. But we still have a problem. You see, all these years Kasid thought that the person who designed the machine was the one who could control it. But that person died a while back. This machine showed up a few days later and started killing people."

Negi snuffed out the cigarette and looked at Raj to see whether he was following. As expected, Raj looked a little confused.

"Was it after someone?"

"It killed most of the people that designed it."

"Why did it do that?"

"Those fools betrayed the man who designed the Cyclone. He was accused of treachery against the country and was subjected to a trial in a military court. The man died of a heart attack in his office. Obviously he was innocent. The machines lay dormant in their storage facilities. But after a while, this Cyclone surfaced. It attacked one of the two plants where the machines were built and killed everyone in it. Those in the other plant tried to run and some tried to fight it. They were all systematically eliminated."

"Did you just say 'machines'? You mean there are more?" asked Raj incredulously

"There is an army of Cyclones." Said Negi

Raj was speechless. Negi lit another cigarette and considered again sharing this information with Raj. But there was no option. Negi went on.

"The Cyclone however, is a machine. It is programmed. This particular Cyclone was programmed to go after specific people. And there was one other purpose."

This, Raj knew was why he had been called.

"You wanted to control that thing. Instead, Yanus got there first. That's what happened, didn't it?" asked Raj

"That is not exactly what happened. And that is not what I wanted. But I admit that you got in the way."

Raj shifted in his seat and waited for Negi to continue. This was getting interesting. Negi was not being clear. And why did he have to keep smiling through all that smoke?

"Jabar Falak, during his last days, linked this Cyclone toYanus. This much I know for sure. But my estimate is that this machine now also holds the key to the Cyclone army. Cyclone R, which was to be the master Cyclone, has become dormant for good and useless."

"All this information seems quite important and confidential. May I ask you why you are sharing this with me?" asked Raj

Negi did not answer and continued to smile. He wanted Raj to come to the conclusion himself.

Raj waited for a while for Negi to answer. Both men stared at each other and finally Negi relented.

"It is not you who I want to have this information. Though I am sure we can talk about that later. It is Yanus who I want to know."

"Then tell him." Said Raj

This time Negi looked out the window. Raj had to agree to it himself.

"You want me to tell him?" asked Raj. Negi nodded.

"I want you to take my offer to him. Tell him I can give him the details of the army that his Cyclone controls. All I ask is that he should work with me. I do not want the control for myself. It cannot be done anyway. A simple give and take relationship that would be beneficial to us both is what I want."

"Assuming I agree to tell him, he might deal directly with Samar Falak. He does not need you. I wouldn't do it if I were in his place." Raj said simply

Negi smiled and answered, "Of course he can. But Samar Falak is the same as Yanus to me. You see, eventually, Samar will not know what to do with his father's legacy. We still don't know why Falak built them. Kasid and I had the same agenda but that was not what Falak had intended. Samar too will need the same offer of help that I now give to Yanus. Yanus has to decide whether he wants to deal with me or he wants me to deal with him and Samar together. I think we both know what choice he will take."

Raj knew that Negi was correct. Yanus would never accept help from Samar if it meant sharing power. Neither would anyone else he knew.

"How do you know so much about this Cyclone?" asked Raj

"That is not important. Will you do this?"

Raj had listened to every word with a lot of care. He had to think more about his next move. Without a word, Raj got out of the car and got in to his own.

Negi didn't waste any more time. Negi was sure that whatever decision Raj took, it would turn out to his benefit. It now remained to be seen whether Yanus would stick to his guns or fall by the wayside.

It had been a terrible night. The medicines had been worse than the fight. But Babur was glad to be alive to complain. No matter how hopeless the odds against life were, every second of it was precious and worth fighting for. Babur sat back and tried to relax. The men around had expressed their concern about his health. Babur had appreciated it and allayed their fears. Operations would be conducted as usual. The men had breathed a sigh of relief as they saw Babur being quite relaxed and not at all tensed about recent events. Babur looked up as Raj entered the room. Raj, like Sunny seemed never to notice or acknowledge other people in the room. He sat down next to Babur and waited.

"Thank you all for coming." Said Babur

It actually meant "I want you to leave." in a different way but the people understood and complied.

Within seconds, Babur was alone with Raj.

Raj explained everything that Negi had told him. Babur listened without interrupting and waited for Raj to finish.

"What do you want to do?" asked Babur

Raj was a little surprised at the question. He had never been asked that before.

"It depends on what you want. Are you still bent on getting Yanus?"

"I was never a fool, Raj. I know it is going to be nearly impossible to get past that thing. What did Negi say?"

Babur listened with rapt attention as Raj explained Negi's offer and the Cyclone.

At the end, Babur shook his head.

"Negi is either mad or playing a very clever game. I am sure he that knows Yanus will never give up that machine. He has a simple idea that he is following. But Negi will never allow Yanus to continue that way. If Yanus is tamed, then he will no longer be a problem. If he is not, even Negi will have no choice but to...."

"Are you telling me that it was not a personal issue you had with Yanus? Isn't that why you sent Sunny to kill him? Now it is okay if Yanus is tamed and gives us no trouble. Now it is just business." Raj sounded annoyed

"Don't get me wrong, Raj. Negi will want to finish Yanus one day, for the same reason that I want to finish him today. Yanus has upset the order of power in the city and is on his way to cause more damage. It is something like what I once did. Many tried to stop me, but they failed. They were all trying to preserve the natural order that I had turned upside down. Today, I am in their shoes and..."

"And Yanus is in yours." Finished Raj

Babur closed his eyes. No matter what he told everyone, Raj could see that the fight with Yanus had severely shaken the old lion. He was nowhere near his old strength or agility. But the voice still had the same timber.

"Thank you for coming back, Raj. I wished you a good life. This is not what I...."

"I never left. But I realise that things will never be the same again without Sunny."

Babur said nothing and simply nodded little. The man looked tired.

"I will speak to Yanus and let you know what I plan to do next." Said Raj and left the room

Babur brushed his moustache with his fingers, like his father used to and thought to himself, *"You're okay, Raj. You will do just fine."*

Raj stood outside the large stone structure. It wasn't a mountain but it was not far from it. Raj could see caves disappearing in to the darkness. There were so many of them. Raj knew this is where Yanus had been for a while. It had taken a while for him to find this place but he had succeeded. Further, he had to wait until it was night time to be sure that Yanus would be there. Though he wouldn't be protected during the day if he ventured out, there was no telling where he and the machine would be. That old man had taught him well. Raj had to know the exact location in this area. Raj squatted down to look closely at the ground for any marks. The man had taught him tracking as well.

Raj jumped to his side as soon as the blue light came on. Raj rolled to his side and looked up.

The two black figures stood side by side. One was taller than the other and gave out the blue light. The other stood looking down at him through dead eyes. The ill-fitting black robes fell loosely to his sides.

Raj put his hands up and approached silently. Yanus jumped from the wall and landed in front of Raj. Yanus made a show looking around.

"Didn't bring your party this time, Raj?" asked Yanus

Raj shook his head. "I have something else for you."

Yanus leaned forward to look in to the eyes of Raj. "What do you want?"

Raj knew that Yanus was itching to command the machine to blow him to bits. He trod carefully.

Raj put his hands down and went back to his car. Yanus watched Raj take out a small bag from the back seat and approach him again. Raj held out the bag.

"What is this?" asked Yanus

"There is something here that you might need."

Yanus snatched the bag from Raj's hands and opened it. Raj was impressed at the boy's guts. He really seemed to have no fear. The machine had nothing to with it. Raj remembered that he had once taken on himself and Sunny and managed to hold them off. There was no Cyclone at that time.

Yanus looked up sharply from the bag.

"What is the meaning of this?" asked Yanus

"There is something you should know, Yanus. I want your attention for a while without the Cyclone breathing down my neck."

"How do you know about...?"

"Please, man. Let's not waste any more time. Can we sit and talk?"

Yanus nodded. "Any smart move and you will burn. Do you understand?"

Raj scratched his head and nodded. Yanus made a gesture to follow him.

The last time, Raj had attacked the machine with the intention of destroying it. The same machine now followed them in to the cave where Yanus was leading them. Raj wondered if he would have been so accommodating if the situation was reversed.

Yanus emptied the bag of medicines and food on the floor and threw the bag out of sight. Yanus studied the medicines one by one.

Yanus sat down on the floor and asked Raj to do the same.

"Thank you for the medicines. But I am afraid; it does not change anything between me and Babur."

"I know that. But what I have to say might. Are you ready to listen?" asked Raj

Yanus nodded a little

"This machine was developed by Samar's father, Jabar Falak. Do you know of him?"

Yanus was stunned. A deep unease began to creep up inside him.

"Are you sure?" Yanus struggled to keep his voice steady

"Have you never wondered where it came from?" asked Raj

"I have wondered why it follows me." Said Yanus

Raj smiled a little. He explained everything that Negi had told him. Yanus stopped Raj at some points and asked questions. Raj did his best to explain Yanus from the conversation he had with Negi. Finally Yanus got up and walked to the Cyclone, addressing it.

"You never told me you commanded an army of Cyclones."

Raj was amazed that the boy could be humorous at a time like this.

"Is this why you came here? Are you afraid that I would turn loose that army on you?"

"Some might think so, but I don't. I understand what you did and why you did it."

"Then why are you here?" asked Yanus

"I want you to go to Samar Falak." Said Raj

Yanus looked at Raj in disgust.

"Are you out of your mind? Why would I want to do that?"

"Sooner or later, they will get you. The Cyclone can't protect you always. You are only one man. There are too many people out there who will make you all sorts of offers to convince you to join them. Trust me, Yanus. Not all battles are fought with violence. You will get lost in that world. How long do you think you can survive here?" Raj gestured around to indicate the caves in the middle of nowhere

"Why are you so concerned about what I do? You know I will not rest till I get Babur."

"That is exactly why I want you to go to Samar. Babur knows about this machine and will take appropriate measures the next time you face him. But that is beside the point. Your presence in our world is causing a lot of trouble. I don't care what plans Falak had when he made that thing follow you. With Samar, you will get to know everything that you need to know. Your life will have a purpose. Out here, you will end up fighting people like Babur. You will have to succeed every time and keep running. They will sit pretty because they have to succeed just once. Your odds, my friend, are better with Samar."

"I know all that I need to know. And I can take care of myself. I was born in the same world that you call your own. I have decided to rid it of all the Baburs I can find. And I will succeed. You can rest assured of that. Samar will have to wait till that day comes. For me, he is not important. If he has anything to say, I am here. Let him find me."

"I can see it is not ego that drives you. You are mad behind your own agendas, even if it kills you. Sunny was like that. But he let ego get in the way too. You are better than that. Will you not consider again? This war with Babur has gone on too long. I could convince Babur to...."

"Was Sunny close to you?" asked Yanus suddenly

"Yes, he was."

Yanus looked closely at Raj. "Tell me, Raj. Is it not true that it is you who does not belong to this world? Why are you here?"

"Why do you care?" asked Raj in a choked voice

"I don't care. But you don't fit beside Babur. How did you get here, man?"

"It is none of your business." Said Raj

Yanus looked at Raj with a sly expression. "I was correct. You do not belong here. But still, why work for Babur?" Yanus was adamant

Raj saw that Yanus was still learning about the world he was born in. And the world that Raj had adopted.

Raj took a deep breath before answering.

"I was working in a company in Mumbai. I had been here for a few years and was going well. I was working my way up for a better life for me and my family. I had a wife and a...son." Raj spoke without much emotion

"It has been many years now, But I still remember it as if it happened yesterday. It was a silly issue that got blown up. One day my wife was molested when she was out shopping for groceries. Some local administrator and his goons were trying to rake in some brownie points with their seniors. He had issues with people from outside the city and was looking for easy targets. But my wife fought back. She slapped the man and pushed him. That night the man visited my house and threatened to kill me and my family. He came with so many people, that my building's area was full of them. No one dared to raise a voice against them. They came in and slapped me and my wife in front of my two year old son. I shouted a lot and tried to fight back. But it was no use. They left as if they had conquered a kingdom, leaving me to console my wife. My wife wanted us to leave the city. But I...I thought that I was too smart. I complained to the police the next morning. They wouldn't even register my complaint. They told me to register it in the jurisdiction in which I was born. I threatened to go the press. I faced numerous threats on the phone. Even the police joined in the fun. My wife was molested and threatened many times when she stepped out. It came to a point that she regretted fighting back. It came to a point where she was afraid to leave our home. But I was too naive and stupid to recognise the danger I had put my family in. I visited a few newspapers and asked them to report my story. I thought I could get some help that way. They agreed but never did anything. I was fired from my job. They were making good on their threats while I still hoped for the system to give me justice. I did not give up and kept nagging the police and even met some influential people in my area to help me get rid of this problem."

Raj seemed out of breath but still went on.

"I got a job that required me to work at night. I was scared and had already decided to leave town. I had given up. But I still needed money. I thought to work for a few months and then leave. I was too late. I got a call early in the morning. It was the police. They wanted me to rush home immediately. My flat had been burned down. My wife and son had been taken to the hospital with serious burn injuries." Raj's tears were flowing freely. He could not stop either his tears or his tale that he had not shared with his closest friend. Tonight he was sharing it with his enemy.

"My son was dead before I reached the hospital. My wife was conscious for a few hours. She mumbled my name and held my hand as I cried at her bed side. She said that she loved me and asked me to remember only the good times that we had shared. My wife died in my arms as I asked her for forgiveness." Raj was silent for a few seconds and Yanus waited for him to go on.

"Around twenty men had broken in to my house that night. They dragged my wife out of the house and brutally assaulted her. My neighbours were witness to all this. They watched and did nothing. It was just a night of entertainment as a woman was abused before their eyes. Once they were done with her, they dragged her broken body back in and set our house on fire. My son was sleeping...."

Raj still did not show any emotion. But his words sent a chill down Yanus's spine.

Yanus's fists tightened as the sick memories of his past threatened to come to the surface. Yanus did not move his eyes from Raj. When Raj looked up, his eyes had a fire in them that Yanus recognised. It was not just anger. It was pure and unadulterated hate. "I realised that some people do not answer to the same God as we do. For some, there is no God. There is only the devil. I had welcomed the devil. I had become him. I went after them. I found each and every one of them. They were not brave and courageous men of war. They were simply opportunistic bastards who had been pumped up by their political masters with a false sense of invincibility. I broke their myth. I killed them all. I made them cry for their mothers before they died. I made them beg for mercy. I wanted them to understand how worthless their life was and how worthless were the twisted ideals they worshipped, but more importantly, I wanted them to feel fear before they died. But you see I was smart too. I did not intend to get caught either. I made each murder look like an accident. Of course, Jadhav knew it was me, but he could never prove it."

"Jadhav?"

"Yes, it was Jadhav who refused to register the complaint and it was he who threatened my family. I got to that politician at the very end. By then, he knew I was coming. He tried to reach me and make peace. He said he wanted a compromise. I gave him peace. He could not protect himself any better than I had protected my family. I cut through his security with incredible ease. He begged me for his life at the end. But all I could see were the burning bodies of my wife and child. All I could hear were the words of love that my wife had struggled with all her strength to whisper during her last moments."

Raj gritted his teeth, "I cooked him alive. He took a long while to die. But it was not long enough for me."

Yanus's throat had gone dry. He unclenched his fist and thought of something to say.

"There were witnesses this time. I was arrested. There was to be a trial. But on the day of my hearing, I was released. It was a case of mistaken identity, I was told with apologies. Sunny had intervened. The last murder had got his attention. I knew I faced the gallows or at least life imprisonment for what I had done. But this corrupt system which had lain idle while my wife and son were being murdered had come to the defence of the one who had mocked it. Money exchanged hands and the matter was dead within a day. Can you believe it? Even the guy who went to prison for me was released after a couple of years for lack of conclusive evidence. I had slaughtered twenty three men and the system was looking for conclusive evidence. This city had proved to me that even death was not enough."

"Sunny saved my life. More importantly, he gave me a new direction. I left Jadhav alive because I wanted him to live in the fear that I might kill him anytime. To this day, he fears that I might kill him. Of course, one day I will."

Raj fell silent. Yanus simply stared at Raj.

"You did not kill just a friend. Sunny was like a brother to me. But like I said, you did what you had to. But now you must listen to me, you must forget about Babur and go to Samar. You have done what you wanted to do. You have proved a point. Now stop before...."

"Can you get back your old job, Raj?" interjected Yanus. Raj ran his hand through his hair and said nothing. Yanus leaned forward to make his point.

"I fully understand what you are trying to say, Raj. I am sorry but I cannot do that. I am sure you understand this. We belong to this hell now though we were not born here. But I intend to become its master."

Yanus had given his answer. Raj had understood that there was nothing more that he could do.

Yanus got up and so did Raj. Both men looked in to each other's eyes for a moment. Then Raj turned and began to walk away. Just before he turned out, Raj stopped and looked back. Yanus was still staring at him.

"Did you take those off Kasid?"

Yanus nodded.

Raj turned around and left.

Raj got in his car and picked up his phone and dialled the number.

"What do you want to do now?" asked the voice on the other end

Raj explained to his boss what he wanted to do. Yanus was out of control. He could not be allowed to live. But a new approach was needed.

Raj started his car and turned in the direction of the city. As the car sped away, a figure rose between the large boulders lining the entrance to the cave where Yanus was waiting with his Cyclone. The figure had patiently waited outside the entrance for Raj to emerge or be blown to pieces. But Raj had emerged in one piece. The figure cautiously approached the entrance.

Yanus had sat back down and held his head in his hands to think about this new development. So it was Samar's father who had developed this machine. The same man who had run the orphanage where Yanus had grew up. And Samar's father had given the control of this machine to him. As much as Yanus wanted to get back at Babur, he wanted to know why the Cyclone followed him.

"Hello, Yanus."

Yanus looked up to see Singh walking toward him. Yanus got up in a rush.

"Singh, what are you doing here? How did you find me?"

"I have to admit that I am impressed. It took me a while to find you. But Raj got here before I did. And I see you have been busy."

Yanus hung his head and turned away.

"Why have you come here?" asked Yanus

"I want you to come with me." Said Singh

Yanus turned around and gave him an exasperated look.

"Do you know who that machine belongs to?" asked Singh

"Yes, I know. That's what Raj came here to tell me. He told me about Samar's father and that army of Cyclones."

Singh rubbed his face with his hands. He knew it. Falak had never been good at protecting all his secrets. Even gangsters knew what he had been doing.

"Samar wants to meet you. I know you both could help each other."

"That is what Raj wanted me to do as well. Why does everyone want me to meet Samar? What is so special about him?" asked Yanus

Singh gave a little laugh. "That is exactly what he wants to know about you. He wants to know why his father gave you that machine. Look Yanus, with Samar, you could figure out the purpose of your life. You can't keep hiding out in caves for the next fifty years."

"I already have a purpose in life...."

"No, you don't. All you have is a vendetta. What is wrong in meeting him? You can walk away if you wish. At least listen to him." Singh tried to make a good point

Yanus pursed his lips and considered.

"When have you ever regretted listening to me, Yanus?" asked Singh

Yanus took a deep breath and got up. Singh was right. What could it hurt? He could ask some of his own questions.

"Okay. I will meet him. But he must come alone. Between here and the next city is another set of such rocks. Ask him to come there tomorrow morning."

"Tell me, what have you planned to do if you decide not to help him? He does have serious problems that may be you could help with."

"I don't care about his problems. But the first thing I will do is get out of here. People come here as if it is a bus station. I need to find a more secure location that is impossible to find." Said Yanus has he walked deeper in to the cave. The Cyclone followed Yanus in to the darkness. Singh watched the odd pair disappear.

Samar stood in the hot sun. Looking around, he noticed that that he could not see the highway where Singh had got off. Samar did not like this at all. This was too vulnerable.

All Yanus had to do was to command the Cyclone to finish him off. There was nowhere to run and Yanus probably knew these rocks better than anyone. Singh had said that Yanus had insisted on this location. This is where he was comfortable. Yanus was obviously wary of meeting in the city. He would have to come alone. But here, he was in his comfort zone. Samar wiped his palms on his trousers. Where was Yanus? Samar decided to wait in the car. Samar turned around and began to walk toward it when a shadow caused him to flinch and look up. Samar was looking in to the eyes of Yanus.

The Cyclone was hovering beside him. Yanus had appeared out of nowhere and was watching him intently.

"An amazing machine, isn't it?" asked Samar

"It is. Your father built it for me." Said Yanus

"I know that. Are you satisfied with its performance? Need any modifications?" asked Samar sarcastically

"I like it just the way it is. Thank you very much. What do you want?" asked Yanus tired of Samar's game

"You know what I want. The question is what you want?" said Samar

"I thought you would know what I wanted. Hasn't Singh told you anything?"

"He told me about Babur." Samar gestured to the Cyclone, "I am sure you will kill him with that. But what will you do then? I know my father built a mean machine. But it can't cook or wash clothes. You can't work, can you? Will you take it to office with you if you ever find a job? That Cyclone will not look good on a job application. Ever thought of that?" Samar came closer with his hands on his waist. Samar walked around Yanus and spoke.

"I have always wondered why my father wanted you to have this." Samar paused at the Cyclone.

"You know, this machine is a lot bigger than the army that my father's team built. But it is smaller than the Cyclone R."

Yanus turned around to face Samar and asked in confusion, "Cyclone R?"

"Of course, this is Cyclone Rx. It was built at the end. Cyclone R was supposed to lead the army. That is what my father intended. But he died before telling anyone who was supposed to lead Cyclone R. Then you show up with Cyclone Rx: The machine that was not supposed to be built...."

"Yeah, I already know this much. A lot of confusion about who was supposed to lead what seems to be in the air. But the fact is that Cyclone Rx is mine to lead. We both know we can't change that."

Samar was seriously annoyed and took a step closer to Yanus. Both men were an inch apart. Where Samar was a little soft and short, Yanus was lean and tall. But both had the same intensity.

"Do you think my father built that for you to play with? Listen to me, that machine has a higher purpose. We both know that we can't change who it follows. But neither of us knows why it was built. What if you die? What if there is a real need for that army and you're off on a humanitarian mission somewhere? Don't you understand?" Samar turned his back on Yanus and continued

"I don't know why it is you and not me. But I trust my father and I have accepted it. I only ask that you respect my father's work."

"I will not...." began Yanus but Samar cut in

"I am not asking you to come with me."

"Then why are you here?" asked Yanus in confusion

"I wanted you to know that if you come to me, we both could find out the true purpose of the Cyclone."

Yanus stood silent and considered the weight of these words. Neither Kasid nor Raj had been able to explain that. Perhaps Samar had a point.

"What will you do if I...." Yanus's words were cut short by the Cyclone.

It had been drifting idly like a referee in a tennis match, but the machine suddenly shot forward toward Yanus. Yanus flinched and fell back before he could balance himself. Yanus thought that the Cyclone was attacking him. But as he fell, he remembered that this was not how it attacked. This was how it defended. No sooner had the thought come in his mind when Yanus heard the ping of metal on metal. The spark and the smoke told Yanus that the Cyclone had come between him and an incoming bullet. The machine had saved his life. Less than two seconds later, the silence of the area was shattered by the sound of rapid firing.

Yanus dived behind the rocks to protect himself. Yanus tried to see where it was coming from but couldn't see anything.

The screech of tires told him that Samar had bolted. Yanus wanted to command the Cyclone to kill Samar for this treachery but first he would make him talk. Then Yanus would show him the true purpose of the Cyclone.

Babur raised his hand. The firing stopped. It had been less than a minute since the first bullet had been fired. Babur looked to the man near him who had fired it. The man's expression told him the truth. The opportunity had been missed. The Cyclone had thrown yet another surprise at them. Babur cursed his luck. This had been difficult to arrange. Raj and Babur had put people to track every movement made by Negi and Samar. These were the two people who would try to reach Yanus. Negi had not moved at all since Kasid's death but Samar had got there eventually. Either his need was greater or Negi was content to sit back and let everyone play their cards first. Try as he might, Babur could not figure out Negi's intention. But Samar had provided an opportunity for Babur to ambush Yanus. But the Cyclone had thwarted that chance.

"We have to get out of here." Said Raj getting up and signalling his men to get back

Raj looked back to see Babur still in position with his gun in hand. "What are you waiting for? We have to leave. Yanus will know where the shots came from. Come on...." said Raj urgently

"I will be the last person to leave the battle. That is what you will do when you lead. Now get back and get these men to safety."

"You're mad. I am...." said Raj in exasperation

"You are wasting time. Get out. I will follow." Said Babur through gritted teeth

Raj saw that Babur was determined. He quickly turned and followed his men beyond the ridge.

"Move out, all of you. Move out now." Said Babur urgently to a few of the old timers who had been dawdling behind to stay with their chief

The idea had been to shoot Yanus as he spoke to Samar. The idea had been to avoid dealing with the Cyclone. Raj and Babur knew that they could not win a fire fight with the machine. They had to escape and wait for another opportunity. Babur knew that the next chance would be more difficult. Now, Yanus knew what they were up to.

The men ducked and quickly ran over the edge to the waiting cars. Babur could hear the engines revving and the tires screeching. He hoped they got away before Yanus knew where they were. They had arrived with nearly fifty men to ensure that they had sufficient fire power if it came to that. Most of them were now gone and Babur got up to leave as well. He could see the last car waiting for him. The men in it patiently waited for their boss to catch up.

Babur flinched as massive blue streak of lightening flew past his head and exploded in the waiting car. The car and its inhabitants were instantly destroyed.

Babur stopped in his tracks and looked back. Yanus was standing on top of the ridge under which Babur's men had positioned themselves to fire. The Cyclone had fired at the car and removed Babur's possibility of escape. Babur was glad that at least Raj had gotten away.

"You really are desperate to kill me, aren't you?" asked Yanus

"You started it." Said Babur

Yanus shook his head. "That is the problem with people like you. You don't even understand the implications of the sick work that you do."

"Back to that, are we? How is your mission to save the children going?" asked Babur

Yanus jumped down and walked close to Babur.

"You look tired old man. Do you want some rest before I kill you?"

"Why don't you let the Cyclone do it for you? That's how you do it, anyway."

Yanus smiled. "Will Raj not come to save you?"

Babur used the opportunity to crash his head on Yanus's nose. Yanus felt his nose break and stumbled backward in pain. But Yanus still laughed through the pain. Babur looked at the Cyclone. It didn't seem to mind. He advanced toward Yanus and kicked him hard in his ribs. Yanus fell to the floor and clutched his sides.

"What's the matter, old man? Is that all?" teased Yanus

Babur used all his strength to hammer Yanus in to the ground. Yanus did not lift a finger to defend himself. But every time Babur put him down, Yanus would get back up. Babur summoned all his power to finish Yanus off. He knew that the moment he pulled his gun, the Cyclone would enter the fight. These were the rules that Yanus had decreed. Yanus had become a bloody mess. Yanus could feel pain in every punch and every kick that Babur landed. Yanus did not fail to notice that every time Babur raised his hand, he found his mark. He never missed. But Babur was still unable to land a killing blow. Yanus ducked and dodged as Babur's reflexes were getting slower. Babur was punching haphazardly and his strength began to wane. Babur tried to choke Yanus but Yanus managed to free himself from the lock. Unlike last time, Yanus had been prepared for it and Babur too was unable to hold on. Finally Babur stopped and put a hand on his chest. The man's knees buckled as his over worked heart started to falter. Babur put his hands on the floor to balance himself and get a breath.

Yanus's feet came in to focus. Babur looked up to see Yanus standing erect in front of him. All the effort that Babur had put in had not had any effect on Yanus at all.

Babur took a deep breath and looked in to the eyes of Yanus. It was his last breath. Yanus rammed his fist on the side of Babur's head. The impact broke Babur's neck and he crumpled to the ground.

Yanus wiped the blood from his face. His body was bruised all over and it was taking a huge effort just to stand. But Yanus walked up to the ridge in the front and climbed it for a better view. Babur's men had disappeared. He had been too late to realise that they were not going to fire anymore and were running. But Babur had stayed back. He had allowed his men to escape while he waited till the end. Yanus walked back to look in to Babur's eyes. He remembered the look in them as he had swung his arm around. In the end, Yanus knew that Babur had repented. There had been no fear. But there had been repentance. Perhaps that is why he had come here. Yanus leaned down and closed Babur's eyes.

Chapter 8

The First Cyclone

Samar had never been this angry before. He could not believe his luck. After weeks of preparation and efforts, he finally had been able to speak to Yanus. It had looked like Yanus was beginning to understand his reason. Samar had felt it. He had seen the spark of realisation in Yanus's eyes. And then those fools had shown up. Yanus must have thought that he had set him up. He was sure of it. Samar was surprised that the Cyclone had not followed him. He had seen Yanus diving behind the rocks and knew that he was pinned. Samar had no option but to take cover himself. For one second, he had entertained the thought of staying and helping Yanus. But that was foolhardy. Yanus could have sensed a trap and would have killed him himself. Samar punched the dashboard in frustration.

"There is no point in beating yourself up. We could never have known...." said Singh who was driving back in to the city

"Who were those people? What did they want with Yanus?" asked Samar loudly

"It could have been anyone. I would have thought that people would be trying to get Yanus on their side." Said Singh

"That didn't look like an invitation to me. They were trying to kill him." Said Samar

"It's simple, Samar. Whoever it was does not care about the Cyclone. They just wanted Yanus." Said Singh

"He will never listen to me after this." Samar bit his knuckle.

"What do want to do now?" asked Singh

"I thought you were leaving." Said Samar in a tone of surprise

"I think I will stay." Said Singh is strange tone. Samar looked suspiciously at Singh.

"Turn right at the next junction."

"Where are we going?" asked Singh

"Hopefully Mani has turned up."

There were all the old faces but some of the new ones were missing. Raj wanted to wait for as long as possible. The news had spread through the city like wild fire that Babur was dead. Everyone had called in to confirm the news and Raj had confirmed it. An explosion had been reported and the police had been called to investigate smoke coming from a deserted area around fifty kilometres from the highway between the two great cities. The police had found the body of Babur and the wreckage of a car with five other dead. It was all over the news. Raj had closed his eyes in sorrow as he mourned the passing of another friend. He did not know how much more of death he could take. Raj had known that it was a risk but Babur had insisted. Raj had devised the best plan that he could come up with. Raj had been worried about the machine and was not sure whether a sniper would work, but Babur had decided that it was the best chance they would get. In the end, the Cyclone had once again surprised them. Raj got the feeling sometimes, that Babur wanted this. He was never one to take a rash decision. But Babur had rushed in to the confrontation with Yanus. Ordinarily in their world, opportunities were never created. You had to wait for them. Raj rubbed the fingers of one hand and tried to make sense of all that happened. His thoughts were scattered and he was having difficulty in focusing. Raj looked up when he heard the door close. The one who had closed the door was one of Babur's oldest men. He looked at Raj and shook his head. That was all. No one else was coming.

Very well, thought Raj. It was all for the best. The ship was being abandoned already. Many had come to hear what Raj had to say. But some had not.

"Thank you for coming in. You know what has happened in the last few hours. I am afraid that I have nothing but further bad news." Said Raj

The men all looked at each other. Babur's death had been a blow, but they were still a team. They had been through this before.

"We are with you, Raj. We know how loyally you served Babur. Every man in this room owes you too much to abandon you. You have helped us all more than once. What manner of men would we be if we do not recognise that?" asked one of them

Raj shook his head. Things had changed. And they were still changing at a rapid pace. Don't these clowns see that?

"I know you men have invested a lot in various operations throughout the city and even in different states, in some cases. You all know the people that work for us in some way or the other. From this moment onwards, these operations are your sole responsibility. The authority of Babur will not pass on to anyone in this room, not even me."

"You can't do that. We have been able to operate because of the protection that Babur gave us." Said another man

"And neither of us is Babur. None of us can work miracles like he did. To assume that position would require immense power. Do either of you possess that power? I know that I don't." Said Raj

The men considered his words. It was true that Babur had found ways around impossible situations. To expect that from someone else would be foolish. It was just another example that true power emanated from the person, not the position. Finally after a few minutes, one of the men got up.

"Are we to assume, that in our respective areas of influence our word would be final?"

Raj knew some would see it that way. He was counting on it.

"This is the last time we will meet." Said Raj not bothering to elaborate

The enormity of Raj's last statement finally sank in. This was to be the last meeting held in the name of Babur.

Raj got up and the men too got up and began to leave. Some looked happy and some looked a little nervous. That was understandable, thought Raj. Not all would survive for long without the protection of Babur and would probably need to look for other alternatives. The manoeuvring for this position would begin immediately.

In the end Raj was alone with the man who had closed the door at the beginning of the meeting. The man had not moved an inch or said anything during the meeting. He had stood beside the door and listened. He had watched the men leave.

"I am sorry Zubin; I have nothing more to say." Said Raj

"I was with Babur all my life. I was there with him through every one of his battles. And now...."

"I know that. I could never fill his shoes. I hope you realise that I did the right thing."

"I don't like it. But I understand it. Babur always thought very highly of you. After Sunny died, he looked upon you as his successor. He knew what you had been through. It was Babur who had wanted Sunny to bring you in. You had shown that you were unafraid to act." The man's eyes were moist

Raj wondered what the world had come to. Babur had brought a lot of suffering in to this world. And here was this man who was sorry that he was no more.

"I am here because I was afraid to act, Zubin. But perhaps the past is best forgotten. It clouds your perception about the future."

"No, Raj. The past reminds us where we have come from and why. There are two points to every journey. If you don't know where you have come from, how will you know where to go?"

Raj nodded and shook the hand that Zubin had extended.

It was time for the final farewell.

Raj locked the door behind Zubin.

"Where will you go?" asked Zubin

"I need to finish some unfinished business." Said Raj

"Best of luck, my friend. Good bye." Said Zubin as he walked away

Raj watched him leave as he made his own way to a different destination.

With every possible scenario running through his head, Samar could not see a way out of this mess. Samar stood with Singh in front of the Cyclones. His face was taut with frustration. Mani had disappeared and there was no one else here who seemed to know anything about him.

Samar punched one of the machines and screamed.

"What are you doing?" asked Singh in surprise

"What have these people done? I can't believe my dad was a part of this. Why did they have to build these machines? What good have they done? Who is going to be responsible for them now? They told me only because they couldn't deal with it themselves. And now...." Samar looked deranged

"Calm down, Samar. All is not lost...."

"Of course not, because all is not lost, not yet. What do you think Yanus is going to do? Those people who attacked him are probably dead too. I am sure of it. As soon as he is done with them, he will come for me. I am seriously thinking of beginning a new life down here. I am sure they will find a use for me. May be I could sweep the floor...."

Singh hit Samar on the head.

"Hey, what was that for?" shouted Samar

"That was to wake you up. Control yourself, boy." Said Singh

Samar shook his head and looked back at the machines lined up in row after row. Samar took a deep breath to calm down.

"Still, what do you make of these, Singh? Do you think they were built for a purpose?" Samar was still rubbing his head

"I agree it is quite a sight. And this is Cyclone R?" Singh pointed to the one standing in the front

It didn't look any different than the others. But the difference was in size. Cyclone R was nearly fifteen feet tall. It had been shifted from its storage facility and moved in with the rest of the army. Samar wanted them all together.

Both men looked at Cyclone R for a while. It was an imposing machine. Singh noticed that Cyclone Rx was about that same size as the other Cyclones. The other difference was that it was completely dark. All the machines here were white in colour.

Singh put his hand on Samar's shoulder and said

"We have to leave, Samar. We can't stay here forever."

"I thought Mani would be here. I thought he would have an answer."

"He is not. Forget about this machine. We have to focus on Yanus and Cyclone Rx."

The two men started on their way out. Again, Samar noticed that no one seemed to care that they were leaving.

"What do you think we should do? I don't want my father's legacy in the control of Yanus. I rather it was destroyed or not put to any use at all. I don't care if they rot here." Samar looked sideways at Singh as he spoke

"As long as Yanus controls Cyclone Rx, that machine will always be a threat."

"Do you think Yanus will take control of the army?"

"We don't even know whether it can. For all we know, Cyclone Rx has nothing to with the Cyclones down below. If that is true, I think you can kiss them all good bye."

Samar walked in silence for the remainder of the way. Could that be possible? Had his father, in anger destroyed his own work? If Cyclone R was the only machine that could control the other Cyclones then Singh was correct in his estimate. No one could control Cyclone R and that would mean that there was nothing to control the Cyclone army. The only Cyclone operational was Cyclone Rx. What had his father actually done? As far as he was concerned, there were two major questions. Out of Cyclone Rx and Cyclone R, which had the key to control the Cyclone Army?

The other question was who controlled Cyclone R? If it was Cyclone Rx that the army followed, Yanus would not hesitate to take that control. He had caused enough trouble with just that one machine. What would he do with an entire army of Cyclones at his command? Samar shuddered. Singh was correct. Whichever way it was looked at, it was Yanus who was the threat.

"Thought of something?" asked Singh who had been noticing Samar for a while

Samar stopped at his car and leaned on the bonnet, a thoughtful expression on his face.

"Well?" asked Singh

"Are you prepared to do what is necessary, Mr Singh?" asked Samar in a casual voice, not even looking at Singh

Singh swallowed. "What do you mean by 'necessary'?" Singh was not sure he was going to like this

"Let me explain...." said Samar as he put his arms around the former soldier's shoulders and took him for a small walk.

Jadhav leaned back as he eyed the woman. She looked in a lot of distress. Of course, a woman walking in a police station in the middle of the night had to be in distress. Jadhav was getting bored with the woman's story. He had been in a happy mood lately. With Babur gone, a huge sword hanging on his head was gone. Jadhav guessed he had Yanus to thank for that. A lot of people who had been a pain for Jadhav had been wiped out courtesy of Yanus.

"Sir, please...please help me." The woman pleaded

"Yes...yes. I want to help you. But I need more information...to begin the investigation. You need to tell me more." Said Jadhav with a little smile that had no hint of sympathy

"I have told you all I could. My husband has not returned home since the last two days. I have looked everywhere for him. None of his friends or relatives...." the woman was distraught and broke down

Jadhav quickly came around the table and put his hands on the woman's shoulder. The woman shrugged the hands off and shifted slightly.

"I understand the problem. But as I told you, we need more information."

The woman didn't seem to hear and continued to cry.

"Your husband disappeared two days ago. And you come to a police station in the middle of the night. Why is that?" Jadhav sat on the table beside the woman. The woman had to look up to see Jadhav leering at her.

"What do you mean? I wanted to make sure that he was not...."

"Would you like to spend some time here? You can try and remember some more information while you wait. I am sure then I will be able to help."

The woman looked a little confused and turned her eyes away.

"How do I know that you haven't killed your husband?" said Jadhav with a little smile

The woman looked shocked. "Please don't say that. I love my husband...I am really looking for..."

Jadhav was really enjoying this. "I don't want to listen to your nonsense. I have to investigate everything, you see. I have to look at all...angles."

Jadhav was struggling not to laugh.

"Please Sir, believe me. I need your help. If you could just...."

"Okay...okay I get it. Wait outside. I will call you."

"But...." the woman fidgeted with her purse. Jadhav had been eying it for a while.

Jadhav raised his hand to silence her and pointed his fingers toward the door.

The woman had no choice but to leave and wait outside.

Jadhav stretched his legs a little. He was glad things were back to normal in at least his station. He no longer had to worry about Raj breathing down his neck. Without Babur supporting him, Raj was nothing but a toothless tiger. Jadhav leaned back even more and tried to get some rest.

An hour later, a constable knocked and entered the office. Jadhav opened an eye.

"What is it?" asked Jadhav

"It's that woman. She is really beginning to panic. Shouldn't we...?" the man began but Jadhav waved his hands and gestured to have the woman brought before him.

The woman entered the room and stood in front of Jadhav's desk with her head bent low.

"Yeah, I have put through some calls for you. There is someone out there who knows where your husband might be. The description you gave fits with someone they found." Said Jadhav rubbing the sleep out of his eyes

The woman nearly jumped in joy. "Oh, thank you, Sir. Thank you so much. I knew you would help..."

"That's not all." Jadhav interrupted. "The person who knows about your husband is not a policeman.

Jadhav pumped up his chest. He is a civilian. And he wants money in exchange for the information."

The woman's face fell. "But I don't have money."

"Then I am sorry. I cannot help you. I cannot force people to give information. We have a difficult job, you see."

"But there has to be another way...." the woman pleaded

Jadhav leaned forward and spoke in a conspiratorial tone, "A few thousand rupees in exchange for information is not a bad deal. I think you should take it. How much can you afford, by the way?"

"I think I could manage some. Shall I get it now?" The woman said in a defeated voice

Jadhav leaned back and relaxed. "Yes, you should. On the way out, ask the constable to file in your complaint."

Jadhav watched as the woman got up and walked out with her head hanging low. Jadhav thought that this was a good beginning to the day. It wasn't even morning yet.

The woman sat down in front of the constable who she had asked to register her complaint when she had first arrived. The man had just begun to write when Jadhav had come out of his office and seen the woman. He had asked the constable to stop and invited the woman in. The constable had feebly protested but Jadhav had not even heard him. The constable now looked at the woman and offered a few words of comfort.

"Don't worry, ma'am. We will find your husband. It's just...." the man seemed to want to say something but then thought better of it.

"What is your name?" asked the woman in a steady voice

The man pointed to his badge, "I am Head Constable Kamble."

The man pointed to the paper. "Let's get this done. You should have registered your complaint when you came in. Tell me your name." Said Kamble

"My name is Sitaji Borey. I am the new Chief Inspector of Police of this area."

Kamble looked in to the eyes of the woman. But the woman's eyes pointed toward something in her hand. It was an identity card; Kamble took it and read it. Kamble's smile was the biggest Sitaji had ever seen. Throughout the night, of all the things that she had seen and heard Kamble's smile was the most perplexing.

"You seem happy to see me?" Sitaji spoke in her slow voice. No one would have guessed that she was a police woman.

"I am sorry ma'am. It's just that this is not the first time such an incident has happened with me. This is in fact, the second time." The man stopped smiling and closed the register book

"When was the first time?" Sitaji knew she could talk to him. She already had the background information on every man in this station. Kamble was an honest man.

"That was in 1977." Said Kamble

"I was not even born then." Said Sitaji

"And like last time, I am sure this too has a purpose." Kamble's tone was professional

"Yes it has." Sitaji drummed her fingers on the table and considered. She checked her watch and decided. Sitaji picked up the phone on the counter and dialled quickly.

The call was answered before the first ring was complete. The conversation was short and cryptic.

Finally Sitaji smiled a little.

"Yes Sir. I will get it done." Sitaji put down the receiver and said to Kamble. "Get two more men over here". Kamble immediately got up and signalled a few men nearby to come to him. Kamble noticed for the first time, that the woman was incredibly tall and broad shouldered. Half the men in the station wouldn't be able to match those shoulders.

"Come with me." Said Sitaji

The men looked to Kamble for an explanation. Kamble explained in hushed tones and that straightened everyone's spines.

Sitaji did not knock and entered the room. Jadhav looked up in surprise.

"Have you got the mo...?"

Sitaji stood at the side of the table. Jadhav looked up at the woman in surprise.

"What's going...." Jadhav had gotten up and had taken a step toward Sitaji when the woman turned to Kamble

"Arrest him."

"What...what are you doing? Kamble...stop it." Jadhav struggled as Kamble pinned his arms behind his back. Sitaji noticed that Kamble applied more force than was necessary.

Jadhav knew the futility of struggling against Kamble. What was going on? And who was this woman?

As if reading Jadhav's mind, Sitaji answered.

"I am Sitaji Borey. I am the temporary Chief Inspector of this unit. Also, in my capacity as an officer of the Crime Branch, I have been investigating your links with known criminals, especially one called Babur. You covered your trails well, Jadhav. But we got enough evidence to put you away for good."

Jadhav was paralysed with fear. That was not possible.

"What are you talking about? You are framing me. I don't know anyone called Babur."

Sitaji held up a hand to Kamble in annoyance. Kamble released the pressure on Jadhav's arms to allow him to stand properly.

"How did you become a policeman? I mean, how can anyone be so dumb? We have always known that you were neck deep with that scum. You and some men of your unit had been taking orders from criminals like Babur for years.

But we needed proof that would hold up in a court. Do you know what I have? I was just sent fifteen videos in which you can clearly be seen speaking to Babur. Even I was shocked at your brazen attitude. Obviously, your masters no longer need you. Or perhaps they realised the same thing that we did. You are just untrustworthy to have around. We don't need to hold back either. Anyways, this conversation will go best during your sentencing."

"Sentencing?" Jadhav thought he would faint

"Of course, this is a case of treachery. You will not be tried the usual way. The verdict is already out. I don't have all the details. Even I don't know how deep they will bury you. I just want you to know that the police force is going to make an example of you. A lesson, you see, for others." Sitaji waved her hand to Kamble

As the men were leaving Sitaji called one of them,

"Constable Munif?"

The young man turned back and stood once more at attention.

Sitaji removed a sheet from a leather folder and handed it to Munif.

"Do you know what this is?" asked Sitaji

Munif read through the sheet quickly. There were names on the document. Looking up, the man nodded a little.

"I have heard good things about you, Munif. You are making quite a name for yourself."

Munif stared at the ground and made no comment.

"I also heard that you are going to appear for your exams, later this year. How is your preparation going on?" asked Sitaji

"I am doing everything I can to prepare. Hopefully I will...."

"You will pass I am sure. But you will never make an officer. Not with your current temperament." Said Sitaji

The man pursed his lips tight and resumed his study of the floor.

"If you want to become an officer, you have to learn to control your temper. Excessive or unnecessary use of force is not something to be proud of. That is what separates us from criminals. You must learn to use your head."

The man nodded and looked up.

"Get that list to Kamble. Go with him and make sure that every man on that list is arrested before sunrise. I don't want this mess to make the papers."

Munif clicked his shoes and marched out. Sitaji sighed and shook her head in amusement. The man was walking around the unit as if he were in a parade. But perhaps that was the enthusiasm that the force now needed. Munif, Kamble, and a few others had stayed clear of Jadhav's filth. There were few, but they were enough. They had proved that the noble ideals of the police force could be adhered to and all that was required was will.

With this stroke, a powerful link between the police and the corrupt had been severed. Sitaji realised that there would be consequences. Such ties were usually endorsed by the high and mighty. But Sitaji was glad that the police was fighting back. They were the final arbitrator of law and order in the city. As long as there was a Kamble and a Munif in the force, they would remain so.

Sitaji wondered who had sent those videos to her seniors and why. Sitaji had seen them and had tried to make out the third person in the videos. But his image was always in the shadows. She couldn't make out the face at all.

Raj was trying to get used to all the smoke. It had been a while since he had lit up and feared that the smoke might entice him to pick up the habit again. On top of it, Negi always offered him a stick every time he lit up. Negi had been speaking for over an hour. Raj had questions. He had asked a lot of questions. This time Negi had answered clearly and without holding anything back. Raj had to use every ounce of his focus to understand the implications. Finally Negi fell silent. Negi had been interested in Raj for a long time. Against what was to come, men like Raj were powerful weapons. And Negi intended to have this weapon. After all was said, Negi let Raj think it over.

"So, Raj, are you in?" asked Negi after a while

"It looks like it. I can hardly go around giving interviews now, can I?"

"Also, it would be pointless." Said Negi

"So you say. You should have told me this the last time we met."

Negi smiled and nodded. He sat back and relaxed. It was just a matter of days. This time Negi didn't feel like lighting up. A storm was coming.

"There is nothing like having your beliefs shot to pieces, is it? I am sure you know that."

"But still...perhaps you should have been a bit more forthcoming... at least with Yanus. You have played an extremely dangerous game." Said Raj

"Whatever risks I have taken are nothing compared to what some others have taken. Or maybe, they were even more helpless to influence events."

"You have put too much faith in Yanus. Do you think he will understand? He did not even want to speak to Samar. What chance...."

"Samar has been a disappointment. But he will make up for it. I am sure. And we hit the point of no return a long while back." Said Negi

Raj sat quietly and considered Negi's words. The whole world was about to be turned upside down. All they could do was to wait and watch their greatest weapon prepare its own recipe for destruction.

Raj made a gesture toward Negi's packet of cigarettes. Negi smiled and took a couple of sticks out. They both lit up and began planning the next stage of operations.

Yanus splashed some more water on his face. It was extremely hot and stifling in this place. He would have preferred the desolate plains with the sprinkling of rocks and caves. But a dense forest had its own advantages. Yanus had spent the last few days resting and recovering. The fight with Babur had taken its toll. The immediate aftermath had been terrible. His wounds had taken a while to heal. His body had been stiff and the pain unbearable, especially at night when it got cold. But he thought that it was lucky that they had come down here before and Singh had taken the time to teach him about healing plants and how to get food. The forest it seemed had the capacity to provide for all the basic needs of life. Yanus rubbed his eyes and sat down. He was not fully recovered. And Yanus was getting impatient. His mind was racing with possibilities. He now understood what Singh had been trying to say. They would never let him be in peace. The Cyclone had attracted too much attention. People had known about it and had desperately wanted it. But Jabar Falak had chosen him. The Cyclone had come to him. And then, there was the army. Thinking about every possibility led Yanus to the army. Is that what Falak wanted? Was that the purpose of the Cyclone? Samar too had insisted that he should come with him. Yanus shook his head ruefully. Even when playing his treacherous game, Samar had let out the truth. He was bitter. His own father had not trusted him. Yanus knew that Samar was jealous of him. Of all the threats that Yanus had so far faced, Yanus realised that it was Samar who was more dangerous. He would stop at nothing to get control of the Cyclone. There was only one answer to this problem. Samar had to be eliminated. Everyone else was immaterial. They could try but they would never succeed. Only Samar understood this power. The others just wanted it.

Suddenly the morning sky lit up with up with a flash. Yanus looked up.

He saw the birds take flight and small animals run out of their holes looking for cover. But he didn't see the large predators. That was the law of the jungle. The most powerful animals did not flee. They fought back to preserve and protect their authority.

Yanus's smile grew as he saw the Cyclone approach him.

Singh hated to do this. He had tried to convince himself that this was not the way. But whichever way he looked at it, there was only one possible outcome. In all the years that he had spent in the orphanage, Yanus had never let his emotions out in the open. But the few weeks since they had escaped from Sunny had allowed Singh to understand Yanus. There was immense frustration and hatred in him. Singh was sure that Jabar Falak had made a mistake. Whatever the purpose of the Cyclones was, Yanus had corrupted it. His cruelty and anger had only increased with the passing of time. He had sensed it on the first night itself. That was why Singh had wanted to avoid the confrontation with Sunny and Babur. He knew that Yanus's mind was vulnerable and it was possible that he would be influenced by the evil that he could not win against. But he had failed. Yanus had begun to understand his strength even before the Cyclone had come to him. But the arrival of the Cyclone had completed the change. With every passing day, Yanus lost his mind a little more until he had become completely stone cold. The fight with Babur and then Kasid had brought the devil in him to life. There was no doubt in Singh's mind. Yanus did not care why Falak had linked that Cyclone to him. But sooner or later, Yanus would take control of the army. And that would be catastrophic.

Samar had worked out his plan perfectly. He just hoped that it didn't take his own life as well. But some risks were unavoidable. Singh crouched down and crept forward. It had taken a while for him to figure out where Yanus would go after Babur had been killed. Yanus was becoming inventive in finding shelter. But this one was more than inventive. It was perfect. Yanus seemed to be attracted to nature and there were few such choices around the city. Singh had found Yanus. And this time he was alone. Singh had walked all the way from the edge of the forest to its centre where Yanus was. As Singh got closer, he inched forward carefully and looked for signs of the Cyclone. Singh checked his gun one last time before advancing. Yanus would not be expecting intruders and didn't need to hide. Singh knew that the element of surprise was going to be his greatest ally. Hiding behind trees and bushes, Singh advanced to a spot where he could finally see his target. Yanus was sitting on a log with his head resting on his hands and didn't seem to be alert. Singh watched him for a while, looking for a sign of the Cyclone. Yanus was completely still and had not detected the presence of Singh creeping up behind the trees. Singh took a minute more to make up his mind.

There was no other way. Yanus was just now realising his taste for power. He would not stop till he had eliminated all those who stood in his way. It would be for the best. Singh closed his eyes for a moment and made up his mind. Singh said a silent sorry to his friend, Jabar, for breaking his oath. Singh had promised to protect Yanus. But even Jabar would not disagree with this decision. Evil had to be stamped out before it grew in to a monster.

Singh cocked his rifle and took aim. All his years in the army and his training could not completely overwhelm those years which he had spent protecting an innocent child. Singh could not block out the image of the child which had grown up in to a man. Nor could he forget the lost innocence, which had suffered and had turned evil to fight evil. Singh shut and opened his eyes again one last time. And then he pulled the trigger.

Yanus lifted his head and felt the bullet whiz past the bridge of his nose. He saw out of the corner of his eye the chips flying off the trunk next to him which the bullet hit instead. Instantly, Yanus jumped backward to get out of the way. But before he could land on his back, Yanus felt a sudden sharp pain in his shoulder. The second bullet had almost found its mark. Whoever it was; was shooting to kill. Yanus struggled through the pain and got back on his feet. Rushing as fast as he could, Yanus got behind a tree and crouched down. The pain in his arm was blinding and he was having trouble thinking straight. Yanus checked his immediate surrounding and decided to run in the opposite direction. Running away just now was the only logical option. He couldn't fight in this condition. Yanus heard a rustle behind and turned instinctively.

Yanus felt the butt of the rifle on his forehead. The blow pushed him backward and Yanus tripped on the low branches, crashing to the ground. Once again, Yanus tasted his own blood.

"Singh?" Yanus could not believe it

"What have you done? What have you done?" Singh brought his foot down on Yanus's chest driving the wind out of his lungs

It didn't matter that Singh had tears in his eyes. Yanus realised that Singh was here to kill him.

Yanus could not move an inch. It was not the pain that took him. It was the betrayal. It was perhaps the shock that paralysed him. Yanus stared at Singh and wondered what he had done to earn this.

"Where is the Cyclone?" asked Singh

The question jolted him only for a few seconds. A smile grew on Yanus's face. His eyes twinkled like that of a child who had been caught with his hand in the cookie jar.

"You know where it is, Singh. I think you have been waiting for this opportunity. I hope you didn't have to wait too long."

"I hoped you would see reason before...."

"I have seen too much reason in the last few weeks. Too many of your pals wanted to reason. It didn't work out for any of them."

Singh raised the gun and pointed it at Yanus's head.

Yanus looked in to Singh's eyes. He wanted to look in to his eyes. Yanus knew that everything else was secondary. Singh's primary aim was to kill Yanus. And he wouldn't want to waste time. Yanus did not blink an eyelid. He would not give his killer that satisfaction.

Moments turned in to seconds. But Singh did not shoot. Singh breathed in and out, his finger itching to pull the trigger. But the mind had the habit of kicking in at the most inappropriate times. It wouldn't allow Singh to kill Yanus.

"What is the matter, old man? You can't do it, can you?" Yanus rested his head on the floor and began to laugh.

Singh's shaking arm lowered the rifle.

"I will not kill you, Yanus. But I will never let you succeed."

"I have already succeeded. You are too late. I will regain my strength. I won't let anyone get in my way."

"Get in the way of what, you moron? What do you want?" Singh knew the answer but wanted to hear it from Yanus.

Yanus took a few seconds and uttered, "I will...rise."

Singh looked in to the eyes of Yanus for one more second. And then he turned and ran.

He had been unable to do it. In the back of his mind, he had known that he would not be able to do it.

The only thing he could now do was to get to Samar. Singh had to get to him, before the Cyclone did.

Samar wondered if Singh had done what he was supposed to. It would not have been easy, if he had succeeded. Samar bent down and tightened his shoe laces. He had been out on the streets for the last two days and tiredness was creeping up in him. He was already missing his bed and good food. No matter what people said, restaurant food was just not good enough. Samar had avoided crowded and populous areas and driven around empty roads looking for a sign. He knew that the Cyclone was fast and probably armed with some lethal fire power. But he would have to deal with it. That was the plan that Samar had come up with. The attack on Yanus would have convinced him that Samar was not going to deal with him. That it was not the truth didn't matter. Samar had accepted his father's decision and wanted to get Yanus on his side. But Yanus had a different idea about the purpose of the Cyclone. He would not care about Samar or his father's work. Samar knew that sooner or later, Yanus would send the Cyclone to kill him. And that was the time when Yanus would be most vulnerable. The only question was when. Samar was hoping it would be soon. Singh too was out there waiting to find Yanus without protection. Maybe he had already found him and waiting for an opportunity.

Singh too had come to the same conclusion. Whatever the original purpose was, it was dead because of Yanus. The only point was to finish Yanus and with it, the Cyclone. It was possible that the Cyclone would continue its hunt for Samar even after Yanus was dead. But that part came later. Samar would think of something. For now, Yanus was top priority. Maybe the Cyclone would get de-activated if its controller was dead. Samar scoffed at the idea. His father would have seen a way around it.

Samar rested his head on the steering wheel and said a prayer. Perhaps, this was the best time to pray. In mortal danger, man usually found God.

"Do we have an agreement?" asked Suri Chetwal in his deep powerful voice. His voice had been subdued for a long while. But the intensity had returned. The purpose had returned. All the pieces had fit in finally. Most of them had fit in a few days after Falak had died. But he had still needed more information. Jabar Falak had indeed played a dangerous game. But Chetwal's respect for the man could not have been any higher.

A small smile came on Chetwal's face. It was all that this small victory could afford in these times of crises. And the madness was yet to begin.

Chetwal had heard what he wanted to hear. It was time to take control. Chetwal crumpled the paper that Samar had given to Mani. Chetwal had finally been able to derive the information that had been hidden in those old and worthless formulae that Falak used to play with when the Cyclone was not even built. If the first bit of information was surprising, the second bit was shocking. But given the current situation, Chetwal realised that Falak must have foreseen it. He must have known what would happen after his death. He had correctly predicted the sequence of events as they unfolded long after his death. Chetwal got up and walked to the elevator and rode up to the main floor. He took a route that he had not taken since Falak had died. Falak stood in front of the giant doors and waited. The automatic sensors kicked in and detected an authorised entry. Gently swaying aside, the doors allowed Chetwal to enter the new holding area of Cyclone R. Its bottom end nestled in a specially designed base to keep it up right. Chetwal stood in front of it and remembered the last time he had stood in front of it. Jabar Falak had stood beside him at that time. Chetwal tried hard to remember what they had spoken about. But all he could recollect was the image. Chetwal wiped the tears from his eyes and spoke quietly but clearly, dimly wondering why Falak had chosen these words to activate Cyclone R.

"Cyclone...Rise."

A deep hum resonated throughout the holding area. Cyclone R rose from its resting place and drifted forward toward Chetwal. Chetwal looked up where he would have expected to find a face on a human being. An intense blue light came on filling the chamber. The massive machine was finally alive.

Chapter 9

The Truth

Samar was lucky that it was night. Had it been during the day, he would never have been able to see the blue light growing in his rear view mirror. Samar started the engine and accelerated at the same time. The engine roared in protest until it found the correct gear. The rear wheels immediately found purchase and the car jumped forward with the front wheels nearly lifting off the ground.

The explosion was deafening. Samar looked back and saw the Cyclone emerging from the ball of fire and gaining speed. So, thought Samar, Yanus had sent the Cyclone after him. Samar looked at the machine and increased his speed. He didn't feel fear at the Cyclone chasing after him. For a few seconds though, he felt pride in himself. He had correctly predicted Yanus's reaction. This meant that Singh now had his opportunity. Samar gunned the motor and shifted in to top gear. The Cyclone was effortlessly gaining on Samar. But it was going to run out of road. Samar pulled the hand brake and turned in the direction of the curve. The car's momentum carried it in the opposite direction for a few metres but Samar checked the drift without letting the car slow down. But the Cyclone blasted the short building in the corner out of the way, cutting through the curve, and emerged almost to Samar's side. Samar was ready for it and knew exactly what to do. The Cyclone missed Samar for the second time as Samar braked and missed the lightening like discharge. The machine was fast but it didn't seem to do well with moving targets. Samar turned while reversing and in an instant was shifting in to the first forward gear as the car spun 180 degrees to face the opposite direction. Samar pushed the engine to its limits as he accelerated like never before in a bid to outrun the Cyclone. He kept an eye on the mirror to check the Cyclone's position. Samar drove out of the road and turned in to a smaller dirt track that offered more protection and better terrain for his sports car. The only problem was visibility. The track led outside the city and toward the mountainous terrain. If Samar lost his headlights, he would be driving blind. The track twisted and turned sharply allowing Samar to dodge the Cyclone's fire. Samar dimly wondered if luck was all that was keeping him alive. Was he that good? The track had opened up again and Samar realised that he had left civilisation behind. The mountain terrain up ahead would provide the perfect cover. Samar knew he could not outrun the Cyclone. The only option was to hide. Samar's hands were sweating and his body was taut with tension. The machine had fired and missed every time. Samar knew his luck would run out. He kept an eye on the machine and swerved every time it fired. He kept gaining and losing ground with every curve and miss. The fear of death pushed Samar to drive like he had never driven before. Samar realised that he was beginning to anticipate every movement of the Cyclone. He knew exactly when it would fire. Samar understood the pattern in which the Cyclone was hunting him. Every time it missed though, Samar thought it was getting closer. Samar prepared to slide through another curve as it approached him on the right. Samar nearly ripped the hand brake off the floor, sending the car in to a nearly 360 degree spin. But Samar accelerated at the right moment and broke the drift. But the manoeuvre cost Samar a lot of speed. Samar saw in dismay the speed of the engine shoot up and the speed of the car drop. By the time the car could get out of the range of the Cyclone, it let loose another shot that landed underneath the bottom of the speeding car. The impact threw the car off track and Samar nearly lost control. The Cyclone fired two more shots that landed perilously close. Samar knew that he could only survive with a combination of speed and dodging the murderous lightening. The question was: for how long? Samar turned left and right to avoid the Cyclone from getting a fix on him. But the machine was incredibly fast and would have got him had he been on an open and straight road. Samar took every curve and turn as fast as he could. But Samar was now driving uphill. That took a load on the car and Samar noticed the speed dropping again. Samar had deliberately driven on roads where the Cyclone could not flank him from the side. But the road snaking along the mountain was open on one side. Samar knew he had made a mistake. The Cyclone bore down on him and prepared to fire. Samar deliberately slowed down allowing the machine to catch up and suddenly braked. The Cyclone fired at the same instant and the lightening sailed over Samar's head and crashed in front of him. The explosion dented the road and Samar knew he could never get past it. Samar had only one option. And that was to go off road. Samar had already turned left and crashed through the barrier preventing cars from going over. The steep incline propelled the car toward the forest below. Samar knew he had to hide. But he couldn't hide in a car. He decided to crash the car as it reached the bottom and jump out at the last moment. Even as Samar thought of the plan, it sounded quite lame. But it was the only plan he had. He had to make it work. The Cyclone didn't bother about terrain as it shot down toward the car. It fired repeatedly but missed as Samar would swerve out of the way. Samar was careful not let the tyres skid too much as picking up speed on loose gravel would be difficult. Samar turned around to check the Cyclone's distance from him. Looking ahead, Samar was relieved to see the edge of the forest. Samar unbuckled his seat belt and unlocked the door. He prepared himself to jump out of the vehicle but he knew he had to time it just right. The incline was about to end and the forested area was coming up fast. Samar checked the Cyclone once again and watched for the lightening.

But this time, instead of the lightening, the Cyclone unleashed an intense blue light that gave Samar no time at all. Just as Samar prepared to jump, the beam hit the car and the explosion threw it way beyond the edge. Samar was thrown from the car before he could jump and landed nearly fifty feet from the burning wreckage. The intensity of the beam had caused a gaping hole where it had crashed in to the car. The car had been completely destroyed. The immediate area had caught fire, but that didn't prevent the Cyclone from approaching the molten mass of metal.

Samar opened his eyes and quickly got to his feet. He had been thrown a huge distance and was surprised that he was still in one piece. Samar got behind a tree to hide and eyed the scene carefully. The Cyclone seemed to be inspecting the car's wreckage. Well, the plan worked. It didn't work the way he had intended, but it had worked. Samar didn't waste any time. Turning around, Samar took a step in the opposite direction to get out of the area. Samar nearly collapsed on his face. He had taken a bad fall and twisted his ankle. Samar tried to get back up without making a sound and hobbled on one leg. Looking back, Samar was surprised to see that the machine was gone. Samar didn't know whether that was good or bad, but decided it was time to get away. Hopping on one foot, Samar began to put some distance between him and the scene of the crash. There was no need to check if the Cyclone had detected his presence. If it did, Samar was dead. He had no hope of outrunning the machine on one leg. The glow from the fire had spread a huge distance and Samar thanked God for at least providing him with visibility.

Samar began to think that he had succeeded. The plan had worked. He looked around and saw that the Cyclone was nowhere to be seen. A smile grew on Samar's face even as he strained his good leg to jump forward. He could not believe it. The planning and the hard work had paid off. Not only had he survived, Singh must have eliminated Yanus as well. All he had to do was get out of here and help Singh get away. He owed Singh a lot. The man had spent a decade and a half protecting Yanus because of Jabar Falak. And now he had killed him. It would take a toll on any man. He would have to ask for his forgiveness. But first he had to get out of here. Samar thought his leg would break with all the jumping and wondered if he was even travelling in the right direction. He had to find a way out, soon.

"Going somewhere?" said a cold voice

Samar froze. Turning slowly, Samar came face to face with his worst nightmare.

Yanus stood in front of him. The Cyclone was hovering beside him. Samar knew he had moments to live.

Judging by the injuries on Yanus, Singh had obviously been at work. But obviously, he had failed; just as he had failed. Singh was probably dead. And he was about to follow Singh. Samar took a deep breath and fought the pain. He lowered his injured leg and put some weight on it. It threatened to give way but Samar forced himself to stand upright. He would not give his enemy the satisfaction of humiliating him.

Yanus walked toward Samar. He too was struggling with each step. Samar smiled a little.

"Find something funny, Samar?" asked Yanus

"What happened to you? Somebody beat you up?" asked Samar

Yanus laughed too.

"Do you know, if it had it not been for these circumstances, we could have been friends." Said Yanus

Samar was still laughing a little.

"I did try to convince you. But obviously...like you said, circumstances just wouldn't give us a chance."

"Are you prepared to die?" asked Yanus. The smile on him had become cold...distant.

"Of course not, but I am not afraid, Yanus." Said Samar defiantly

Yanus blinked slowly and nodded. "Good bye, Samar."

Singh had seen the lightening discharges as he had run toward the other end of the forest. He had thought that perhaps it was going to rain. But then he heard the explosion and that sound had not come from the sky. It had come from behind him. Even when facing the other way, Singh had seen for an instant the sky light up with an intense blue light just seconds before the sound. Singh stopped running and faced the direction from where he had come. How was that possible? Singh recognised that light and that intensity. It had the characteristics of that intense beam of light that the Cyclone unleashed. How could it be? But then Singh saw something else. Toward what seemed the edge of the forest, Singh saw the sky glow red. Singh cursed loudly and started running again.

Jumping over low bushes and pushing aside loose branches, Singh ran recklessly. Singh began to feel the heat of the fire and could smell the burning wood up ahead. Whatever it was that had caused the explosion had to be close. Singh picked up pace as the ground began to clear up of obstacles and there were fewer trees around. Singh realised that he was approaching the end of the forest. Over the din of the raging fire Singh heard something that made his blood run cold. Someone was laughing. Singh slowed down to a walk and followed the sound. Then he heard another voice which was strong and clear. It was Samar. Singh came to a small crest that rose up a few metres off the ground. Crawling up on his belly Singh espied the scene below. Singh thought he was having a nightmare. How did Samar manage to do this? He was supposed to be in the city. There was no time to lose. And there was definitely no time to play games. There was nothing he could do to save Samar. He could walk away, he supposed. Singh smiled to himself. Obviously, he knew he wouldn't. His failure to kill Yanus was going to cost Samar his life...and probably his too. Singh took out his pistol and flicked the safety off. It had been a long time he had handled this fire arm. Singh pocketed it and got up. Singh gathered his courage and walked over the crest to face Yanus one last time.

"I should have killed you, Yanus." Said Singh loudly with genuine regret

If Samar gave a start, Yanus was not surprised at all.

"I was beginning to think that you had gone. That entire ruckus must have caught your attention, huh? I was just about to introduce the Cyclone to Samar." Yanus was as fearless as he had been when Singh had nearly killed him an hour ago.

"What are you doing, old man? This is between me and Yanus. Get out of here." Said Samar

"It's too late for that. He had his chance. But he chose to come back." Said Yanus

"He's right, Samar. I guess I have to pay for letting this monster live." Said Singh with a lot of venom

"Yes, that is true. I have learned that the hard way, Mr Singh. Inaction can have serious consequences." Said Yanus

Yanus turned toward Samar and spoke softly.

"Singh here has managed to injure me and I am not in the mood to fight you both. So you will have to do with the Cyclone. Since you are the boss, you get to decide. Will you go first, or....?" Yanus was unable to finish his sentence.

Singh took his chance and as fact as he could, withdrew the pistol. At point blank range, all he had to do was to fire at Yanus. He would have succeeded too. But the Cyclone was faster. It shot the bullet out of the air. Singh had only a second to jump out of the way as the Cyclone responded by unleashing a deadly discharge of lightening at Singh. Yanus too jumped sideways and took cover. Singh was on the ground and looked up at the machine. He knew he could not jump out of the way a second time. There was no place for Singh to take cover and neither could he run. Samar screamed Singh's name, knowing that he too was about to die. Yanus screamed as loud as he could, "Kill them."

The Cyclone had never needed that command as it had already decided that Singh and Samar were threats. It fired a third time and this time it fired directly at Singh. Singh instinctively put his hands up to shield himself. His knew it would do no good and knew it was over.

But this time, Cyclone Rx's lightning discharge was met by another bolt of lightning that caused it to explode before it hit the target.

Yanus, Samar, and Singh turned to see what had caused it. From the direction of the fire, drifting just like Cyclone Rx, approached Cyclone R. Yanus seemed to be in a shock.

Cyclone Rx instantly recognised an enemy and unleashed an intense blue beam that hit the Cyclone R at its centre. But the Cyclone R continued its drift toward Cyclone Rx. Samar recognised the massive machine and knew what was about to happen. Samar ran as fast as he could and pushed Singh and himself to safety. An instant later, Cyclone Rx fired another shot at Cyclone R. But this time Cyclone R responded with an ear splitting and ground shaking bolt of blue lightning that blew Cyclone Rx to pieces.

The shock wave of the fire from the much larger Cyclone R had blown everyone off their feet. Nearly every tree in the vicinity toppled over and the ground shook for a while after the discharge.

Singh was the first to recover. Yanus was still screaming and seemed to have lost his senses. Singh rolled over to his side and took aim. It had to be now. Singh fired at Yanus. But once again, fate intervened.

Cyclone R let loose a thin beam that shot the bullet before it hit Yanus. Singh screamed in anger. Yanus was on his feet and advanced toward Singh. But almost instantaneously, Cyclone R fired another thin beam at Yanus which hit him squarely in the chest. Yanus took a few more steps before realising what had happened. Clutching his heart, Yanus crumpled to the ground.

Samar ran toward Yanus but Singh put his arm out and blocked Samar from approaching Yanus. Yanus's feet twitched for a few seconds and then became still.

"Stay here." Singh said to Samar

Singh strode toward Yanus and bent down to check his pulse.

"Hold it, Sir. You are not authorised to do that." Said a cold and snide voice

Surprised, Singh stood up straight and took in the weird looking man in a weirder costume. Singh looked around. There were more of them materialising all over the place.

"Hey, who are you?" Samar ran toward the men. They lifted Yanus's body and quickly put it in a bag.

"They are your employees, Samar." Said a deep voice

"And who the hell are you?" asked Singh

"Oh! I am his employee too." Samar and Singh looked at each other

"My name is Suri Chetwal. And Mr Samar Falak, I believe I owe you an explanation." Said Chetwal as he stood beside the Cyclone R

"Who are you, man? And how did this thing come to life?" asked Samar pointing to the Cyclone. Samar decided that the machine looked a lot deadlier when alive than when in the storage facility.

Singh pointed to the men who were collecting the pieces of the fallen Cyclone dumping them in a box.

"And what are they doing? Where are they taking Yanus's body? Why are the police not here?" asked Singh

"Did you call the police?" asked Chetwal

"No, I didn't. I mean shouldn't they be the ones to...." Chetwal raised a hand to silence Singh.

"You have been of immense help. Ordinarily, I would not be sharing this information with you, but...given the circumstances, I think I will have to. All I ask for is your patience."

Samar looked at Singh and motioned him to be silent. He wanted this man to talk.

"My name is Suri Chetwal..."

"We got that bit." Said Singh still eyeing the men collecting the Cyclone Rx parts

Chetwal eyed the man with a little annoyance and went on.

"I was second in command at your father's company." Said Chetwal

"What did you have to do with the Cyclones? I never saw you at the facility." asked Samar

"I...was busy and thought that the time was not right. Besides, there was Mani."

"And what about this?" asked Singh pointing to the Cyclone

"If you allow me, I will explain." Said Chetwal

"I have all night, man. Go ahead. And you owe me another car." Said Samar

Chetwal looked at Samar and took a deep breath.

"Your father and I started this company many years ago. We were young, enthusiastic and your father had some money. We had been educated well but we wanted to try out our hand in business...we had dreams of becoming rich. Working for someone else was not something we were interested in." Chetwal started walking as he spoke.

Samar and Singh joined him to listen. Singh finally tore his eyes away from the men who were in the process of putting Yanus's body in a van.

"Within a few years, Falak and I were raking in huge profits in transport, restaurants, garments, and a lot of other ventures that struck our fantasy. Everything that we touched, we turned to gold. Our businesses were not unique and we never meddled in anything new. All of our ventures were simple, tried and tested ideas. But then everything changed." Falak seemed to be recollecting his thoughts. Singh and Samar walked without saying a word.

"It had been around five years since we had founded FS Industries. By that time, we were already in to manufacturing and exporting of electronic and hydraulic equipment. We were successful in getting clients in and around the country. That's when your father first spoke of the Cyclones."

"FS stands for Falak and Suri, doesn't it? I thought it stood for Samar." Said Samar ruefully

"You were not born then. How could your father name something after someone who was not even born?" asked Chetwal

Samar nodded his understanding and motioned Chetwal to go on.

"We were to build a machine that would be the ultimate fighter and..."

"Just like that? What were your motives? Why the sudden interest in weapons? You were not in that field." interrupted Singh

"The motives are not important. Your father designed it and we had the resources to build it."

"An entire army of Cyclones?" asked Samar incredulously

"And where did Samar's father get that technology from? What was Yanus's role?" asked Singh

"Jabar Falak was a nationalist. We were still reeling from the Emergency and things were looking bleak for our country. There was talk of war on all sides along with the constant fear of an atomic strike. Falak and I had nothing to do with the armed forces or anyone else for that matter. We were simple businessmen plying ordinary goods. But Falak had the technological know-how. We realised that we could...contribute. We thought about it just like many of our generation who had nationalistic fervour. But we had the resources to turn our ideas in to reality."

"Contribute?" Singh asked with some sarcasm

"Yes, contribute. You see, our army was large and had courage. And many had given the ultimate sacrifice to keep our country safe and our borders intact. We had already seen a few wars. This was common knowledge and many of our generation wanted to emulate these men. We wanted to be the ones to take the nation on the route to glory. Of course, as the years have gone on, such ideas have become outdated. Anyway, our short comings were in the field of equipment. Our armed forces did not have superior technology compared to some of our enemies. During those days, when the cold war was at its height, there was a lot of focus on technology. We were not even in the race. While our aggressive neighbours were far ahead in this field, we were unable to provide hi tech weapons and equipment to our brave soldiers. Falak and I were still young and decided that we could change that. And so the concept of Cyclone was born. For many years, Falak worked on the design while I took control of our daily operations. Money was needed to finance this project as we did not want any outside help or interference. Falak travelled far and wide and met enterprising people who were intelligent and had a lot of information that contributed in the building of the Cyclone. Falak was an extremely clever man. I suspect that he had been working on the design since we were very young. He was extremely secretive and did not trust anyone. He never revealed his sources and never shared his thoughts with anyone. Within a few years, the design of the Cyclone was ready. He had worked it out. The metal to build the machine, its weapons, its shape, its colour, and every other aspect was perfected in his head. When I first saw the blue prints, I realised that I was seeing something far ahead of our time. If built, this machine would be superior to anything that was built or be built for another hundred years. Still, it was not all Falak. There were people in the most unlikely places who contributed in the most unlikely aspects. You will not believe the alternatives people had thought up to replace the internal combustion engine...and that too in places where you would least expect to find such innovations. The advent of computers and software in the eighties revolutionised our work. Falak re-designed its capabilities to seek, to hunt, to detect, and to understand commands. Falak re-designed the manner in which it would react to threats. Falak designed an extremely advanced system to allow it to drift, to fly, and to manoeuvre at high speeds..."

"What powers it?" asked Singh

"Yeah, how come it never requires any charging or re fuelling? Some...technological innovation?" asked Samar

"Solar power had been given up as being inefficient as it could never match the output of a conventional engine per unit size. Falak worked on that for many years. Today, each Cyclone has a body that absorbs heat and light from its surrounding and converts it in to energy, an unmatched piece of technology that Falak perfected after a lot of research. Such a design allowed it to function without an exhaust or without the need to refuel. Even the slightest light in the atmosphere is enough to keep it activated. Of course, if kept in the dark for too long in extremely cold conditions, the Cyclone will not function. But that will take time and the Cyclone will not allow it happen."

"Why not?" asked Samar

"Whoever is linked to Cyclone R will not allow it." Said Chetwal

"Ah! I think we really want to know about that." Said Singh

"Cyclone Rx was linked to Yanus and Cyclone R was linked to me."

"We noticed that, but why?" Said Samar

"Falak wanted the machines to be used only for defence and not as a war making tool. He feared that in the wrong hands, the machine would wreak havoc. This too, I think he learned from what was happening on the international stage. Therefore, the machines would remain under the control of FS and would be used in case the civilian leadership felt it was needed. It was to assist our armed forces, but would not take orders from them."

"So what happened?" asked Singh

"Cyclone R and the army were easier to design on paper than to build in reality. We suffered many setbacks. Falak began to think that his theories concerning the power source and its weapons systems were flawed. Falak just couldn't get it to work. The damn things would not even lift off the ground. For nearly a decade, we struggled with getting them activated and functioning. Obviously, we were not getting any younger. The threat of the cold war diminished. But our potential enemies had gotten even more powerful. They outnumbered us and their technological advancements in weaponry were now further ahead of our own. By that time, Falak had been married and you were born. He knew that the machine would only become reality long after he was past his prime. And that is exactly what happened. You were all grown up when the machines finally began to satisfy our requirements. But as the machines neared completion, a newer threat began to take shape. It was this threat and our inability to solve it that led me in to the biggest mistake of my life. It was a mistake that I know I will regret for as long as I live."

Samar knew what Chetwal was talking about. Chetwal had betrayed his father. There were doubts in his mind about what Chetwal was saying. How had his father designed a machine whose technology was perhaps two hundred years ahead of its time? Nothing he knew could match the Cyclone Rx for power and speed. Cyclone R seemed even more powerful and seemed to surpass the Cyclone Rx.

"During the final stages of construction, we had brought in many experts belonging to different fields. Most of them were untrustworthy and had their own agendas. But Falak did not care about the internal security. No matter how hard I tried to convince him that we must have stricter controls, Falak remained ignorant of this problem. We both regretted our inaction. Details of the project were leaked to Kasid. Kasid was a young politician still making his way up in the world. But he knew the value of information. Kasid had spies in nearly every union in the city. His network had infiltrated some of the highest level of corporate hierarchies in the country. We were similarly unable to prevent this breach. But for us, the consequences were severe. What Falak and I had built to protect our country was seen as a tool of leverage over enemies by opportunistic politicians. Kasid shared this information with his seniors and provided them with proof that such technology existed. Of course, the support of such powerful weapons would...."

"What did Kasid do?" interrupted Samar

"He approached your father. He offered him a position in the party and a lot of money. It seemed that simple to Kasid. When your father refused, he tried to intimidate your father in sharing the command of the Cyclones. Your father refused. Falak was not a man to be intimidated by thugs.

But your father had been shaken by how simple it was for someone to reach him and make daft offers in return for the Cyclones. The very principle on which the Cyclones were based on was thrown out of the window. I tried once again to convince Falak that someone was leaking information from within the team, but he was focussed entirely on the getting the machines ready. That was when I began to realise that Falak had lost it. A week later we received another jolt. We were formally approached by officials from the army who literally demanded that we allow them to inspect the Cyclones and if they thought it was worth it, they would take command of it. They cited clauses and used terms like national security to make their point. Their audacity and reach was unbelievable. I was in no doubt that the security of the Cyclones had been shot to pieces."

"Exactly what kind of politician was Kasid?" asked Singh

"I told you. He was no one of importance in his party. But in the last decade, his primary focus had been on the Cyclones. He accrued a lot of clout in his party because of this. He never wanted responsibility, just power."

"You seem to know a lot about him." Said Samar

"I...had my own network. After the army posted a liaison in our team, I was fed up. I too used every bit of resource I had to find out exactly who knew what about the Cyclones."

"Liaison? Who are you talking about?" asked Samar

"What did you think Mani was? Did he look like a technician or a scientist to you?"

"Mani is from the army? Are you serious?" Samar couldn't believe it. All that time Mani had avoided telling Samar exactly what he did at the Cyclone facility.

"He was from the army. Falak convinced the army high command that the Cyclones were not ready and would take a while to be functional. The army knew that Falak was lying. He never intended to share command. So they sent Mani to keep an eye on us. We couldn't do anything about it. As time went on, Falak began to get past the technical issues that were holding up the Cyclones. Mani reported everything to his seniors. Our work was being shadowed by forces we could not match. And that is when the real trouble started."

Chetwal seemed to have run out of breath. He settled down on a fallen log and wiped the sweat from his brow. Samar and Singh stood on each side and waited for him to go on. Singh noticed that Cyclone R did not follow Chetwal the way Cyclone Rx had followed Yanus. It had remained back where it had attacked Yanus.

"This trouble started when you betrayed my father, didn't it?" asked Samar without any anger

"I never betrayed Falak. But I admit I made a huge mistake in not taking a tougher stand against Mani. I failed to save your father. You don't understand, Samar...Falak had completely isolated himself.

Falak had told me that he had chosen a child to take command of the Cyclones when he grew up. Though I had known this from the start he never even told me the child's name. It never occurred to me that the child was in of the orphanages run by FS. Anyway, Falak intended this child to command Cyclone R and this machine in turn would direct the other Cyclones."

"But that is not what he did, did he?" asked Samar

"Your father was playing an incredible game of deceit with Kasid and Mani. I too was trying to convince your father that he must reveal the boy's location, but your father refused. I was at my wit's end. But I realised that the pressure on Falak must be immense. And then Mani threw a bomb. He accused Falak of making a deal with a politician. Whether Mani knew of Kasid or not I never knew but your father was threatened with prosecution in a military court. Many in the team believed Mani and I knew that was the last straw for Falak. He had been gored by his own indifference...."

"You watch your mouth, old man...." Samar was noticing for a while the condescending tone about his father and decided to keep Chetwal in check

"I am saying it like it is. Your father would not let me help him. If he had told me about Yanus, I would have thrown Mani out that instant. I never thought that that we needed to entertain Mani once the machines were ready. But I too began to doubt in the Yanus theory when your father would not tell me who or where the child was, even after nearly twenty years. I began to think that there was no one and Falak intended to keep control for himself. When I asked your father whether he had met someone, he said 'yes' but wouldn't elaborate. What was I supposed to do?"

"You mean Mani was right?" asked Singh

"Not really. Your father had designed the Cyclones and only he understood the threat. He was not worried about the machines. He was worried about Yanus. He had lied to fool Mani and Kasid to keep Yanus safe. He wanted to ensure that Yanus was safe when eventually he took command of the Cyclone. This task he had entrusted to a man, whose name, along with mine was hidden in that document you gave to Mani."

Samar looked shocked.

"That man was Negi. Negi had the same information I did. He knew about the Cyclones. He knew about Cyclone

R. He knew that there was a person who would control it. Falak wanted Negi to protect Yanus when he was ready. And Negi was therefore looking for Yanus ever since he was arrested by the police."

Samar nodded his understanding. He spoke to himself as he pointed in the air

"Yanus was supposed to take control of Cyclone R. Mani and Kasid wanted control of the machines for their own agendas but Dad wouldn't give it to them. Dad must have thought that he was running out of allies, so that's why he contacted Negi. He wanted to ensure protection for Yanus after he was gone. Dad was not keeping well, he must have known...."

Singh put a hand on Samar's shoulder. But Samar jerked the hand away and walked up to the old man.

"I will tell you what happened next, you moron. When dad realised that no one in his team would help him, he turned to Negi. In the meantime, he built Cyclone Rx and linked that Cyclone to Yanus. He knew that he could not rely on Yanus reaching Cyclone R with so many staking a claim to it. So he linked Cyclone R to you. You had failed him, but he still trusted you. He hoped that if and when the country needed these machines, by then you would have realised that he was innocent. By then you would have figured out that he specifically built the Cyclone Rx not just to root out those betrayed him, but so that the machine would lead you to Yanus. Instead of me, Babur and God knows who, it should have been you out there trying to speak to him. My father must have hoped that you would get to Yanus through Cyclone Rx and then...." Samar was nearly in tears

"Cyclone Rx never had the control of the army. It was always Cyclone R. You are right. When your father realised that he had been isolated from his own work and couldn't count on Yanus reaching Cyclone R, he devised this strategy. I only wish that he had told me about Yanus sooner and I could have convinced him. But Yanus was obsessed with Babur and by the time I got to know about Cyclone R's link to me, it was too late. Even if that document had been...."

"He probably put those papers in the locker before he died. He knew I would have to go through all the documents to understand the operations. He left so much to chance because you fools wouldn't trust him." Samar wiped the tears from his eyes

"Cyclone Rx showed up a few days after your father died. Falak must have built it in secret and kept it hidden in the other facility. This was where your father was spending a lot of time...before his death. The Cyclone was programmed to eliminate Falak's team and then to link up with Yanus. At first I thought the machine was after everyone, but Falak knew who had betrayed him and who had not. Falak must have activated the machine and commanded it to execute the program if it did not receive any communication from him for a specific time frame. It killed every one in that facility and more than half in the one where you met Mani."

"Where is he now?" asked Singh

"Deactivated." Said Chetwal simply

"I hope my explanation has answered your questions." Said Chetwal as he stood up

"What now?" Samar asked

"I want you to go home and get some rest. We will meet again soon. I am sure you will have more questions. The more you think about this, the more you will need to know."

"Why did...?" Samar began but Chetwal interrupted

"Please, Samar. I know you have questions. But you must wait till you understand what I have told you tonight. Rest assured that there are more surprises." Said Chetwal smilingly

"With Yanus gone, my father's work has been destroyed. What does it matter now, anyway?" said Samar as he began walking in the direction of the waiting car

Chetwal put his hand on Samar's shoulder and turned him around to face him.

"Your father was the most devious man I ever met. His genius was beyond the comprehension of most minds. Falak invested nearly all his life in developing the Cyclones. Trust me, this is not over."

Samar nodded and turned away once again.

Singh and Samar got in to the car.

"Where are you taking the Cyclone?" asked Samar through the open window

"It will go back where it belongs. I will come and see you soon. Take care and think hard. I want to hear some difficult questions when I see you again." Said Chetwal as he gestured to Singh

Singh took the cue and drove away.

Chetwal immediately turned around and walked up to the Cyclone.

"We are ready to leave." Chetwal looked at the technician who had spoken to him

"Is everything cleared?" asked Chetwal

"Every bit of Cyclone Rx has been collected."

"What about Yanus?"

"Yanus is secured." Said the man

"Take him to the Cube."

The man nodded and rushed to follow the orders of Suri Chetwal. Chetwal turned to the machine.

"Go to the Cube." Said Chetwal and stood back

Cyclone R shot in to the sky without a sound. Chetwal lost the machine in the morning sky as it streaked in the direction of the Cube.

Chetwal took in the forest floor and contemplated the next task. It was finally time to go see him. He hated doing this. But Falak Jabar had left him no choice. If he had known that this was the real reason why Falak wanted to build these machines then he would have quit and run back home.

High in the most forbidding mountain ranges in the world are places which are lost or forgotten. There are caves, rivers, stones, and valleys that have a tale to tell and secrets to reveal, of times that have come to pass and those that will be. Nothing is certain and yet everything is inevitable. To face the inevitable and to learn new secrets, three men had journeyed from far. For these are not places for those who are weak of heart and no heart is stronger than the one that has felt pain, that has broken, that has touched death...and survived.

Raj checked his footing again and hoisted himself. Negi followed him up with a lot more difficulty. Heavier and with lesser lung capacity, Negi had a difficult time getting to this height. Negi straightened up and looked at Raj. Raj was already on the path leading up to the cave. Negi shook his head in disbelief. What was that? Is that where someone lived? Negi looked back and saw the view below. It was absolutely stunning. And it was killing. Negi wondered how he was going to get down. First things first, thought Negi and ran to catch up with Raj.

The cave was a lot warmer compared to the weather outside. It was getting hotter with every few steps. Raj walked in front of Negi as it was a narrow passage and wouldn't allow two people to walk beside each other. The cave was deep but there was yellow flickering light coming from within. Raj clenched his fist and sped up. They were late.

"Welcome." The voice sent an eerie chill through Raj

Raj had never heard a voice like that. Raj knew the man whose back was facing him. It was Suri Chetwal. This was the man who had called Negi. But it was the man who was facing him that had spoken.

In the silence that followed, Chetwal did not turn to look. Raj and Negi looked at each other and sat down on the floor on each side of Chetwal. The fire in front of them had thrown the features of the man facing them in to light. Raj had never seen a man who was more frightening in his entire life.

This was Pandit Taraj. An extremely large man with powerful muscles and an equally thick neck, Pandit Taraj had long flowing hair that fell to his waist. His eyes were unlike any that Raj had ever seen.

The man glared at Raj and Negi, similarly sizing them up.

Without a word, Taraj put his hand in the fire and withdrew two stones and flung them behind him.

"You have strength." Said Taraj to Raj

"I know. Thank you."

"I do not mean the strength of your body or your mind."

"What then?" asked Raj wondering why he always attracted such conversations? Did he look like a philosopher? He had to stop wearing Polo neck shirts.

"Your soul."

Raj thought the heat and solitude must have muddled this man's mind.

"You can see my soul? How does it look? Nice?" asked Raj. After spending so many years with Babur, no man on Earth could intimidate him.

"Not in the conventional way." Replied Taraj

Raj nodded. He did not understand at all.

"I am Taraj."

"I am Raj and this is Negi."

"I know who you are. I have known your souls for far too long now. But it is a pleasure to meet you at last."

Raj and Negi looked at each other. Had the man not been so big, Raj suspected Negi would have burst out laughing. This was seriously funny.

"I am sorry about your wife, Raj." Said Taraj

Raj turned to Taraj and his eyes became slits.

"How do you know…?"

"I told you. I have known your soul. The first time I met your soul was when she died. I am sorry."

Raj closed his eyes and nodded.

"Have you explained them?" asked Taraj

"I have. But I…." Chetwal began but could not finish

"What is it?" prompted Taraj

"Falak could have survived. Why did you not…?"

"I told you before. Falak's time was up. Nothing you or he could have done could avert it. We must have faith in Him and what He chooses for us all. All that happens is inevitable. We must be prepared.."

"Is that true?" asked Raj

"You will know soon enough. I want you all to understand that whatever role you will have to play in this; you must have faith in each other. A difficult time lies ahead, and your trust in each other might save your life."

Taraj looked at Chetwal and tried to look in to his eyes. Chetwal seemed ready to spit fire. Unlike Raj and Negi, who were new to this environment, Chetwal had a little experience.

"What troubles your soul, Suri?" asked Taraj

"My soul? I am concerned about my work. It was you who sent Falak to look for Yanus. It was you who wanted him to be sent to the orphanage. All these years I thought Falak designed the Cyclones to defend the country. But you and Falak never told me the real reason. My friend was harassed to the end of his days. He died alone all because you would not disclose the real purpose of the Cyclones. Why did you do it? And why did you hide the truth about Yanus. I supported this venture from the start. And yet I was not told the truth. Why was Yanus not taken in to confidence when he grew up? Why did you allow him to go through that hell?"

"I thought you knew...." interrupted Raj looking at Chetwal

"Falak met Taraj many years ago when Falak was on one of his tours. It was Taraj who told Falak how to build the Cyclones and....why to build them. Falak shared the 'how', but lied about the 'why'. And about Yanus, all he told me till the very end that there was a boy who would control the Cyclones when he grew up. Falak never intended to control the machines. His primary focus was to develop Cyclone R and the army, and to ensure that Yanus was protected till he was ready. He had hidden Yanus well and the development of the machines was on track. But Mani and Kasid disrupted his plans. He had not been keeping well. Perhaps he knew he was running out of time. So he took two further precautions. He got in touch with Negi and told him about the Cyclones and Yanus." Chetwal looked to Negi

"Falak told me that there was a boy named Yanus who held the key to an advanced combat machine. He made me promise that when this boy surfaced, he should be protected at all costs. My only priority was to prevent Yanus from joining any individual or agency. He told me that one day I would be contacted by his...only friend in the world. That would be when Yanus was where he belonged. He mentioned something...some cube or...I am not sure..." Negi tried to remember but Chetwal joined in

"The Cube. But I bet he must have assumed that Yanus would arrive at the Cube in one piece, not half dead."

Taraj looked at Raj more than he looked at Negi. Taraj tried his best to read Raj, but Raj was more difficult that any man Taraj had ever met. And Taraj had met many of the best...and the worst.

Chetwal however did not move his eyes from Taraj. He wanted an explanation.

"What was the other thing that Falak did? You mentioned that he took two precautions. Negi was one. What was the other?" asked Raj

"The other was Cyclone Rx. Falak was being hounded by Mani and shadowed by the minions of Kasid. He was trapped. He probably feared that if they found about Yanus they would kill him or influence him. And Falak's health was failing him too. Mani had succeeded in turning Falak's team against him. Falak knew it was a matter of time before Mani completely shut him out of his own project. With what little time he had, Falak built Cyclone Rx. It was not as potent as the Cyclone R, but it was enough for the two specific purposes it was built for: To hunt and eliminate all those who had turned against him and then to protect Yanus. Falak must have thought that the machine would go to Yanus when he would be in the orphanage. And that is what the Cyclone must have done. Only, Yanus was not there. He had escaped with Singh. Falak also left a code in his office. It was a code we used when we were at college. He put it on one of the initial plans he had drawn up when the machine was still in our imaginations. Samar knew it had something to do with us. But he did not know of the code, and neither did Mani. The code revealed to me that it was I who had the control for Cyclone R. The other bit it revealed was Negi's name. I had known that Falak had contacted a politician. He had admitted it to me. But he never told me why. Of course...." Chetwal had become so tired that he wanted to sleep

"So when you got Negi's name, you contacted him. And Negi told you exactly why Falak had asked him for help. He had known that neither you nor he could stave off a politician of Kasid's calibre. Only another politician could keep Kasid at bay, especially after he was dead or incapable of influencing anything to do with the Cyclones if this Mani had got his way. These two factors were his insurances. Of course, Babur spoiled the party." Said Raj stroking his chin

"And you were no less deep with that filth." Said Chetwal

"Of course, I was." Said Raj

Chetwal was a little disappointed to see that Raj had not taken the bait. He turned his attention to Taraj who was listening intently. But Negi spoke first.

"Why did you hide so much from Chetwal? He was supporting Falak. Had he known everything from the beginning, Chetwal would have ensured better protection for the Cyclones and for Yanus. It would have freed Falak to focus on the machines."

"Yes, let's hear your reasons." Piped up Chetwal

"When I first met Falak, he was young and enthusiastic. But he carried out every task I asked of him with great efficiency. Few years later, he told me about his health. I had known about it, but I wanted him to tell me when he was ready. It was his personal decision and I did not want to trouble him. He had enough on his mind already. Falak and I were the only ones who knew about this threat. But when we both realised that Falak's days were numbered, it was Falak who nominated Chetwal to take his place when he was gone. We didn't know when it would happen. Falak was an extremely determined man and he fought for his life valiantly. But in the end the illness coupled with his stress proved too much for his weak heart. I contacted Chetwal only when Falak died. Of course, that was when Chetwal found out about the real purpose of the Cyclones."

"But why did you not tell me where Yanus was? I could have gone to him. I could have spoken to him then. Negi knew, didn't he?" asked Chetwal annoyingly

"Negi's purpose was to keep Yanus safe. And Babur's was to train Yanus."

Chetwal got up in a rush.

"What did you say?" Chetwal nearly shouted.

Negi was aghast. He thought he hadn't heard right. Negi put his hands on his head. This was insane.

Only Raj showed no emotion. He had guessed that was it. It was the training that was necessary.

"Yanus had seen many hardships in that orphanage. He had a lot of frustration in him that was seeking an outlet. This usually happens to people when they suffer too much and cannot fight back. Yanus had the capacity to fight, but his tender years could not comprehend what needed to be done. Eventually he realised that he had to fight to survive and simply hiding was not enough. It was a path that I

chose for him because I knew what waited for him there."
Said Taraj

"Babur and Sunny." Said Raj

"And you. I wanted Yanus to test his strength. I wanted Yanus to understand his capabilities and even more importantly, his limits. I wanted him to channel his frustration and unleash it in the form of his anger. Had I told you where he was, then undoubtedly this carnage would have been avoided but Yanus would not be prepared. He has proved that he not only has the guts and strength, he has the intelligence and cunning to face graver threats. Not one man I know or ever knew of could beat a man of Babur's power. Even I could not see a chink in that man's armour. The almighty created that one to remind us of what awaits us in hell, should we deserve to earn a place. Babur was a man who could put the fear of God even in the devil's heart. The only reason Babur was outwitted and defeated in the end was because he had become old and had lost the will to survive. It took such a man to force Yanus to use every ounce of his intelligence and his courage. Any other mortal and it would have been too easy for Yanus. That is why I did not tell you about Yanus. I wanted him to understand. I wanted him to learn. And for that, he had to stay out on his own and learn how to use his own head."

Chetwal turned away from Taraj and looked at Raj. The fire seemed to have gone out.

Taraj had watched each man during the conversation and what he had seen was enough.

Taraj got up and walked through the fire. Taraj passed each man in turn and led the way out.

Coming out of the cave, Taraj turned to Chetwal. "How long before he recovers?"

"He will recover. For now, that is enough." Said Suri Chetwal

Raj and Negi stepped out and stood beside Taraj and Chetwal.

"Do you think it will happen?" asked Negi

Raj looked sideways at Taraj and waited for the answer.

Taraj looked at the heavens.

"It will happen. It is just a matter of time." Taraj clenched his fists and took a deep breath

"And when it does, we will be ready." Said Raj

The four men took the path that led to the bottom of the mountain. Their destination was the busiest city in the world where the Cube's two new guests waited for their arrival.

Cyclone R and Yanus